DIAMOND IN THE ROUGH

FOUR KINGS SECURITY BOOK 4

CHARLIE COCHET

CONTENTS

Diamond in the Rough

** Please note this novel contains scenes dealing with sensitive issues that may trigger some readers, including the trauma of military service and loss of brothers-in-arms.

ACKNOWLEDGEMENTS

Thank you to everyone who joined the Kings on their adventures. It's been incredible, but the ride's not over yet! To everyone who helped bring this book together, thank you. And to my besties who continue to support me, lift me up when I'm down, and overall just make life even more amazing. Thank you.

FOUR KINGS SECURITY UNIVERSE

WELCOME to the Four Kings Security Universe! The current reading order for the universe is as follows:

FOUR KINGS SECURITY UNIVERSE

STANDALONES
Beware of Geeks Bearing Gifts - Standalone
(Spencer and Quinn. Quinn is Ace and Lucky's cousin.)
Can be read any time before *In the Cards*.

FOUR KINGS SECURITY
Love in Spades - Book 1 (Ace and Colton)
Ante Up - Book 1.5 (Seth and Kit)
Free short story
Be Still My Heart - Book 2 (Red and Laz)
Join the Club - Book 3 (Lucky and Mason)
Diamond in the Rough - Book 4 (King and Leo)
In the Cards - Book 4.5 (Spencer and Quinn's wedding.)

FOUR KINGS SECURITY BOXED SET
Boxed Set includes all 4 main Four Kings Security novels:
Love in Spades, Be Still My Heart, Join the Club, and
Diamond in the Rough.

BLACK OPS: OPERATION ORION'S BELT
Kept in the Dark - Book 1 (Standalone series can be read
anytime)

THE KINGS: WILD CARDS
Stacking the Deck - Book 1 (Jack and Fitz).
Raising the Ante - Book 2 (Frank and Joshua)
Sleight of Hand - Book 3 (Joker and Gio)

THE KINGS: WILD CARDS BOXED SET
Boxed Set includes all 3 main The Kings: Wild Cards
books: Stacking the Deck, Raising the Ante, Sleight of
Hand, and bonus story In the Cards.

RUNAWAY GROOMS SERIES
Aisle Be There

SYNOPSIS

For Ward "King" Kingston the role of protector, forged by fire and tragedy, is one he takes seriously. When King is asked to safeguard the son of a four-star general and friend, he is pulled back into the world of government black ops on a mission that raises painful memories from his past. The moment King meets Leo, amid the chaos of a lockdown at a secret black site, it's clear he's never faced a challenge like this—one that will test his unwavering sense of control.

Leopold de Loughrey is a misunderstood genius whose anxiety and insecurities are sent into overdrive when he is forcefully recruited to work on a top-secret project. Terrified of what his role as invaluable asset means, Leo's stress leads to disappearances, arguments, and blowups that threaten the project and Leo's future. King's arrival is a calm in the storm for Leo and his frenetic thoughts.

King and Leo couldn't be more different, yet as they navigate the dangers of a secret multi-agency operation and face unknown threats, their differences could be what saves them. Neither man believes happy ever after is in the cards, but their hearts might just prove them wrong... if they can survive a deadly betrayal.

ONE

THE PROBLEM with doing favors was that they had a habit of coming back to bite King on the ass. His current situation being a perfect example.

Years ago, King decided he was out for good. He'd served his country, made sacrifices, and allowed them to turn him into someone he barely recognized. While deployed, he'd lost his parents and hadn't been able to bury them or even attend their funerals. Another chain added to the ones already wrapped around his heart, weighing him down. Then he lost his brothers-in-arms, and he was done. He loved his country. He did not love the men who asked for his loyalty and sacrifice but gave none in return, only empty promises. It was King who'd looked after his broken brothers on their return, not the men in Washington who'd turned their backs on them, offering hollow words of sympathy and condolences. He neither needed nor wanted their prayers. What he wanted was for them to stop using soldiers as their playthings, or at least have the decency to take care of their toys.

Yet here he was being escorted through a cold windowless concrete corridor by half a dozen armed soldiers at an undisclosed location in the middle of God-Knew-Where, Florida. Anyone who believed black sites on US soil didn't exist was living a fairy tale. They were everywhere, belonging to various government agencies—some buried deep, some hidden in plain sight. This particular one was in plain sight. At least the top floors were. King had been to more black sites than he cared to think about.

No time for regrets.

King had given his word, and he *never* went back on his word. Had it been anyone else, he would have walked away the moment those armed soldiers approached him on the tarmac at the airport. Instead he'd allowed them to escort him to one of several government Suburbans lined up waiting for him. But it wasn't just anyone who'd needed him. He and the General shared too much history, had suffered great loss, and were bound by a secret few people outside the two of them and the remaining members of King's Special Forces unit knew about.

A dark-haired man in a black suit, white shirt, and black tie approached King. He had government spook written all over him. The guy extended his hand to King.

"Mr. Kingston. I'm Agent Ross Bowers. Thank you for your service."

King nodded in appreciation as he shook the man's hand. "Please, call me King. CIA?"

"No." Bowers's smirk said it all. NSA. He motioned for King to walk with him. "I'll be your point of contact for this operation. I've been asked to brief you on the situation and escort you to the asset."

The asset.

Leopold de Loughrey was twenty-five years old, a free-lance software engineer, and a coding genius. He had the misfortune of being the son of four-star United States Army General Leon de Loughrey. The misfortune didn't lie with who Leo's father was, but rather *what* he was—an Army General in a position of power within the United States government. The fact it took Washington this long to discover such a powerful asset had been right under their noses for years was a testament to the General's love for his son, because there was no doubt in King's mind it was the General who'd managed to keep Leo off government radars.

Until now.

"I've been informed you know the identity of the asset and his relationship to General de Loughrey," Bowers stated.

"Yes."

"What else do you know?"

Like with every classified operation, King knew only as much as he needed to know to perform his duty. Nothing less, nothing more. "I know who the asset is, that he's working on something for our government, and that I've been brought in because there have been... complications."

Bowers nodded. "The General trusts you. He believes you'll be able to provide insight."

Insight. Interesting choice of words. Then again, King supposed the General wasn't about to tell his own government he'd brought in outside help because he didn't trust them with his son.

"The code name for this operation is Avengers, and for unsecured communications, the asset is to be referred to as Spider-Man. You are Captain America."

King stopped and turned to Bowers. "I'm sorry, what?"

Bowers's lips curled up in the corner. "You heard me."

"Captain America? The guy who fights with a shield and wears a giant star on his chest?"

Bowers appeared far too amused for his own good. "Fan, are we?"

"Not particularly." The Kings had provided an important client with security for his son's tenth birthday party. It was superhero themed. Unfortunately, the guy the event company sent to play Captain America had food poisoning and spent most of the gig puking in the bushes. King had been the only one who fit into the costume. He was pretty sure Ace had more fun at that party than the kids did. There were pictures and everything. King had been cheerfully informed he would never live it down.

Bowers shrugged. "Quite frankly, we could care less what the asset chooses to name the op if it means his cooperation. What he's working on is groundbreaking and could mean a significant advantage in counterterrorist measures for our government. Operation Avengers is a joint op between the Pentagon and multiple intelligence agencies."

King let out a whistle. "Wow, you boys are playing in the same sandbox?"

"Yep, and we're playing nice and everything. That should tell you how important this is. We need the asset—"

"Leo," King corrected. "We're in a secure location. We can call him Leo." Calling Leo an asset allowed those involved to detach themselves from the young man, making it easy for them to forget they were dealing with a human being, a citizen of their country, and not a faceless object or threat. King was familiar with the process. He wasn't about to make it easy for them with Leo.

Bowers paused, studying him before nodding. "Okay. We need Leo to cooperate, and right now that's not happening."

"He's refusing?"

"Not quite. The asset—I mean Leo is... well, a unique

case. It takes a certain type of individual to be able to do what he's capable of doing. Leo's file didn't prepare us for the real thing. We've brought in several experts in the hopes our people could learn how to effectively interact with him, but that only made things worse. Then there's the disappearing."

King frowned. "Disappearing?" When the General first approached King, he'd mentioned something about his son disappearing, but King figured he meant Leo kept leaving his station, not that he was actually vanishing. "Are you telling me that somehow Leo is disappearing from under the noses of the military and NSA?"

"Trust me, I'm as confused as you are. I don't know how the hell he does it, but he does. Then he just wanders back in like nothing happened. Every time he disappears, we risk exposure because security protocol has to be initiated and everything is locked down. It's a goddamn mess."

"What about surveillance?"

"That's the thing," Bowers said as he stopped walking and faced King. "Every time he disappears, something happens to the cameras."

"Are they being tampered with? I mean, the guy's a computer genius after all."

"Nope. We've had the footage screened and analyzed by our guys. No one has tampered with the cameras or the footage. During one incident, we found one of the camera lenses covered in strawberry jelly."

King squinted at him. "I'm sorry, did you say strawberry jelly?"

"That's correct."

"How the hell did strawberry jelly get on the camera?"

"We have no idea. One minute the kid's there, the next minute he's not. When we check the security footage, no one seems to be where they're supposed to be when the kid walks out. We've investigated, and each time there's a legitimate reason for the guards not being at their post, which makes this whole thing even stranger. We've noticed it seems to happen whenever he's anxious, which quite frankly is most of the time. Kid's jittery as hell. It doesn't help that he and the team of analysts brought in to support him and the project don't see eye to eye. He... um, he keeps correcting their work."

King held back a smile. "I see." He had to admit, he was curious. But if the NSA couldn't keep track of Leo, what exactly did the General think King could do? He needed to meet Leo and assess the situation.

They reached a solid steel door and Bowers stopped. He pulled a black cell phone out of his pocket and handed it to King. "All communication is to be done through that phone. Leo has been on site just over two weeks, and he's barely started the project. He spends more of his time questioning and correcting the analysts' work than coding the damned program. As you can imagine, the higher-ups are getting antsy. They need to see some progress."

And if they didn't, it would only be a matter of time before they lost their patience and instead of treating Leo like the son of a General, started treating him like the asset he was. Leo would be moved somewhere out of his father's reach, and the General would be lucky to see his son again. Leo wasn't a soldier or a government agent. They would break him, and there was little chance he'd come back from the hell they'd put him through. King clenched his jaw tight to keep from saying something he'd regret. He'd promised the General he would look after his son, and that's what he would do.

"I'll get you everything you need inside, along with

documentation for you to read through. If anyone on your approved list calls your cell phone, the call will be forwarded to the phone I just gave you."

King nodded. Depending on how quickly Leo got things done, King could either be here anywhere from a few weeks to several months. Not exactly how he wanted to spend his holidays. It was in both their best interests that Leo get this done as quickly as possible so they could both go home. At least that was the agreement King signed and had been informed Leo had signed. Once Operation Avengers was complete, they were both free to return to their lives. King had no doubt he'd be cut free, but Leo? Just because the government promised to let him go, didn't mean they would. If Leo was as valuable an asset as Bowers said, the government would find a way to keep him, and King couldn't let that happen.

"The system only recognizes those persons authorized by the General himself, and for the door to open, it requires three forms of identity verification: fingerprint scan, retina scan, and voice match. If even one of those doesn't correspond with what's in the system, the person will be locked out and armed personnel will arrive to investigate."

"I assume there's some kind of emergency evac plan in place?"

"Three, actually. One by land, one by sea, and one by air. Emergency transportation is on standby should you need it. As soon as you meet the asset—I mean, Leo, you'll receive a secure tablet with all the information you'll need to perform your duties. Should someone suspect your involvement, which is unlikely, considering your name is in no way connected to this operation, the FBI has conveniently made our lives easier by providing the appropriate digital and paper trail showing you never left England and are there on vacation. Don't worry, the rest of that case has remained sealed."

As far as the world knew, King was still abroad. As per his insistence, the only ones authorized to know he was back in the country were Ace, Red, Lucky, Jack, and Joker. That was the extent of their knowledge on the matter. The less they knew, the safer they would be. King was under no illusion this whole thing couldn't go sideways at any time, considering the parties involved. The security measures taken with Leo provided all the evidence King needed to know how important this project was to their government.

The door opened, and they stepped into what resembled a command center, albeit a secret one, located in a huge underground bunker. Before King had a chance to scan his surroundings, they came to a halt so as not to get mowed down by the half dozen soldiers charging past them.

"What the hell? Christ! Stay here. I'll be right back." Bowers took off, and King remained where he stood. He crossed his arms over his chest and pressed his lips together to observe what could only be described as a clusterfuck of epic proportions. Military personnel in and out of uniform darted from one place to another, some on cell phones, others on radios. A small group of what were clearly analysts stood arguing. Not exactly the kind of situation he'd been hoping to walk into.

A soldier hurried toward him, and King caught him before he could whiz by.

"What's going on?"

The soldier looked him over, and King held up the ID hanging from the lanyard around his neck. "Ward Kingston. I've been brought in by General de Loughrey. Could you show me to the asset?"

"I'm afraid I can't do that at the moment, sir."

King cursed under his breath. "Let me guess. Leo's gone for another walk."

The soldier nodded before excusing himself.

Every security job came with unique challenges, but he could say with absolute certainty that none of his previous jobs revolved around someone pulling a Houdini act several times a day. Leo had to know the danger he was in, so why take such a risk? To anyone, this sort of environment would be daunting, and rather terrifying, but Leo was the son of a General, and King recalled plenty of instances when the General had mentioned having his son with him.

After the loss of his wife, it would have been easy for General de Loughrey to leave his son and daughter with someone while he was away doing his duty to his country, but he kept his children at his side whenever possible. If they couldn't be in the same room as their father, they were still somewhere in the building or safely hidden away close by. How the General managed it, considering his position, was beyond King, but he'd done it, moving heaven and earth to take care of his grieving children. From the beginning, however, it became clear to King that the General was far more protective of his son than his daughter—not because the General loved one more than the other, but because according to the General, Leo was different.

From their friendly conversations years ago, King learned Leo was a soft-hearted boy whose vast intelligence made him vulnerable. He had difficulties socializing and communicating with others, and while he could do things at a level most adults couldn't even fathom, he had trouble with smaller mundane tasks, leading to him being home-schooled by the best tutors so he could learn at his own pace. And more importantly, to keep him safe. One thing King remembered above everything else was the love and pride pouring from the General when he spoke of his children. King looked forward to his interaction with the mysterious and fascinating young man. But first, they'd have to find him.

"Hey."

Turning, King frowned down at his new guest. Where had the guy come from? "Hey."

"Goldfish cracker?"

King stared at the guy and the little bag of—did he say Goldfish crackers?

"They're not stale, which I guess is the most you can hope for, considering how often that vending machine is stocked up. Not a lot of people are the Goldfish cracker type, but hey, more for me, so I can't complain." The guy shook the bag at him. "Goldfish cracker?"

King shook his head, his brows drawn together as he tried to figure out what he was dealing with here. Could this be Leo? If it was, surely Bowers would have returned, and the chaos around them would have come to an end. From the looks of the younger man, King guessed he was one of the analysts. He was cute, just under six feet, with messy brown hair poking out from beneath the blue beanie on his head. His eyes were big and brown, his lashes long, eyebrows thick, and his mouth pink and wide. The little mole to the right of his lips drew King's attention. He was in his mid-twenties at most, wearing trendy black-framed glasses, gray skinny jeans, black Chucks, and a yellow T-shirt under a navy cardigan of which only the center two buttons were fastened. He was lean, with a sinewy body. Oddly, the guy wasn't wearing any kind of ID.

"Would you like a Goldfish cracker?"

"I'm sorry, what?"

The analyst seemed awfully serene, considering the chaos happening around him. "Goldfish cracker."

"No. Thank you."

The guy shrugged. He popped a cracker into his mouth, drawing King's attention to his pink lips.

"Let me guess. SEAL?"

The word snapped King's attention from those plump lips back up to his pretty eyes. The young man's assessing gaze had King rounding his shoulders. What the hell was happening right now? Who was this guy? This was neither the time nor the place for him to be distracted by a pretty face. Not to mention, he was *never* distracted by a pretty face. It wasn't something he did. King opened his mouth to reply, but the guy put a hand up to stop him.

"No. Don't tell me." He snapped his fingers. "Green Beret. Special Forces, am I right?"

Interesting. Then again, King supposed the analysts spent a lot of time around soldiers and military personnel. "I was. Yes."

"I knew it. You give off that Green Beret vibe." He wiggled his fingers at King and his general person.

King arched an eyebrow. "Green Beret vibe?"

"Yep. Also, it's in your purpose."

"Sorry?" Were the rest of the analysts so... peculiar?

The guy's smile was wide, sweet. "Your purpose. You have a purpose. You're not about to move, so everyone who comes near you senses that and they go around you. Anyone who gets in the way of that purpose has no one to blame but themselves when they end up on the floor. That's amazing. That would never happen to me. Most people don't even notice me. I could be standing right next to them, and they'd have no clue."

King doubted that. "I'm sorry, who are you?"

The analyst opened his mouth to speak up, but King reacted, throwing his arm across the guy and taking two steps back with him just as a soldier stumbled forward, hit the floor, and skidded several feet past them.

"That looked painful," his companion muttered, though it would have been more painful had the soldier stumbled into him and taken him down with him. He beamed up at King. "See. Green Beret." He waved the bag at King again. "You sure you don't want a Goldfish cracker?"

"I'm sure." King's frown deepened. The guy's smile was bright, open, and friendly. "Why won't you tell me your name?"

"I never said I wouldn't tell you. What's *your* name?"

"Ward Kingston, but everyone calls me King."

The guy tilted his head. "Why King?"

"Long story." One he was certainly not about to get into with a stranger, and here of all places. Though he surprised himself by discovering he wanted to know more about his odd little companion.

"I bet it's fascinating."

"Why do you keep distracting me from getting your name?" This whole situation was bizarre. How did he not have this guy's name, position, and clearance level already? He wouldn't be too hard on himself, considering he was in a secure location and wasn't officially on the clock yet since the person he was supposed to be working with had disappeared. Normally he would have joined the search the moment he'd been told Leo was missing, but he had no idea what Leo looked like. The General—and King was certain several US intelligence agencies—had done a stellar job of erasing any trace of Leo from the internet. They left just enough details not to arouse suspicion, but there were no photos of Leo, no descriptions of him. Due to the classified nature of the op and Leo's involvement, King had been given little to no information about him. That was to come after he met Leo.

"I'm distracting you?"

The guy's startled words snapped King out of his thoughts. Why did he sound so surprised?

As if reading his mind, the analyst spoke up. "I've never distracted anyone before. Like I said, most people don't even realize I'm there, much less find themselves distracted by me." His wide smile lit up his face, and King sucked in a sharp breath. Whatever was happening had to stop. Now. King was about to demand answers when Bowers appeared. He thundered toward them, his murderous glare on the analyst and intent in his eyes. What exactly Bowers was going to do, King had no idea, but he wasn't about to let it happen. He instinctively put himself between Bowers and the young man, ignoring the fingers curling around his forearm or the searing heat from the touch.

"Leo!"

"Shit," the guy muttered from behind King.

"Shit," King repeated, looking over his shoulder at Leo, who was now sporting a sheepish grin. "Leopold de Loughrey?"

Leo worried his bottom lip with his teeth and waved. "Hi."

Fuck my life. Of course it was Leo. He should have known.

"Christ's sake, Leo! How many times do we have to do this?" Bowers growled, trying to get around King to Leo, but King kept himself between them.

Needing to defuse the situation, and quickly, King put his hands up in a nonthreatening gesture in the hopes of soothing Bowers. "It's okay. He's okay. Take a breath."

Bowers's nostrils flared, but he reined it in and breathed like King suggested. When Bowers spoke to Leo, the anger was still there but controlled.

Somewhat.

"Where the hell were you?"

Leo held up the bag of Goldfish crackers, and Bowers's eyes nearly bugged out of his head.

"You broke protocol and sent everyone into a panic for a goddamn snack? You little—" He snatched the bag from Leo, but King caught his wrist, and Bowers's expression went from furious to stunned.

King narrowed his eyes. "Not how to handle this." He gently took the bag from Bowers and returned it to Leo, his gaze never leaving Bowers's. "Why don't you take five and let me talk to Leo."

"Fine," Bowers spat. "He's your headache now."

Before King had a chance to respond, Bowers stormed off. Definitely not how he'd expected this to go. King turned, finding everyone watching them—more specifically Leo. They weren't so much watching him as they were glaring at him. Leo's fair skin burned red with embarrassment, his eyes on his feet.

"Get back to work," King barked at the room, his scowl fierce.

Everyone jumped to it, scrambling away to get back to whatever they'd been doing.

"Wow. They just... they didn't even question who you were, just did it. You were an officer, huh?"

"Warrant Officer 1."

Leo nodded. "I'm, uh, sorry about all this."

"Is there somewhere we can talk?" King asked, needing to speak to Leo away from all the prying eyes. Hopefully King could put him at ease. Leo's anxiety was showing in the way he shifted from one foot to the other and tapped his fingers against his leg.

"Yeah, sure." Leo nodded behind King, and they walked past the rows and rows of workstations where analysts huddled in front of multiple monitors. Each station looked like a small hurricane had hit it, with several strewn laptops, more wires than King had ever seen in his life, various pieces of hardware, and stacks of manuals.

The place looked like any government pop-up cyber command center, with one wall covered in huge screens monitoring who knew what and another wall lined with servers. A lone workstation sat at the far end of the room against the third wall, and he figured it was Leo's, being the only one unoccupied. The lighting from the high fluorescent beams hanging from the ceiling was low, and the room was mostly lit from the dozens upon dozens of screens. The walls and floor were the same cold gray concrete as the corridors outside.

Beyond the command center was a closed-off area where armed soldiers took one look at Leo and nodded, letting him through before checking King's security clearance. Once he was identified, they turned right at the end of the short hall and entered one of only two doors. Inside, the room resembled a typical Army barrack setup for one person, with an iron-framed bed King was all too familiar with, a plain wooden nightstand, matching desk, and wardrobe. Opposite the wardrobe was a tiny bathroom. The place was bare, cold, and cramped with two people in it. Leo took a seat on the edge of the bed, looking tragically out of place, small and alone. The nightstand beside the bed was occupied by a small lamp, a tablet, a couple of chargers, a black handball, and a Funko Pop figure of a little guy with brown hair and black eyes wearing a blue science school shirt.

"Who's this?" King asked, picking up the figure.

Leo's smile was timid. "Oh, um, that's Peter Parker."

"Why not Spider-Man?"

Leo shrugged, his hands clasped between his knees, fingers laced together. "I like to be reminded of the guy beneath the mask. I mean, Peter's a regular guy, you know? Yeah, he's a superhero, but really, he's this awkward, antisocial science nerd with self-esteem issues who's trying to do the right thing and figure himself out along the way. He didn't ask to be a superhero. To have all that power and responsibility thrown at him. Underneath the heroics is a guy who's trying to get by in life, and despite all the tragedy he's faced, he finds a way to keep moving forward, cracking jokes along the way."

King gently placed Peter Parker back on the nightstand. "Sounds like my kind of hero."

Leo's head shot up, his cheeks going a lovely pink. "Really?"

"What superhero would you have picked for me?" King smiled knowingly. "Captain America?"

Leo brushed some imaginary lint off his jeans. "I didn't know what you looked like, only that you were a soldier. You kinda remind me more of Oliver Queen than Steve Rogers. I didn't figure you for the superhero type."

"Oh?" King took a seat on the mattress next to Leo, making sure to leave enough space between them.

Leo lifted his gaze to King's, his brows furrowed. "Because you're the real deal."

King's heart stumbled. "I'm sorry?"

"A real hero." Sadness filled Leo's eyes. "I'm sorry for whatever happened to you out there."

Leo's words took King by surprise. "What makes you think something happened?"

"You would still be serving otherwise, wouldn't you?"

"Maybe."

"What happened?"

King stood and shoved his hands into his pockets, the question a stark reminder of why he had to keep his distance, not just because of who Leo was, but because of what King had done, or rather failed to do. Before he could politely steer the conversation back to the reason he'd asked to speak to Leo in private, Leo jumped to his feet.

"I'm sorry. That's personal."

"Did your father tell you anything about who I am or why I'm here?"

Leo nodded before resuming his seat on the edge of the bed, his knee bouncing. "He said you were a friend, which means he trusts you. I can count on one hand how many people he trusts, and two of them are me and my sister. He said you were a soldier, part owner of a private security company, and that you were here to help. I'm not really sure what that means. Help with what?"

King leaned against the wall opposite Leo, arms folded over his chest. "Tell me about the Goldfish crackers."

Leo blinked at him. "Um, they're delicious."

The seriousness with which Leo said the words caught King off guard, and he let out a bark of laughter.

Leo smiled tentatively. "What?"

"I'm sorry." King shook his head at himself. What was it about Leo that put him so at ease? It was a confounding sentiment and one he couldn't afford right now, especially with Leo.

"Why are you sorry? Because I made you laugh?"

"Because you were being serious."

"I was," Leo agreed. "You don't have to be sorry because I made you laugh. You have a really nice smile, by the way. It makes your eyes light up and little lines form at the corners."

King forced himself to get serious again. He was going to have to be careful around Leo. It wasn't so much that Leo ignored King's defenses—he seemed oblivious to them. It was the strangest thing. *No time to think on it now.* "What I meant was, tell me what happened. How did you get past all the security, and why?"

"Pretzels aren't crackers."

"No, they're not," King agreed.

"I mean, it's pretty obvious. One doesn't look remotely like the other. The textures are different, and despite sharing their cute fishy shape, they taste different. There's also the very distinct lack of cheese in the latter. If I'd wanted pretzels, I would have asked for pretzels. Do they really expect me to believe they're capable of running a highly classified black op from a black site, involving multiple intelligence agencies along with the military, but they're incapable of distinguishing between a cracker and pretzel?"

"Absolutely."

Leo peered at him. "Anyway, they gave me pretzels."

"So you decided to go find some Goldfish crackers." King motioned to the tablet on the nightstand. "Can you bring up the floor plans of this building?"

"Pfft." Leo grabbed his tablet, turned it on, then entered a security code followed by a scan of his finger. He tapped away at the screen before turning the tablet to hold it out to King. Leo had managed to not only evade security in the bunker, but the rest of the building, and King wanted to know how. He wasn't even going to think about how easily

Leo brought up the building's floor plans, minus the secret government facility of course.

"Where's the vending machine with your crackers?"

Leo tapped the tablet before showing King. "Employee lounge. Thirteenth floor."

How in the hell...? "You got to the thirteenth-floor employee lounge without anyone seeing you? How did you even know where the employee lounge was or that they had your crackers?"

"Well, Harold—he's one of the analysts on the project and a jerk—he came in eating them yesterday afternoon because, like I said, he's a jerk, so I knew there were some in the building even though he wouldn't tell me where. I mean, who doesn't share that kind of information? It's not like I was going to steal *all* the Goldfish crackers. He doesn't even like them! But he knows they're my favorite, so he went out of his way to get them and eat them in front of me. Who does that? A jerk, that's who. Never trust a guy who home brews his own kombucha."

"I don't know what that is," King murmured.

"And you don't want to know. Hey, to each his own, right? But you don't gotta be a—"

"Leo," King stated gently but firmly to get him back on track.

"Right, so I checked the occupants of each floor, ruling out the accountants, lawyers, architects, brokers, and HR department for some big retail chain—although they could have Goldfish crackers in their vending machine, considering the stress levels in that place—but my money was on the thirteenth floor. Video game testing. Much more likely to have fun snacks of the animal or nonanimal-shaped variety."

"You couldn't have found another way to check?"

Someone with Leo's skills could have easily discovered where to find the crackers without guessing.

Leo looked almost affronted by King's question. "Of course. A few key strokes and I could have pulled up every vending machine in the building and what it contained."

"So why didn't you?"

Leo frowned at him. "Just because I can, doesn't mean I should."

King's brows shot up. He hadn't expected that. Except for his friend Jack, King had met plenty of computer guys who'd jump at the chance to show off their skills. Leo had been brought to a black site to create something for their government, yet he wouldn't abuse his power to look into vending machine snacks. King tucked that little bit of insight away for later. "How did you get there without anyone seeing you?"

"Combination of stairs and elevator, cutting through the third, eighth, and eleventh floors. The third floor is under renovation, the eighth is available for lease, and the company on the eleventh floor is hosting their annual employee picnic today. They just landed a big account. Good for them."

"How did you get that information?"

Leo's smile was wide. "Google."

"Right. And how did you get out of the bunker?"

Leo shrugged. "I walked out the door."

"You...." King squinted at him. "What do you mean you walked out the door?"

Leo darted his gaze around the room before his eyes landed back on King again. "Um, I opened the door and walked out." He moved his fingers in a walking gesture. "Oh, there were stairs. I took the stairs up. Is that what you meant?"

"Where was security?" King had to get through several layers of security checks to get into the building, much less down the corridor, and Leo had walked out?

Leo shrugged. "I didn't see any. Maybe they were busy?"

That was not possible. King would need to look at the security footage. There was no way Leo moseyed on down the corridor and walked upstairs without help or anyone spotting him. First things first.

"Leo, I'm here to help you in any way I can, but I'm going to need you to trust me. I know it will take some time, but I'm confident we'll get there."

Leo studied him. "What exactly did my dad hire you for?"

"Your dad didn't hire me. I'm here as a personal favor to him."

Leo looked puzzled. "He's not paying you?"

"He's a friend who needs my help. I don't take payments from friends."

"How are you helping him?"

"The government is providing around-the-clock security. It's their job to keep you safe. It's also their job to see this project completed by any means necessary. Their interest is in the project. My interest is in you. I'm here for you, not them. I'll make sure you have what you need to do your job, then get you home safely."

"So what you're saying is they're Team Uncle Sam and you're Team Leo."

King quirked his lips. "Something like that."

Leo's smile was dazzling, and King found himself returning the gesture. Jesus, what the hell was happening? King schooled his features and straightened away from the wall, ignoring how it bothered him when Leo's expression dimmed. Something about Leo brought out a fierce sense of protectiveness, one reserved for those closest to King. A strangely quick response, considering he'd only just met Leo.

"Let's get you back to your workstation. I need to be brought up to speed before I can make a full assessment. We'll talk again after."

King didn't warm to people easily, if at all. He could be personable and charming when he wanted to be. Handling people was what he did. Knowing how to make people feel at ease came naturally to him, and it made his job easier. It was different with Leo. King found himself simply reacting to Leo, and that disturbed him greatly. Whatever this odd feeling was, it ended now.

TWO

TRAIN WRECK. Otherwise known as *his life*.

Leo followed King out of the room, doing his best not to get caught sneaking glances at the man his father had sent to help him. Anyone else might have been furious by the gesture, but not Leo. His family always looked out for him, took extra measures to ensure his well-being, and although at times Leo chastised himself—he was a grown man, after all—he'd also resigned himself to the fact he wasn't like most people, and if he needed a little extra help, he shouldn't feel bad about it, should he?

King's presence alone made more of a difference than the man could possibly know. Earlier, when Leo stepped back into the bunker, it had been chaos. Things had certainly escalated quickly after his short excursion for his favorite fish-shaped snack. The madness had been all encompassing, from the analysts arguing to the numerous soldiers darting from one place to another. It wasn't like he'd gone far, or even left the building. If they'd just brought him his Goldfish crackers like he'd asked, none of it would have happened. How was he supposed to concentrate when he'd been given pretzels? He'd been tempted to walk back out and wait until it was over. There'd been too much noise, too much movement happening all around him. It was always followed by anger, frustration, yelling, and lecturing, which Leo ended up tuning out, and that just led to more anger, frustration, yelling, and lecturing, the cycle repeating itself until he felt like Bill Murray in *Groundhog Day*, without the benefit of escaping via creative demise.

Then he saw King. The calm in the storm.

King had stood there, beefy arms crossed over his wide chest like some ancient god carved out of a mountain. Despite being bigger than Leo, he wasn't an extraordinarily large man. There were soldiers in the bunker who were bigger and wider, but something about King gave off an air of solidness. Leo had pegged him for a soldier right away even without a uniform. He was a very handsome man with stunning blue eyes. Tall, roughly six foot two or three, over two hundred pounds, blond with matching stubble on his chiseled jaw. He was all rippling muscles, dressed in black tactical pants, boots, and a black henley with the sleeves shoved up to his elbows, revealing corded forearms. The man had barely blinked as he'd stood observing his surroundings. Even when someone headed in his direction, looking like they might run into him, they had quickly swerved, as if they'd known he wasn't about to budge. Like a human wall. Leo had been fascinated and a little bit awed. He'd thought, whoever the man was, he appeared immovable. Something about him set Leo at ease, which didn't make sense considering they'd only just met.

Now as they neared Leo's workstation in the command center, Leo's pulse sped up and his nerves kicked in. He took a seat in his chair, his frown deep.

"What's wrong?" King asked, clearly aware of the many

curious gazes focused on them. Who couldn't feel the stares burning into the back of their shirts? King lifted his head, and everyone's eye darted to their monitors.

"Nothing." Leo glanced over his hunched shoulders at the rows of analysts before turning back to his station, his knee bouncing. How much longer could he do this? Every day his anxiety got worse.

"Why don't we turn your station around?"

Leo's head shot up, and he stared at King. "Move my station?"

"Having people hovering over your shoulder, or feeling like they are, can't be comfortable. Let's turn your station around and see if that helps."

Leo dropped his gaze to his fingers, his cheeks burning. "I didn't think of that."

"Your job is to focus on the project. Don't worry about the rest." King placed a hand on Leo's shoulder and gave it a gentle squeeze. "I'm here to help, remember?" He caught the attention of a couple of soldiers and motioned them over. Together the three of them helped Leo turn his workstation around so he had the wall to his back and his desk provided a good shield from prying eyes. "Thanks, fellas."

The soldiers nodded and left. What was it like to command that kind of power? To simply say something and have people not just listen but do as asked? When King turned back to Leo, his smile amused, Leo realized he'd been gawking. *Shit!* He swiveled his chair so fast he ended up spinning awkwardly, the chair slowly coming to a stop as it reached King so they were facing each other again. *Oh my God, seriously?* Could he *be* any more awkward? Movement from the corner of his eye had Leo turning, and he'd barely managed to suppress a groan when Bowers approached.

The guy was clearly still pissed, and he didn't even pretend he wasn't ignoring Leo.

"I apologize for my outburst earlier," Bowers said, shaking his head. "That kid's going to give me an ulcer."

Um, hello? Was he a mirage? Leo was right here. *Unbelievable. Story of my freaking life.*

King's scowl was epic, and Leo took a tiny bit of pleasure in the fact that Bowers cowered enough to take a small step back. Who was he kidding? Leo took *great* pleasure in knowing Bowers was intimidated by King.

Bowers handed King an armored case with what looked like a biometric lock. He pointed to the lock. "Fingerprint and the access code on your ID. Inside you'll find the tablet we discussed. The information is encrypted, and the encryption keys auto-generate every hour. The tablet can only be accessed by you via retina scan and handprint scan. If anyone who isn't you tries to access it, the information will corrupt itself. You'll also find a SIG Sauer M18 in there, along with extra ammunition."

King arched an eyebrow at him. "You're issuing me a sidearm?"

"Considering your military history, current career, and the General's glowing reference of your character, there was a likely chance you might pick up a weapon during this operation. We'd rather it was one of ours and not one of your own."

In other words, if things went south, it would be easier for them to sweep King's involvement under the rug. Did they think King was stupid? The guy had been Special Forces. Leo snorted, earning himself a daggered look from Bowers and a lip twitch from King. At least Bowers was no longer ignoring him.

"Any questions just call me. Your bags were cleared and delivered. They're in the barrack next door to the asset's."

The asset. So personable, these spooks.

King nodded. "Thanks." They exchanged a few more pleasantries before Bowers wished him luck and headed off. King turned to Leo, who couldn't stop his knee from bouncing again. He laced his fingers between his knees and stared at the screen before him. The black screen. The black, empty screen. The black, empty screen projecting what the inside of his coffin would look like if he didn't get this damned program done. *Wow*. That went to a dark place quickly. Maybe it was time for some more tea.

"Everything okay?"

Leo bit down on his bottom lip and nodded. "Mm-hm." *How about we not reveal what a complete and total freak we are to the hot soldier guy? Not hot.* Obviously hot, but Leo shouldn't be thinking hot. Ones and zeroes. That's what he should be thinking. Ones and zeroes and sixes, or was that eights? Six-pack or eight-pack?

"Leo?"

"Eight."

"I'm sorry?"

Leo's jaw went slack. *Holy shit*, he'd said that out loud! He promptly shut his mouth, eyes wide. Something banged somewhere, and he flinched. Lifting his gaze, King scanned the room, his expression turning pensive, like he was trying to figure something out. For Leo, it was easy. *Noise*. It filled the room. Clicking of keyboards, talking, whirring of equipment, and movement. The hostility that rolled off some of the analysts like little clouds of doom didn't help either.

"I'll be right back," King said before he headed toward the analysts.

Leo followed King's movement as he walked down the rows of workstations until he seemed to find what he was looking for. With a warm smile at Heather, one of the first analysts to be recruited, he pointed to a pair of heavy-duty noise-canceling headphones. He said something that had her blinking up at him, and he checked her ID before his next words were followed by him putting his hand to his chest. She raked her gaze over every inch of him—*way to be subtle, Heather*—and her cheeks went pink before she lifted her wide eyes to his. Leo wouldn't have believed it if he hadn't seen it, but she visibly sighed. Like a dreamy sigh, not the frustrated "why do you have to breathe the same oxygen as me" sigh she'd given Leo that morning when he'd asked to borrow a highlighter.

Heather nodded, and King took the pair of large headphones from her desk, then returned to Leo, Heather's gaze never leaving him, or rather his ass. Leo narrowed his eyes at her, and when she realized she'd been busted, she started typing away at her keyboard like she was Sandra Bullock in *Speed* and her desk would blow up if she typed under fifty words per minute.

"Does anyone actually ever say no to you?" Leo asked.

King chuckled and handed him the headphones. "You'd be surprised. My family certainly has no problem giving me a piece of their minds. Noise-canceling headphones. Why don't you use these for now and let me know which brand you prefer, and I'll be sure to get a pair brought to you right away."

"How did you know?"

"One of my brothers-in-arms, Jack, handles cybersecurity for Four Kings Security, and when he's working on an important project, he puts on headphones to block out any noise that messes with his concentration. Usually it's when our other brother, Ace, is in the same building."

Leo couldn't help his smile. "King, Jack, Ace? I'm sensing a pattern here."

"Nicknames given to us during our time in the service. Lucky, Red, and Ace co-own Four Kings Security with me. Jack and Joker head their own departments in the company."

Leo's expression fell. "I'm so sorry for your loss." Leo's dad had worked closely with Special Forces units years ago. From the little King had said, and how the brightness in his eyes dimmed when he spoke about his time in the service, it was obvious King had lost brothers-in-arms, especially as he'd yet to mention the remaining six men Leo knew would have made up the other half of King's unit. He quickly wiped the wetness from his eyes. "Sorry. I can't even imagine what that must have been like for you and your brothers." A tear escaped, and King shifted, as if he'd been about to move closer but refrained. Leo wiped at his face and let out a breath. "Geez, I'm sorry. I'm such an idiot, getting all emotional. Like you don't think I'm enough of a freak."

King crouched down in front of Leo and gently placed a hand on his knee. "That's a bit unfair, don't you think?"

Leo blinked at him, wondering what he'd said wrong. "What is?"

"You presuming to know what I'm thinking."

"Sorry." Leo turned his face away, embarrassed. It was a bad habit born from years of unpleasant experiences with people who'd been quick to judge his peculiarities.

"No more apologizing. I don't think you're a freak, Leo. I think you're a very gifted young man with a big soft heart. Thank you for your kind words."

Leo nodded. King was a nice guy, and he'd been sent to help Leo get the job done, which meant putting up with

Leo's weirdness and acting like it was no big deal. It was still nice to hear, though, so he smiled softly at King in appreciation.

As if shaking himself out of his thoughts, King stood. "Why don't you get to work. I'm going to catch up on a few things and check on my bags. I'll be right back. If you need me, I'll be in the room right next to yours."

After turning back to face his station, Leo logged into his interface and put on the headphones. They weren't the same as his, but still a very good pair. On the monitor to his right, data coming in from the analysts scrolled through several windows, highlighting names, IP addresses, keywords, and every piece of information that existed linked to those individuals, all from foreign territories.

How had he gone from being a freelance software engineer working from home to working on a government project from a black site? He closed his eyes, inviting the silence to swallow him up in the hopes of starting his process. Were this any of the projects he worked on at home, he would have just put on some music and gotten down to it, no sweat, but for this? He needed to completely lose himself. To open up hundreds of tabs in his mind's browser as he worked through the limitless algorithms until he discovered the ones that would work.

This project was huge, consisting of several moving pieces with a revolving door of code that expired from one heartbeat to the next, and if he wasn't quick enough locking in that piece of code, he'd have to start again. And again. And again. It was akin to conducting a symphony. Each instrument on its own provided its own unique sound, a beautiful but incomplete piece. It was his job to bring them all together to create one harmonious work of art.

A shake to his shoulder jolted him, and he jumped from

his chair, removing the headphones to hear Harold snarling at him.

"Why can't you do your damn job?"

Had the guy not noticed that's exactly what he'd been trying to do before he decided to be a dick? Leo dropped the headphones onto the desk and started to pace, tapping his fingers against his legs. Why did they always have to get angry and shout? If it was as easy as they believed it was, wouldn't he be doing it? Wouldn't they have gotten anyone? Given the choice, of course he'd love to dive right into it, but his brain didn't work that way. It never had.

When he was five, he and a group of other children had been presented with a piece of fruit, and when asked what they saw, the other kids said "an orange." Leo didn't say "orange" because when he looked at the sliced fruit, what he saw was rind, pulp, zest, juice vesicles, seeds—everything that made up an orange. They had asked him what he saw, not what the fruit was called. The rest of the children had looked at him like something was wrong with him. A recurring theme throughout his life.

As a little boy, he'd pray to God like his mom had taught him and asked to be like all the other children. His prayers were never answered, though he imagined part of it had to do with the fact that even at such a young age, he struggled to come to terms with a big man in the sky looking down on him. Quite frankly, it had scared the heck out of him, and he'd burst into tears until his mother reassured him that God was more about faith than a giant strange man watching his every move.

Faith had been a foreign concept, one he'd tried so hard to dissect and make sense of. He'd told his mother as much when he turned seven, and he never forgot her response. She kissed his cheek, hugged him close, and told him not to look with his mind but with his heart. Leo missed her so damned much. She'd been the only one who understood him, who knew what to do and what to say when he became frustrated with the world around him. No one had defended or protected him as fiercely. His father and sister were incredible and far more patient than anyone should be, but they'd always looked at him like he was something precious in need of protecting, and that wasn't necessarily a bad thing, but they never really understood him.

"Hey, I'm talking to you."

"No, you're shouting," Leo muttered as he paced. "There is a distinct difference between talking and shouting. The volume level alone should give you an indication that you're—"

"Christ, what the hell is wrong with you?"

A lot. There was a lot wrong with him according to most people. Why couldn't he sit down and get to it like everyone else? They were all very smart individuals. The fact they were here said as much. The problem was, he was smarter, vastly smarter. That wasn't a slight to them, but it made things difficult for him, always did, because he didn't know how to communicate with them. He'd tried to tell Bowers when he'd been recruited—more like drafted—but Bowers had assured him everything would be fine. How could it be fine? Nothing was fine. Everyone was staring at him, glaring at him, whispering to one another, and then there was Harold, shouting at him, cursing him, calling him names.

"Are you fucking listening to me?" Harold grabbed his shoulder, and Leo jerked away from him.

"Don't touch me! I don't like strangers touching me."

"You're a freak, de Loughrey. I don't give a shit who your daddy is. Man up and get this shit done."

Man up? What the hell did that even mean? Was he

supposed to beat at his chest and piss on his workstation to mark it as his territory? That because he was a man it translated automatically to bravery and toughness? Could a woman man up? Was that supposed to help him, encourage him? He didn't get it.

"What the hell is going on?"

Leo released a shaky breath at the familiar booming voice. It washed over him, easing some of his tension. It was okay. Everything would be okay. He didn't know why he felt that, but he did.

King put himself between Leo and Harold, his steely blue eyes narrowed at Harold. "Is there a problem here?"

"Yeah, he's the problem," Harold spat, trying to get around King whose expression Leo couldn't see but which stopped Harold in his tracks. Harold's face went ashen, and he took a quick step back.

"Why don't you go back to your station."

It wasn't a suggestion.

Harold hesitated before briskly walking off, his intense glare trying to set Leo on fire. King turned to Leo, his expression softening as he stepped closer. Leo didn't move away like he would have for everyone else. Instead he found himself moving closer to King's warmth, to the calm he gave off.

"Talk to me, Leo," King said quietly. "What's going on?"

Shit. King was going to think he was so stupid. A diva, or worse, he'd think what everyone else did. The thought of King looking at him like the others had Leo pacing again. God, he hated this. Hated that he'd let himself get trapped. He should have known better. His father had taught him better. Now he was stuck here, trying to find a way out without alerting them. His life hadn't been perfect, but it had been *his*. Did they think he was stupid? That he would buy the bullshit they were trying to feed him? There was no computer he couldn't get into, no part of the dark web he hadn't seen. The world was a terrifying place, and he was an insignificant spec in the grand scheme of things.

The government wanted him to believe he was doing good, but the reality was they would take what he built and mutate it into something monstrous, unless he found a way to ensure they didn't, but the thought scared him. There was no such thing as safe in this world anymore. He was never safe, and with his father sent God knew where, and his sister halfway across the world, Leo was utterly alone.

They'd isolated him.

"Oh God, I can't," Leo whispered, wringing his hands. It was getting harder to breathe. He was going to have a panic attack. They'd taken the first steps. They were going to throw him in a hole where no one would ever find him, take him from his father and his sister, force him to do horrible things, and if he refused, they would—

"Leo."

The soft-spoken word had him looking up, and he lost himself in the deep blue pools of King's eyes. King breathed in through his mouth and released the breath slowly through his lips, the movement drawing Leo's gaze to his full mouth. Without thinking, Leo followed King's lead, breathing in through his mouth, then releasing the breath. He lost track of how much time went by while they did nothing but breathe.

"Come with me."

Leo didn't question the gentle order. He simply did as King said, walking beside him, aware of King's solid strength, and feeling the tension leaving his body. It was as if King was surrounded by an invisible shield, one that encompassed Leo if he was close enough, a protective bubble that kept the outside world away from Leo. He focused on nothing but King, barely aware of the bunker, the noise, the stares he was surely getting. Inside the concrete box doubling as his room, the desolation of it had the world crashing down on him again, and he gasped for breath.

"What do you need?" King asked, coming to stand in front of Leo.

He wouldn't let anything happen to Leo, would he? That's why his dad had sent King. He must have known. Who was Leo kidding? Of course his dad knew; he had been in the military for decades. He was a general. He'd known, and he'd sent someone he trusted, someone he could entrust Leo with. Safe. Leo would need to feel safe, so his father had sent him King. *Safe. King. Safe. King.* The words repeated in his head on a continuous loop.

Leo was surrounded by strangers, dangerous people he didn't trust, who didn't care about him or his family, who wanted to use him and what he could do. "I'm sorry," Leo murmured, tapping his fingers against his legs. "I'm so sorry. You're probably regretting this already."

"Leo."

Leo slowly lifted his gaze, expecting to see frustration or annoyance on King's handsome face, but instead he found a tenderness that warmed him from the inside out, making his heart stumble and fall over itself. How was King so calm? Leo supposed it was the soldier in him. The ability to summon calm amid the chaos. There was something else, though, something Leo couldn't quite put his finger on, but it soothed him. He let out a shaky breath. Leo added *calm* to the loop. *Calm. Safe. King. Calm. Safe. King...*

"You're doing it again," King said gently but firmly.

"Doing what?" *Being stupid? Weird? Obnoxious?*

"Making assumptions about what I'm thinking. I don't regret being here, and believe me when I say, you would know if I did. I won't mince words with you. If you're worried about what I'm thinking, just ask."

Could it be that easy? Leo considered King's words and searched his gaze. King's eyes were filled with only sincerity. "Okay."

"Now tell me what's wrong. Is it your blood sugar? Do you need something to eat?"

What? The suggestion completely threw Leo. He shook his head, ready to tell King he was fine when King put a finger to his own lips. They were very nice lips, but then why wouldn't they be? The man was easy to get lost in. King tapped his ear, and Leo figured he was trying to tell Leo not to say anything in case someone was listening. He held a hand out to Leo, and Leo stared at it, hesitating for a heartbeat before he placed his hand in King's larger one. King's fingers wrapped around Leo's—they were long, calloused, rough, but his grip so amazingly tender.

"Um, yeah. That's probably what it is." Heat from King's touch flooded through Leo, and his face burned. He'd never had this kind of reaction to anyone before, but then he'd never been touched by a man like King. *Jeez, he's holding your hand, not inviting you for sex.* Why was he even thinking about sex? That was so wrong. As if a guy like King would ever find him attractive anyway. The guy was gorgeous, like one of those handsome actors playing super-heroes on the big screen. Leo wouldn't even know what to do with the guy. The few sexual encounters he'd had were more often than not quick, awkward, disappointing, and ended with his sexual partner taking off faster than he'd come—pun totally intended. Some of them didn't even bother asking his name. Which was fine. They were random hookups. Scratching an itch.

King didn't strike Leo as a random-hookup kind of guy. Then again, it wasn't like they knew much at all about each other. Maybe the man was a player. Shit, he probably wasn't even into guys. Leo thought he'd felt *something* spark between them, but now that he thought about it, King was most likely doing what he'd promised Leo's dad he'd do. Man, he was such an idiot. King being a nice guy was an added bonus. It did *not* translate to King wanting anything from him other than to fulfill his promise. Whatever ridiculous thoughts were trying to worm their way into Leo's head needed to go away. Love wasn't meant for guys like him. After this, there was a good chance he'd always be on someone's radar, always watching his back, and he had to face the fact he was pretty shit at taking care of himself. Who'd want that? Who'd want a guy that needed constant protection or looking after?

King opened the door to Leo's room and peeked out before pulling Leo with him into the room next door, then locking the door behind them. It was an exact copy of Leo's room, with the exception of the large black duffel bag and black laptop bag on the bed. Leo stood mesmerized as King released his hand and went digging in his duffel bag, then pulled out what appeared to be a tablet in its case. To Leo's bewilderment, King removed the case and started taking it apart. Leo's eyes widened as he realized the case was hollow. King removed a black object resembling a business card. He pressed something and a tiny red light blinked before King began sweeping the room. Leo's jaw dropped. He wasn't sure what concerned him more, that King believed their rooms were bugged, or that he carried a sweeping device with him hidden in his tablet case. Then again, King had been Special Forces and now worked in private security.

"I think I have a protein bar in my bag," King said, mouthing the words "outside pocket" and pointing to the right side of the bag. Protein bars weren't really on Leo's list of enjoyable snacks, but he did as King suggested, unzipping the pocket and removing a large resealable bag with over a dozen protein bars wrapped in cellophane. Were these homemade? With King's nod of approval, Leo removed one, unwrapped it, and took a bite while King continued to sweep the room, ducking his head inside the now open wardrobe.

"Oh God, this is so good," Leo said with a moan. Maybe it *was* his blood sugar. He let out another moan, but a loud *thump* and growled curse startled him. He leaned over to look at King, who was rubbing his head as he pulled back from the wardrobe.

"You okay?" Leo asked through a mouthful of protein bar.

"Yep. Room's clear."

"Did you bump your head?"

"I'm fine," King grumbled.

"Okay. Thanks for the protein bar. This is amazing. I've never tasted anything like it. I don't normally eat protein bars. They usually taste like dirt or freeze-dried cardboard. Not that I know what freeze-dried cardboard tastes like, but I imagine it's not all that different from protein bars." Maybe he should shut up now. Leo took another bite and tasted chocolate, macadamia nuts, a hint of coconut, healthy oaty stuff, and a few other ingredients he couldn't quite discern, but it was good.

"My sister makes them. She and her husband own a café in St. Augustine Beach."

"Cool." Leo sat on the bed, his brows furrowed. "Do you think they've bugged my room?"

"It's possible. I'll give it a sweep later, but if it's bugged, we can't tamper with it in any way, or they'll know we're onto them."

Leo nodded. He guessed he couldn't complain about having his privacy invaded when he was creating a program that would do just that on a much grander, scarier scale. King moved his bags to the floor and took a seat beside him.

"Want some?" Not feeling very hungry, Leo held out the remaining piece of protein bar. He swallowed hard when King smiled warmly and took it from him before popping it into his mouth. Leo really needed to get ahold of himself. Developing a crush on the sexy soldier was a very bad idea. The guy could knock him out with one punch.

"Do you have a girlfriend? Or, um, boyfriend?"

Wow. And you wonder why you don't have a boyfriend.

King let out a choking sound before he started to cough violently into his hand, his face turning red.

"Shit." Leo looked around the room, grabbed the water bottle on the nightstand, twisted the cap off, and handed it to King, his eyes fixed on King's throat as he gulped down the liquid. Wiping his mouth, King handed the bottle back to Leo, who capped it and returned it to the nightstand. "Sorry." Because awkward questions weren't enough, now he was trying to kill the guy.

"No, it's fine," King wheezed. He blew out a breath. "There's no one."

Well, that didn't help.

"But if I did have someone," King said, picking up the pieces of his tablet's case, a deep frown on his face, "it would be a man. Is that going to be a problem?"

Leo blinked at him. "Why would that be a problem? I'm gay."

"What? Wait a second." King turned to face him. "I remember talking to your dad and him saying you had a girlfriend."

Leo's brows shot up near his hairline. Well, that was news to him. "When was this?"

"Um, 2002, I think."

King remembered a conversation he had in 2002? Leo couldn't remember what he had for breakfast. Oh, wait. Now he remembered.

"Dude, I was nine. Sarah Lieberman invited me to her birthday party and declared I was her boyfriend. The first Spider-Man movie came out in theaters the same day of the party, so unless she was a dude dressed in blue-and-red spandex, I wasn't interested. Pretty sure she figured as much when she asked me to kiss her and I presented her with my pet tarantula, Spidey. They did not hit it off."

King stared at him before letting out a bark of laughter that had Leo smiling like a dope. The guy had a great laugh, and an even better smile. Leo couldn't help but be drawn in. Whatever ridiculous thoughts were trying to form in his annoying brain had to stop. God, King was so, so pretty. A sigh slipped out before he could stop it, and Leo froze as King's laughter faded, those intense blue eyes focused on him. Thankfully, King didn't address Leo behaving like a schoolboy with a first crush. King didn't so much as hint at knowing what Leo was thinking. Instead, he busied himself putting his tablet case back together.

"Do you want to talk to me about what happened out there?"

Shit. For a moment, Leo had been so lost in King, he'd forgotten all about where he was and what he was here to do, which in turn made him think of what would happen if he didn't get this project done and what would happen after. What would happen to him when this was all over and King went home? Were they really going to let Leo walk away? They promised they would, but that was like leaving a baby gazelle with a lion that had just eaten. Sure, the lion might ignore it while it had a full belly, but the second it got hungry again, *chomp!* No more baby gazelle. Okay, he needed to stop being so morbid.

"Leo? What's wrong?"

Leo jumped to his feet and started pacing, his fingers tap, tap, tapping away at his leg. "Everything is wrong. This whole place is wrong. I can't even hear myself think. The constant noise, the people, the talking, the yelling. I know you got me headphones, and I appreciate that, I do, but it doesn't change the fact that they're there. I know they're there, looking at me, talking about me, all of them so angry and frustrated.

"It's not like I'm doing it on purpose. I want to work on it. It terrifies me, but I know I have to or—I don't even want to think about what'll happen if I don't, but I can't snap my fingers and make it happen. It doesn't work that way. I told them that. I told them it would be hard for me if I wasn't in my own environment. I know that sort of thing doesn't matter to most people, but most people aren't in the sludge like I am. They're just circling it, observing it. I'm the one that has to be in there, in the dark, with the monsters." He was rambling like a lunatic, but he couldn't stop. "I never wanted this. This wasn't supposed to happen, but now I have no choice, and if I don't do this, who knows what they're going to do to my dad. I mean they're already forcing him to retire because of me."

King was on his feet, his hands on Leo's shoulders,

bringing his pacing to a stop. "Wait. They're forcing your father to retire?"

"Yes, his punishment for keeping me 'hidden,' like I belong to them or something. My dad was never going to tell them about me. He'd been preparing me for this since I was a kid, always telling me to be careful, not to leave any traces on the internet, and I *was* careful, but they laid a trap, and I fell right into it."

"How?"

"I'm a freelance software engineer. It gives me the freedom to work from home and not have to... people. Whenever I got a job to design something for someone, I was very careful. I did only what they asked me to do, nothing over-the-top or crazy that would draw attention to myself. It was hard. So hard. Some of these programs needed so much improvement, I had to recreate the whole thing on my computer the right way just to get it out of my system. I hated that I couldn't give them something way better than what they asked for, but I knew I couldn't do anything outside some minor upgrades, nothing any other decent software engineer wouldn't do.

"Designing video games is a hobby of mine. It's video games, right? I figured it was safe. I was part of a game design forum, where members helped each other out during the various design and programming stages. It wasn't like anyone was going to ask how to get into the Pentagon or anything. I hid my identity. I was careful, or so I thought. There was a guy in the forum I chatted with all the time. I'd known him since the forum launched back when I was at MIT. One day he messaged me privately, begging me for help, panicking about his sister being in danger. I didn't even know he had a sister. He never talked about her, but then no one talked about their real lives in the forum.

"Anyway, he said some guy was harassing his sister, but that the police weren't taking her claims seriously. She was starting to get scared, fearing for her life, but no one could do anything because this guy was some bigwig in her company and there was no evidence because someone kept deleting the messages he was sending her from the company's servers. He asked me if I knew anyone who could get into the servers and find the messages this guy was sending. It sounded pretty straightforward. Get in, get out." Leo started pacing again.

"I knew I shouldn't have, but he was so scared for his sister. I thought about my sister, and what if she were in the same position? I told him I'd have a go at it." Leo rubbed his eyes. "I was so stupid. So careless. I should have known when I hit the first firewall. The company's security wasn't like your average company, and that should have been my first red flag, but I told myself it was probably a financial institution or something similar. I kept digging deeper and deeper. Something was seriously wrong, and then I found information that shouldn't have been there. Advanced coding and intel referencing government operations. By the time I realized what I'd stumbled across, I knew it was too late."

"The guy you'd been talking to hadn't been your friend."

Leo shook his head. "I shut my laptop and was about to leave the Starbucks I was in, when a bunch of suits walked in and asked me to come with them." Leo blinked the wetness from his eyes. "I'd never been so scared in my entire life. I mean, I spend most of my days behind a computer screen, trying not to draw attention to myself. Blending in with a crowd has never been a problem for me. No one ever gives me a second glance, but online? I've been covering my tracks for years, knowing that if I wasn't careful.... In that moment, I knew I'd messed up. They'd been throwing that net out for years, waiting to catch their white whale, and they finally did. They tried to make it sound like I should be proud. No one else had made it to the middle of their little maze except me. I'd be doing my father proud, protecting my country, using my gifts for the greater good, fighting terrorists, catching the bad guys before they hurt innocent people. One of them looked me in the eye and said I could be a real superhero. Patronizing asshole."

Cursing under his breath, King wrapped his arm around Leo's shoulders, pulling him close. Leo shut his eyes when it struck him that he hadn't recoiled from King's touch, not once. There was something about King that made Leo feel comfortable in his own skin. He didn't have to pretend to be something he wasn't around King, didn't have to put on a brave front. Leo wanted to turn and bury his face against the man's chest, inhale more of his scent, the fabric softener and whatever woodsy shower gel King used. His body was warm, and Leo wanted more. As if sensing his thoughts, King pulled away. Leo couldn't blame him. Who wanted to take on a wreck like him? High-maintenance didn't begin to cover it. Weird eating habits, health oddities, general weirdness, neediness, social anxiety, and constant need for vigilance.... Yeah, he was a real catch.

"I don't want to end up like Codey Cat."

"Who?"

"This coder I met on the dark web a few years ago. They were nicknamed Codey Cat because whoever they were always slipped in a little coded cat face. Anyway, they were good. Like *me* levels of good. We used to chat and try to out-code each other. Then one day, they disappeared. Rumor was they'd somehow been picked up by the spooks.

It happened all the time. I don't want to end up like Codey Cat."

"Leo—"

Too afraid of what King was going to say—like maybe King was having second thoughts about being here, or that Leo needed to suck it up and get on with it—Leo pasted a smile on his face and quickly spoke up. "You know what? It's okay. I'm okay. Early-morning nerves, you know? Thanks for hearing me out. I'm good to go."

"Leo, you don't—"

The genuine concern on King's handsome face was too much, and Leo spun on his heels and left the room before King could stop him. "Really. I'm better now. Let's get to work, huh?" He'd get this damn project done if it killed him. It wasn't fair to King. He didn't ask to be brought into the mess that was Leo's life. Soon as he was done, he'd disappear for a while in case Bowers and his superiors got any ideas about keeping him on. King would go back to his life, and Leo would forget those kind blue eyes. Didn't matter that King looked at him in a way no one in his life ever had. Getting attached wasn't an option. Not unless he wanted to get his heart broken. Nope. From this moment forward, he'd focus on the job and nothing else.

"Leo, wait a second."

Leo turned, his heart practically bursting out of his chest to throw itself at King when King presented him with a bag of Goldfish crackers, a warm smile on his face.

"In case you need a snack."

He was so doomed.

THREE

KING SPENT the next couple of weeks shadowing Leo and doing reconnaissance. In that time, he'd given Bowers a list of items to get for Leo, including a thirty-two-ounce refillable water bottle, which Leo was expected to drink two of a day, a giant box of Leo's favorite cheesy Goldfish crackers, multivitamins with extra Vitamin C, a lumbar pillow for his back, tea, and a host of other items meant to make Leo's time here more bearable.

Bowers had given King as much information as he was going to, which amounted to fuck all, so King took care of it himself. While Leo tried to get on with it, King got familiar with Leo, their environment, and the people in it. He greeted each and every analyst, soldier, and suit who worked in the bunker, discreetly getting their names, clearance level, and roles. He paid attention to what soldiers were on what shifts, when they changed over, and every move Bowers made. King did what he did best. He carried out his mission undetected, inspecting every corner of the bunker, noting every exit, every movement until he had everyone's schedule and routine memorized.

In that time, he also reviewed the bunker's security footage from the times Leo had disappeared. He'd watched it several times, unable to believe what he was seeing. Leo had been right. Whenever he made it to the exit, there was no one there. Each and every time, something happened to take the guards away from their posts, leaving Leo to walk right out. It was one hell of a coincidence, but King couldn't see anything out of the ordinary otherwise. It was mystifying.

Leo had been quiet since the day they'd met, and it was obvious he was trying to avoid King for some reason, but King wouldn't let him. He was there to look after Leo, so from the moment Leo left his room, King was at his side. The only times he wasn't with Leo was when Bowers called him in to tell him off for something or other. King quickly figured out that since Bowers couldn't yell at Leo, King was the next best thing. As if he could do something about Leo not working fast enough. This morning, he'd stood by Leo's room, same as every morning before then, and waited for Leo so he could accompany him into the command center. Whatever was going on wasn't good. Leo was growing more jittery by the day, evident by his constant tapping of his fingers against his leg, but no matter how many times King asked him, Leo brushed him off with an "I'm fine." It bothered King.

He had never felt so off-balance. It had been years since he'd had a relationship, and even then, he hadn't felt this... whatever *this* was. Christ, he couldn't even put a name to it. His previous partners hadn't been able to handle his intensity, the commitment to his family and brothers, the job. He'd never had a problem walking away. If someone didn't want him around, he wasn't going to waste either of their time. Because of his ability to cut people off at the drop of a hat, he'd been accused of being cold, heartless, but if someone wanted him gone, he was gone. The only people he made exceptions for were those close to him. He'd heard it all before from the men he'd tried to get to know, how he was too unforgiving, too serious, repressed, domineering.

Granted, King wasn't the easiest man to get along with, and in a relationship, perhaps he was several of those things he'd been accused of, but only because he hadn't found the right person to change any of that. His entire life was about control. He ruled with his head, not his heart. His partners were often men vouched for by friends, and although the sex had been good, they'd been incompatible. His ability to read people was a trait he considered invaluable. Where his romantic relationships were concerned, it was somewhat of a hindrance, because from very early on, he could usually tell the new guy wouldn't work out. Why was he even thinking about his past relationships or lack thereof?

The answer to that question tripped over his untied shoelaces and would have fallen face-first onto the hard floor if King hadn't caught him. King steadied Leo, enjoying the pink streak that appeared across his cheeks when he was embarrassed, a pleasant color King was quickly growing fond of.

"Sorry," Leo muttered.

King didn't think about his actions. Next thing he knew, he was down on one knee, tying Leo's shoelaces for him with a neat and tidy double knot. He stood, ending up in front of Leo, their bodies mere inches from each other. Leo had to look up, his body all but getting eclipsed by King's. He wasn't small, roughly four or five inches shorter than King, but certainly leaner. That tiny mole to the right of his lips kept drawing King's eye, and he shoved his hands into his pockets, too afraid of what his treacherous body might do if he didn't.

"Thank you," Leo said, taking a step back and walking around King.

Something was off, but King got the feeling Leo would just turn him down yet again if he asked. Was it something he'd said? As he followed Leo into the command center, he played back their conversations in his head but couldn't think of an instance where he'd done or said something that would have Leo pulling away from him. Leo had been chatty when they'd first met. What changed?

Leo headed straight to his workstation, took a seat, and put his headphones on. He closed his eyes, and King left him to it. Someone had moved the conference room chair King had confiscated and placed by Leo's workstation, and he scanned the room to see if it was close by. No chair, but there were several futons lined up along the walls opposite the servers and across the back of the command center. King headed over to a futon, lifted one end to test its weight —pleasantly surprised the wood was very light. He picked it up and carried it over to Leo's station. After placing it on the floor, he then pushed it up against the wall, and turned to sit, when he found Leo staring at him, eyes huge.

Leo moved his headphones off his ears. "Dude, you just picked up a couch and carried it across the room."

King cringed. "Shit, was I not supposed to?" Why was Leo staring at him like he'd sprouted a tail or something?

"What? That's not—never mind." Leo spun back to face his desk. "Sure. No sweat. I mean, what can a couch weigh? It's probably like picking up a poodle."

King chuckled. Leo was fascinating, no doubt about it. Removing his tablet from one of the deep pockets in his tac pants, King logged in while Leo got to doing his thing, which included closing his eyes for several minutes. There was a process involved, one that seemed to involve some kind of meditation. King didn't know much about coding, but he could see Bowers's concerns. For someone who was supposed to be coding, Leo spent more time staring at the screen than typing, as if Leo were hesitant to work on it at all for some reason, one not entirely connected to his anxiety. King wished there was something he could do to help, but whatever Leo was working on was way above his clearance level. Harold cursed loudly, jumping from his seat, glare aimed at Leo. He took a step forward, and King narrowed his eyes at the guy as he approached. Not being a complete idiot, Harold glanced his way, caught King's expression and subtle shake of his head.

Don't even think about it.

Seeming to think better of whatever he'd been about to do, he spun on his heels and headed right back to his desk, then dropped into his chair with a grumble. The guy really had a hard-on for Leo. King would have to keep an eye on him. He didn't like the way Harold watched Leo. After several instances of Harold getting up to refill his water bottle from the water cooler, his gaze always going to Leo, King tucked his tablet into his pocket and stood. When Leo glanced at him, King shook his head, his smile reassuring. He made a drinking motion and headed for the water cooler where Harold quickly averted his gaze.

King shoved his hands into his pockets and turned away from the command center, his voice quiet. "There a reason you keep staring at him?"

"I don't know what you're talking about," Harold muttered.

"How about this. You so much as think about laying

another finger on him, and typing is going to become very difficult for you."

Harold turned to sneer at him. "Are you threatening me?"

King met his gaze and leaned in, his next words coming out low and menacing. "Absolutely. Touch him again, and I will break your fingers."

"You... you can't do that," Harold murmured, his Adam's apple bobbing nervously.

"I can, and I will. Very easily. I don't work for them, Harold, and I don't follow their orders. Now clean that up. You've made a mess all over the floor."

Harold dropped his gaze to the floor and water spilling down from his overflowing bottle.

Leaving a cursing Harold to clean up, King returned to Leo and resumed his seat. He spent the next two hours rereading the bunker's security protocols and evac plans. In that time, nearly every analyst—except for Harold—interrupted Leo to tell him off for something he'd done. How the hell was Leo supposed to get any work done if they interrupted him every five minutes? And why couldn't they simply discuss the matter with him rather than go on the defensive, demanding to know why he'd changed, deleted, or rewritten their code? They believed he was doing it because he thought he was better than them. Which he was. That's why he'd been brought in on this project in the first place. But Leo wasn't correcting them because he felt he was better. Their coding affected his work. From what King could understand of their tech speak, what they did checked Leo's work and tested each strand of code, and according to Leo, their coding wasn't just testing, but letting in hidden code. It was also obvious from the arguments, that a fair number of the analysts were trying to impress people like Bowers and those he worked for.

All the analysts were young, about Leo's age or a few years older, but not by much. They were ambitious, and King didn't hold that against them, but many of them were being blinded by whatever shiny promises Bowers had made. Promises King was certain Bowers wouldn't come through with. He'd seen it plenty of times before. In the end, they'd receive the usual "I'll see what I can do" or "I'll be sure to put in a good word," and then they'd be sent back to wherever they came from, feeling lost, wondering how they were supposed to go back to their old jobs after having experienced all this. King felt for them. They were made to feel special, but they weren't. Not enough to keep. In that, lay the problem with Leo. He *was* special. But no way was King going to let them keep him.

A man in a gray suit approached, and King shut off his tablet. Now what? For an agency that wanted to get this project done as quickly as possible, there sure were a lot of interruptions.

"Mr. Kingston. Please come with me."

"What's going on?" Leo asked, removing his headphones.

"Bowers would like to see you," the man told King as if Leo hadn't spoken.

King pressed his lips together, doing nothing to disguise his displeasure at the man's complete disregard of Leo. Standing, King turned to Leo and smiled warmly.

"Don't worry. I'm sure he just wants to check in. I'll be back as soon as I'm done." Or as soon as Bowers was done yelling at him some more.

Leo didn't look convinced in the slightest, but he turned back to his desk nonetheless, his body tense. He put his headphones back on and started typing again. Following the suit, King was led to the glassed-in boardroom at the end of the short hall where the barracks were. Inside, Bowers sat at the head of the table, and King congratulated himself on not rolling his eyes. The whole my-dick-is-bigger routine wasn't lost on him, and quite frankly it was getting old. He'd never been a fan of the game, and he wasn't about to start playing now. He took the seat Bowers indicated to his right.

"It's come to my attention that you've been... approaching our analysts."

King's suspicions were correct. It was *that* kind of meeting. Again. Whenever the urge struck, Bowers dragged King into a "meeting" to remind him who was in charge, in case King had forgotten. Because of Bowers, King had been stuck in this room from morning until just after lunch time. Did the guy have nothing better to do? "If by approaching, you mean threatening, then yes, I've been *approaching* your analysts. Or rather, one analyst in particular."

Bowers sat back in his chair and observed King. "I respect you, King. You're loyal, fiercely protective. It's how you're built. Green Beret, Special Forces, warrant officer. Now you command your own little army in the private sector. You boys have done really well for yourselves."

"Why, thank you," King said pleasantly. "That means a lot coming from you. I especially appreciate the condescending tone."

Bowers's expression darkened.

"Oh, I'm sorry. You thought I was being sincere. My fault entirely. The guys are always telling me I need to work on my delivery."

"I don't like you, Kingston."

"That's okay. You're not my type."

Bowers snorted. "Fucking Green Berets. Always so damned cocky."

Better cocky than an asshole. King didn't have to say the words; he was certain his expression said it for him.

Bowers leaned in, growling at King. "You stay the hell away from my analysts."

"Sure." King shrugged. "As long as you keep your analysts away from my guy."

"*Your* guy?" Bowers laughed. He jammed a finger against the table for emphasis. "Until he delivers the program, he's ours. You're a smart guy, Kingston. You don't need to watch the news to know we're in the middle of a cyber war. We've got spies on our shores and in our computers. If we're going to win this, we can't just even the playing field. We have to own it, and Leo's our secret weapon. This program has six moving pieces, two of which no coder has ever managed to complete. Until now. We're positive Leo can do it, but he hasn't even completed the first piece yet, and he's been here a month already. We need him to get this done."

King stood. "Then tell your analysts to back off and let him do his job."

"Where the hell do you think you're going? I didn't say this meeting was over."

King headed for the door. "If Harold harasses him again, you're going to be down one analyst."

A soldier threw the door open, and King's heart slammed in his chest. Something had happened to Leo.

"We have a problem."

"What happened?" King asked, already moving past the guy.

"The kid just fainted."

King took off toward the command center, ignoring

Bowers's anger-fueled orders. A group gathered around the couch King had been sitting on earlier.

"Out of the way," King barked, marching down the path they cleared for him. Leo lay on the couch, his face pale. Anger flared through King as he took a seat on the edge of the couch beside him. "What the hell happened?" He checked Leo's pulse. It was slow but steady. His skin was sweaty, but he was breathing.

One of the suits frowned down at him. "I don't know. Someone said he went to stand up, looked like he got dizzy, and sat back down. A couple of minutes later, he fainted on his keyboard."

King scanned Leo's workstation. "Has he had any water?"

Harold shrugged. "How the hell would we know?"

"Easy, has he moved from his desk?" King snapped.

Blank stares.

"Jesus H. Christ. Are you telling me none of you have paid even the slightest bit of attention to him?"

"We're not his babysitters," Harold said with a scoff.

"You don't seem to have a problem paying him attention when you're arguing with him." King turned to one of the soldiers. "Get me a cool damp cloth, a bottle of water, and a bottle or can of something sugary. Bring it to my room." Gently, King lifted Leo into his arms. Normally he wouldn't have moved Leo, but he wanted to get him away from there, from all the people staring at him, judging him. King carried him into his room rather than Leo's, since an earlier sweep revealed a listening device installed into the base of Leo's bedside lamp.

Carefully, he laid Leo on the bed, then placed a couple of extra pillows from the wardrobe under his legs to elevate them and get more blood flowing to his brain. He thanked the soldier who brought him what he'd asked for, then locked the door behind the man. It wouldn't be long before Bowers barged in demanding answers. He'd talk to the guy after he made sure Leo was okay.

Taking a seat on the edge of the mattress beside Leo, King placed the cool cloth on Leo's forehead. He understood now why the General had sent him. Leo wasn't just in danger from foreign threats. King had seen power struggles before, and he knew there were those who resented General de Loughrey for one reason or another. The man didn't get to where he was without making enemies, several within his own government, and definitely within this operation. By now, it was likely common knowledge in the intelligence community what the General had done, his attempt to hide his son from them. The government had a long memory, and those in positions of power were often the most petty and vindictive.

Punishing Leo for his father's actions was deplorable and doing it because they knew Leo would make an easy target was even more vile. Not anymore. This ended now. King brushed his fingers down Leo's soft cheek. "Leo. Wake up." If Leo remained unconscious for much longer, King would call in a medic. No sooner had the thought crossed his mind than Leo's long lashes fluttered, and he slowly opened his eyes. His brows drew together as he stared at the ceiling.

"What happened?"

"You fainted," King replied. "Let me help you sit up so you can have something to drink."

Leo groaned and shut his eyes tight. He put a hand to his head. "I feel like the Hulk is smashing my skull in."

"You're dehydrated." King stood and slipped his arm under Leo's shoulders, then gently helped him sit up. Leo carefully pushed himself back to sit against the headboard.

"Great. Because they don't hate me enough."

"They don't hate you," King said, handing Leo a bottle of water. "They simply don't understand you."

Leo glanced at him but didn't respond. He took the bottle of water, placed it to his lips, and took small sips at a time, like King instructed.

"When did you last eat?"

"Um, I had those Goldfish crackers you gave me this morning before your meeting."

It had become King's way to try to tempt Leo to get out of his shell. Every morning he had a packet of Goldfish crackers waiting for Leo when he emerged from his room.

"I mean a full meal."

Leo's cheeks turned that lovely shade of pink King was so fond of. *Wait.* King narrowed his eyes. "Have you not eaten anything today besides your crackers?"

Leo winced.

"What's the last meal you ate?"

"Um, dinner yesterday."

"What?" King snapped, then held his hands up in apology when Leo flinched. *Control.* He needed to center himself. *Calm. Control.* "Why?"

"Because they ordered sandwiches for lunch today, and I asked for no tomatoes, but I guess they forgot. I know I could have taken it out—they wanted me to take it out—but I can't. Sliced tomatoes make me feel sick. It's the slimy factor. I can't eat slimy food. Once the tomato was in there, sliding all over my food, I couldn't. I should have said I was allergic. It's easier that way, but I thought it would be okay. There were potato chips, but they were barbecue instead of plain, and they don't really sit well with my stomach, so I couldn't eat those either. I'm sorry."

"Don't apologize. It's perfectly understandable. I feel the same way about oysters. And okra. Don't care how it's cooked."

Leo looked up at him, his hopeful smile breaking King's heart, like maybe he wasn't such a freak if King felt the same way about food. "Really?"

"Yep. Not a fan of liver either."

Leo made a face. "Does anyone outside of Hannibal Lecter actually *like* liver?"

"What happened with breakfast?"

"Um...." Leo opened his mouth, the denial written all over his face until King gave him a pointed look. With a heavy sigh, Leo shook his head.

"Tomato?"

A nod.

"So you didn't eat? Why didn't they get you something else?"

"Because the first day they got my order wrong, Bowers got all pissed off and made a big production about it. Like I was some precious princess for daring to want what I ordered. I have issues, I know, and that translates to my food as well. I'm picky about what I eat, but I'm not unreasonable. There are certain things I won't or can't eat. Anyway, it was embarrassing, so I didn't ask again after. They seem to get my order wrong. A lot. When you showed up it stopped happening. Except when you're in a meeting."

Calm. Control.

Breaking Bowers's nose would feel great but getting arrested for it wouldn't help Leo. Speak of the devil. A fierce pounding at the door made Leo flinch, and King once again found himself in need of centering. He stood and unlocked the door, barely having enough time to step out of the way before Bowers thundered in like a charging bull.

"Are you fucking kidding me?" Bowers fumed. "Fainted?"

"Of course he passed out," King growled, putting himself between Bowers and Leo. "He's dehydrated and hasn't eaten anything since dinner yesterday. What the hell kind of operation are you running here, Bowers?"

"Hey, we buy him food. If he doesn't eat it, that's not my problem. What? You want me to feed him now? He's an adult."

"Who's being targeted by a bunch of petty, bitter individuals. He didn't ask to be here." King let the words hang in the air, and Bowers met his gaze. *That's right. I know what you did.* "You and your organization are the ones who want him here. *You* brought him into this, so it's your job to make sure he has what he needs to do it, whether it's equipment or food. If he asks for something, your job is to get it for him, no questions. I suggest you and your team sort yourselves out and stop fucking this up. Without him, there is no project, so it's time for *you* to get. It. Done."

Bowers gritted his teeth, his hands balled into fists. King remained silent and calm, waiting for Bowers to make the first move. He would not hesitate to put Bowers on the ground if that was how he wanted to play this. Nostrils flaring, Bowers snarled at Leo.

"Get back to work."

King crossed his arms over his chest. "That's not happening."

"Excuse me?"

"I'm sorry, were you not present for the conversation that just happened? Because I'm pretty sure your mouth moved and words came out. You're going to send someone to get him some food that he can eat, and then when he's feeling better, he'll get back to work. I would suggest that whoever deals with the meals around here pays better attention."

"Are you telling me how to do my job?"

King shrugged. "Do I need to?"

Bowers opened his mouth, but King cut him off, his voice low.

"Choose your next words carefully."

"You think I can't have you removed?"

It was an empty threat, and they both knew it. King removed his cell phone from his pocket and held it out to Bowers. "I have the General's personal cell phone number if you'd like to give him a call and let him know that the man he insisted be here to look after his son, and rightfully so, is being removed because he asked that you provide his son with food he can eat."

Bowers spun on his heels, left the room, and slammed the door behind him. With a heavy sigh, King turned, cursing under his breath when Leo got out of bed, a wave of dizziness almost knocking him over. King caught Leo and held him up. "What are you doing? You need to stay in bed until you've eaten and are feeling better."

"I need to get back to work," Leo insisted groggily. "I'll be fine."

"You can barely stand."

Leo sighed and let his head fall against King's chest. "I've caused you enough trouble."

"First of all, you haven't caused me any trouble at all. Second of all, you haven't done anything wrong, Leo. What you're asking for isn't outrageous. They should be taking better care of you." He ran a hand over Leo's head, his fingers slipping into the soft brown locks now that Leo's hat had fallen off when King had laid him down. Leo clutched at King's shoulders as King wrapped an arm around his waist and held him firmly. King felt Leo tentatively place his fingers on King's waist before he slipped his arms around King. It was almost as if he were afraid of getting too close to King. What was Leo afraid of?

Maybe the same thing you're afraid of.

King swallowed hard and tightened his hold around Leo. That's not what this was. He was just concerned for Leo. His affection toward the young man had nothing to do with personal feelings. He'd been sent to look after Leo, and that's what he was doing. Nothing more, nothing less. His duty.

"This op has been a disaster from the start," Leo murmured.

"Bowers probably wasn't the right guy for this assignment."

"Bowers?" Leo tilted his head, his big brown eyes searching King's for something. Why did Leo have to gaze at him like that? Like King held all the answers, could do anything, make everything better. No one had ever looked at him in such a way. Like he was everything they needed.

"Yes. Something like this requires patience, the ability to understand and adapt, which you'd think someone in his position would have spades of, but—"

"He's never met someone like me."

King laughed softly. Talk about an understatement. "I'll bet he hasn't." He shrugged. "His loss."

Leo's smile was radiant, and it thawed something deep inside King. Not wanting to let his thoughts wander into such dangerous territory, he opted for remaining silent.

"Thank you, King." Leo buried his head into King's chest. "I'm glad you're here."

King closed his eyes. What the hell was he doing? Putting his trust in anyone outside of Leo would be foolish, but the question he worried about most was, could he trust himself? "I think you should sleep in my room." That certainly wasn't a step in the right direction. Jesus.

Leo's eyes were so huge they looked like they might pop out of his skull. "What? Your room? Why?"

"For one, your room is bugged. Two, outside of you, I don't trust anyone here, which means I don't want you out of my sight."

Leo licked his bottom lip, and King stifled a groan. *Control. Calm. Control.*

"And, uh, where are you going to sleep?" Leo asked, his voice almost a whisper.

"Floor."

"What?" Leo's scandalized expression was sweet. "It's concrete."

"I've slept in worse places, believe me."

Leo frowned at him, his expression resolute. "No."

"No?" King tilted his head, puzzled. "What do you mean?"

Leo peered at him. "I mean, no. I'm not sleeping in your room if it means you sleeping on the floor."

King arched an eyebrow at him. "Where else am I supposed to sleep?" The bed was barely big enough for him, much less both of them, and why the hell was he even contemplating the possibility of sleeping in the same bed as Leo? Bowers would love that. March in here and find King spooning Leo. Christ, he wasn't helping himself *at all.*

"What if we bring in my mattress?"

King blinked at him. "Your mattress?"

"Yeah. You sleep in your bed, and I'll sleep on my

mattress on the floor. Deal? Great." Leo beamed up at him. "You have the best plans."

"Wait, what just happened?"

"We came up with a plan."

King's lips quirked up in the corners. "Is that what that was? Seemed like *I* came up with a plan, you shot it down completely, came up with your own, insisted it was my idea, and now we're bringing your mattress in here."

Leo squeezed King's biceps. "Actually, you'll be doing the heavy lifting. I mean, it's just a twin mattress. Not like it's a couch or anything."

King's laughter echoed through the room. He helped Leo over to the bed, shaking his head in amusement at him. "All right, smart guy. Sit your butt down. You need to rest." King pointed to the end of the bed. "You mind if I stay?"

"You want to stay?"

Why did Leo sound so surprised? Did he not believe King when he'd said he didn't want Leo out of his sight? "If that's okay with you. I want to make sure you're okay and that they bring you the right food order."

"Oh."

King peered at him. "That sounded like a disappointed *oh*. It's okay. I can go and come back once you're up."

"No, that's not it. I'd like you to stay."

"Okay." King sat at the end of the bed and pulled himself back until his back hit the wall. "So why the sad-puppy look?"

Leo grimaced.

"Talk to me, Leo."

"Nothing. It's stupid. I was kind of hoping you wanted to stay because of me." His eyes went wide. "I didn't mean that how it sounded. I meant maybe you wanted to spend time with me, like hang out. Oh God, that sounded even worse. How lame is that? Like, hey, do you want to come over to my house and play video games? Man, I suck at this."

"At what?"

Leo flailed his arms. "At this whole peopling thing." He winced and put a hand to his head. "Ow."

"I'm people?" King asked, holding back a smile. Did Leo have any idea how damned cute he was? He was nothing like any of the guys King had ever been with. Leo reminded him a little bit of Jay, his executive assistant. They were about the same height and build, but Jay was far feistier and sassier. People often underestimated Jay, believing his slighter frame and pretty features made him an easy target, until they pissed him off. By the time they realized they'd been messing with a tiger and not a kitten, it was too late. King hadn't seen Leo's fierceness yet, but he knew it was in there. There was a hell of a lot more to Leopold de Loughrey than even King knew about. *Yet*.

"Well, yeah. No, I mean, you're not regular people," Leo stammered. "Not that you're not normal or something, but what is normal anymore? I meant, you're... um, I'm not sure. What were we talking about?"

"How about we start with friend?"

Leo smiled. "Okay. Um, friend?"

King chuckled. "Yes?"

"What if you need to go to the bathroom in the middle of the night?"

King moved his gaze to the small patch of floor where the mattress would go, between Leo's bed and the bathroom. "Well, since you're going to be on the bed—did I forget to mention that in *my* plan? No? Anyway, try not to step on my head."

Leo blinked at him before bursting into laughter, the sound warm and infectious.

"Now get some rest. I'll be right here if you need me."

With a nod, Leo lay curled up on his side, his back to King, and within seconds, his breathing evened out and he was asleep.

Outside of his family, King had never felt so at ease around anyone. His head told him it didn't make any sense —Leo was a stranger—but his heart told him that wasn't true at all. Leo wasn't a stranger. King had been hearing about him for years. It was as if the young man had grown up around him without actually being there. Over the years, since King and his remaining brothers had returned, the General kept in touch with King. He was the only one who checked up on them, who offered to help in any way he could, the only one King believed when he expressed his deepest regrets. King hadn't accepted the man's guilt or his offers to pay medical bills, but he accepted stories of his family because they always lifted his spirits.

Even now, thinking back on those conversations made him smile. When King had been at his lowest, when the darkness seemed ready to swallow him up, as if knowing, the General would call and regale him with tales of Leo's latest adventures. The General had invited King to his home in Michigan several times, but as much as it pained him, the General was part of his past, a past he'd wanted to leave buried where it belonged. Never in a million years would he have expected to find himself here, with the young man who'd brought brightness to his days without even knowing it. Leo had been an extraordinary little boy who'd grown into an amazing man.

Leo let out a little sigh as he rolled onto his back, straightening his legs and draping them over King's. His lips were slightly parted as he slept, his hair a mess, and he'd forgotten to remove his glasses. King leaned in and gingerly removed them so they wouldn't get crushed. He closed one end and stuck the other into the collar of his shirt. Looking at Leo, he was just a regular guy. Brown hair, brown eyes, a slightly crooked grin, which made him appear younger than he was. But inside was a brilliance that could outshine the sun. Leo was kind, sweet, awkward, and... scared. He needed King, and King would do everything in his power to see Leo through this.

FOUR

DON'T STARE. Don't stare. Don't stare. And definitely don't drool!

Was this a test? It had to be. Had he expected King to sleep in his tactical pants and boots? He hadn't been thinking about it when King went into the bathroom with a change of clothes. It really wasn't fair. How was Leo supposed to think, much less sleep, when King was dressed in a snug long-sleeved gray henley and loose pajama pants that very clearly outlined his perfectly rounded ass. His feet were bare, and his hair was a mess from having washed it when he showered. King looked up, saw him, and stopped in his tracks. His eyes traveled over Leo, and Leo could have sworn he felt the caress as if it had been King's fingers. He shivered, despite not understanding the reason behind King's reaction. It couldn't be because of Leo. He wore what he always wore to bed, a comfy baseball tee and charcoal-gray pajama bottoms. King was the one obscenely dressed. Okay, not obscenely, but definitely distracting.

What did it say about Leo's social life that today had been one of the best days he'd had in forever? Maybe not that whole fainting incident, but everything that came after. As instructed, lunch had been brought to them, and the food had been amazing. All stuff Leo liked. They ate on the floor picnic-style and talked. King told him about his brothers—the four Kings, Jack, and Joker. Leo couldn't remember the last time he'd laughed so much. He'd never known anyone who was as easy to talk to as King. Leo didn't have to try to explain himself. Somehow King knew what he was trying to say, and making King laugh quickly became Leo's newest mission in life. There was something about seeing those little lines appear at the corners of King's bright blue eyes that brought Leo inexplicable joy.

After eating, King insisted Leo take another nap. If Leo were honest with himself, the one thing that made this whole experience bearable was in the form of a no-nonsense ex-Green Beret with a stare that could freeze the balls off you, and a smile that Leo could fool himself into believing appeared around him.

Earlier that afternoon, once Leo was feeling better, he'd gone back to work, and as promised, King never left his side. Even when Leo had to go to the bathroom, King accompanied him, waiting outside for him. He'd become Leo's shadow. No one harassed Leo, and Leo was able to finally immerse himself, coming out of his trance when he got thirsty or hungry, and then whatever he needed was there, King made sure of it.

The rest of the day flew by, and Leo would have stayed at his desk into the wee hours of the morning like he had every day before King's arrival had King not brought him out of his mind cave with a gentle touch to his cheek. Leo had blinked up at him, and at King's soft "Time for bed," Leo stood and followed him without hesitation. He hadn't even been fully awake, but he hadn't questioned King. Leo would follow him anywhere. And that was the problem, wasn't it? He didn't know anything about this man, only what few details his father had given him. No, that wasn't true. In the short time King had been here, Leo had learned more about King than he'd learned about the majority of the people in his life outside his father and sister.

King cleared his throat, snapping Leo back to the present. He really needed to stop daydreaming about the guy.

"I'm sorry, what?"

"I said the bathroom is all yours if you need it."

"Oh, um... thanks." Leo went into the tiny bathroom and closed the door behind him. When he finished his business, he washed his hands, brushed his teeth, and splashed cold water on his face. How was he supposed to get any sleep with King mere inches away?

Okay, get ahold of yourself. It's no big deal.

He was supposed to be keeping his distance. Squaring his shoulders, he stood tall and left the bathroom, his resolve flying out the window at the sight of King on his hands and knees, his ass in the air as he tried to get something from under the bed. *God bless America.* Why did he get the sudden urge to salute? He must have made some kind of noise, because King gave a start, and Leo winced as King hit his head against the underside of the bed. Cursing under his breath, King crawled back out. That image was forever seared into Leo's brain.

"You okay?"

"I'm fine."

"You keep saying that, and yet...."

King rubbed the back of his head. "Did you need something?"

Leo tried very hard not to smile. The guy was an

adorable grump. "I finished with the bathroom and was just going to get into bed. As much as I appreciate you checking under my bed in case Bowers is lying in wait to smother me in my sleep, it's not necessary."

"I dropped my phone. It bounced off the mattress and skidded under the bed." He waved the cell phone at Leo before placing it on the nightstand. "Ready to go to bed?"

Leo's stupid heart skipped a beat, and he didn't trust his voice to be steady enough to speak, so he simply nodded. He climbed into the tiny twin bed with creaky springs. Man, he missed his king-size mattress. *King-size.* He snickered.

"What?"

"Nothing. It's dumb."

"I'm sure it's not," King said as he lay down, his head facing the direction of Leo's feet, so Leo had an unobstructed view of King's face.

"I was just thinking about how I missed my bed, and how it's *king-size.*"

King's brows shot up near his hairline, and Leo's face burned.

"Wait. That came out wrong. I wasn't implying I want you in my bed," Leo said quickly. "Not that I wouldn't want you in my bed, because who wouldn't? I mean, look at you. Oh God." Leo pulled his blanket over his head with a groan. "That sounded way different in my head."

"I'm sure it did."

King's voice sounded... off. Taking a chance, Leo sneaked a peek from under his blanket, then threw it off with a gasp. "You're laughing!"

King lay on his side, turned away from him, his shirt stretching over his impossibly wide shoulders, shoulders that shook with laughter despite him very clearly shaking his head. "Nope."

"You totally are." Leo grabbed a pillow and hurled it at King's head, but all that did was make the handsome jerk laugh harder. King rolled onto his back and wiped a tear from his eye. Leo arched an eyebrow at him. "It wasn't that funny."

"I'm going to have to disagree with you on that. It was cute."

Leo sniffed. "Because that's what every guy wants to hear."

"You don't like to hear that you're cute? What's wrong with cute?"

"Has anyone ever told *you* that you're cute?"

King seemed to think about it. "In a nonsarcastic way?"

"Yes."

"No."

"See?"

"But I'm not cute. I'm scary."

It was Leo's turn to burst into laughter. "*What*?"

King stared at him. "I am."

Leo's snort was not delicate. "Okay. If you say so."

King sat up. "Wait. I don't scare you?"

"Why would you scare me? I mean, you've got this whole pouty, grumpy thing going on, but it's hardly scary."

"I don't pout."

"Oh my God, you so do! You're doing it right now."

King scoffed. "I think you've been staring at that computer screen for too long." He lay down, rolling his eyes at Leo's snicker.

At the silence that filled the room, Leo turned to check King hadn't fallen asleep. He was gazing up at the ceiling, lost in thought.

"I really don't scare you?"

"You can be intense at times, but usually that's when someone's being an ass-hat. I feel safe around you. Isn't that part of your whole reason for being here with me? I don't think my dad would send someone to look out for me who scared the crap out of me. He knows me better than that."

King's lips spread into a wicked grin. "Like the time he sent one of his men to pick you up from his office after his meeting ran late, and you punched the guy in the balls."

Leo barked out a laugh. "Oh my God! Poor guy. In my defense, I was twelve, and my dad sent freaking Sven the Gargantuan Viking to pick me up. I mean, the dude walks up to me and growls 'Leopold de Loughrey?' And my little twelve-year-old brain goes into overdrive, thinking this guy's about to kidnap me and sell my organs or something, so yeah, I screamed and punched him in the nuts." King was laughing again, and Leo joined in before turning to face King. "Wait, my dad told you about that?"

"Does it feel like we've known each other longer than we have?"

"Now that you mention it...." Leo hadn't wanted to bring it up, thinking it was just him being stupid.

"My familiarity with you, Leo, comes from years of your dad telling me stories about you."

Leo bolted upright. "What?"

"Yep." King smiled warmly, his gaze on the ceiling. "Your dad and I used to talk all the time, especially when I got back. He'd call to check on me and the guys, and I'd mostly listen. I think it started because I didn't want to talk about what happened, or anything else, for that matter. I think he felt I needed to hear... something. So he'd start talking about you."

His dad had talked about him to King? "I'm not quite sure how to feel about that."

"Far be it from me to tell you how you feel, but if I were you, I would feel pretty damn good."

"Oh?"

"You helped me heal."

Leo lay down, his hand under his cheek as he studied King. He couldn't imagine the guy being anything other than fearless. Indestructible. How had hearing about Leo's weirdness helped? As if reading his thoughts, King spoke up, his words low and rough.

"Could you turn off the lamp?"

"Sure." Well, guess that's that. Leo turned off the light, and after a moment, King spoke up again.

"When we got back, it was rough. We were all so angry, in a world of pain, on our own. I knew I had to do something. Watching my brothers tear one another apart, tearing themselves apart, was too much. I'd already lost men I cared about. I wasn't going to lose my best friends. I went to each of their places—had to actually break into Ace's apartment because he wouldn't let me in—and pack their shit up. Red tried to punch me in the face when I showed up at his place."

Leo cursed under his breath but remained silent. This couldn't be easy for King to talk about, and Leo had a feeling he didn't open up about those years with just anyone. His heart squeezed, knowing King was telling him.

"I went one at a time, forced them into my truck, and drove them to my house. I made my sister stand guard at the door, because as angry as they were, I knew they would never hurt her. According to Ace, *she's* the real scary one. Anyway, I got them all in my house and told them if they tried to make a run for it, I would shoot them in the leg. I wasn't kidding either. Red was a medic; he could patch them up."

King let out a heavy sigh Leo felt down to his bones. He blinked back his tears, unable to imagine what it must have been like.

"The months that followed were some of the hardest in my life. Maybe even harder than our time in the service. Red's PTSD was getting worse, and he was refusing treatment. Ace and Lucky were at each other's throats all the time. Joker was a ticking time bomb waiting to go off, and when he did, things got bloody. He's small, but he's dangerous. Jack got quiet. Too quiet. He'd lock himself in his room and not come out. It terrified me that he'd try and hurt himself while I was trying to keep the other four from killing one another."

"What changed?"

"I took them to see the families of our fallen brothers. Don't get me wrong, they were livid with me about it, but at that point, I'd had enough. Months of burying what I was feeling was taking its toll. I told them that we didn't leave our brothers behind while they were alive, so what made them think we'd leave them behind in death?"

Leo wiped at his eyes and sniffed. "What did they say?"

"I think that's when we realized that we may have survived, but we weren't living. Our brothers were gone, their families grieving, willing to give anything to have them back, and what were we doing with the gift of life we'd been granted? We were hurting each other, cursing the world and everyone in it. After that, Red let me help. He still wasn't happy about it, and tried to quit several times, but I wouldn't let him. The rest of the guys started getting help as well, and we were finally using our words instead of our fists. From there, life improved for us. During all that, your dad would call, usually when I was at my lowest, as if he knew, and he'd talk about you." King's voice was so soft Leo had to strain to hear him. "When it felt like the darkness was closing in on me, there you were."

The room went quiet, and Leo knew King had fallen asleep. He closed his eyes, his words a whisper in the darkness.

"I'm still here."

———

BLARING alarms and a beaming red light startled Leo awake. He would have fallen out of bed had two strong hands not grabbed his arms. Not fully awake, Leo opened his mouth to scream when King put a hand over his mouth and leaned in, his now familiar scent soothing Leo.

"Shhh, it's just me," King whispered hoarsely, turning the lamp on. He handed Leo his sneakers. "Quick, put these on."

"What's going on?" Leo's heart pounded fiercely in his ears as he grabbed his sneakers from King and pulled them on, his eyes going wide when King lifted the gun Bowers had given him and checked the magazine. Why would King need a gun? "What's happening?"

"I don't know, but we need to get you out of here."

"What? Why?" Gunfire made Leo jump, and he scrambled out of bed, nearly tripping over the blanket he was tangled in. King caught his arm and steadied him, then pulled Leo behind him. He edged them to one side of the door before turning and putting his free hand on Leo's shoulder.

"Stay close to me, and whatever happens, you do exactly as I say, okay?"

Leo nodded fervently, his pulse skyrocketing when King raised his weapon. This couldn't be happening. Swallowing hard, Leo stayed close to King as he cracked the door open, the terrifying sound of gunfire and screaming meeting Leo's ears. King put a hand to Leo's chest and gently pushed him back. Taking the hint, Leo moved farther into the room.

"What is it?"

"It looks like they've gathered the analysts into the boardroom. There's an armed guard keeping watch. He's not one of ours. Stay here. I'll be right back."

"King, stop," Leo urged, grabbing King's arm. "You can't go out there."

"It's okay, Leo. This is what I do, remember?"

"That right? People shoot at you all the time at the day job, do they? I bet your vibranium shield comes in real handy when you take that slow-motion swan dive into a shower of bullets. Must be nice being an enhanced supersoldier. Oh, wait."

King arched an eyebrow at him. "Sarcasm. Really?"

"It seemed appropriate. You're not going to listen to me, are you?"

"I promise you, I'll be right back. Lock this door behind me, and don't open it for anyone but me."

Before Leo could protest further, King took off. Leo should have listened, but he couldn't stand the thought of King going out there on his own. Peeking out, he watched, mesmerized as King placed his gun in the waistband of his pants. He ran in a crouch while the gunman was turned away, then hid behind the covered section of the boardroom's outside wall. After edging closer to the door, King opened it and paused as if to check whether the guy had seen and would charge out to investigate, but the guy was still turned away. King peeked in, then moving silently, he sneaked up on the guy and grabbed his head. In a violent move Leo had only ever seen in the movies, King snapped the man's neck before the guy even knew what was happening.

Leo stifled a gasp as King caught the dead man and dragged him off to the side so he couldn't be seen from the open door. He snatched up the automatic rifle, said something to the analysts, locked the door, closed it behind him, and hurried back to Leo, his scowl deep.

"Didn't I tell you to stay inside and lock the door?"

"I was worried about you."

King sighed. "Leo—"

"What about them?" Leo asked, motioning toward the roomful of analysts.

As King removed his cell phone from his pocket, Leo wondered who he was calling at a time like this.

"Bowers? We can argue about it later. The analysts are in the boardroom. The guy guarding them is dead. Of course he wasn't one of yours. Because I know what I'm doing, and that includes getting Leo out of here. I need you and your guys to cover us. You'll see us." King hung up, then tucked the phone back into his pocket. He motioned for Leo to follow him into the empty corridor.

"You killed that guy."

"Before he could kill any innocent civilians."

"Why didn't you just put him in a choke hold or something?"

"Because I didn't want him firing his weapon, sounding the alarm, and getting people shot in the process."

Made sense. What the hell was happening, and why were they going toward the shooting?

"King?" Leo asked, feeling like he was going to be sick. It suddenly registered why they were heading toward the danger. The evacuation exit was on the other side of the command center. But King wasn't wearing a vest or any kind of protection. What if he was hurt protecting Leo? What if he was *killed*?

Leo tried to push down the fear that threatened to cripple him. He followed King as he moved toward the command center but made the mistake of peeking around King's shoulder to see the group of armed men flooding through the main door. Oh God, those men were here for *him*. The reality of what was happening was enough to freeze Leo in his tracks. If those men took him, he'd never see his family again. He'd never see King again. Hell, he would never see the light of day again. They would torture him or find a way to force him to do what they wanted—like use people he cared about.

"Leo." King dragged Leo against the wall. "Breathe, sweetheart. We need to get you out of here."

Terror spread through Leo. "I won't go with them. I'd rather die."

"That's enough," King snapped, startling Leo. "I won't let them take you, but I need you to help me out here."

"There's so many of them." Leo closed his eyes and tried to breathe. How had they gotten in? It was wrong, all wrong. This wasn't supposed to happen. They'd given him their word, stated that this was the most secure place for him. He should have known better. How many times was he going to fall for their lies? Then it hit him.

Someone had betrayed them.

It was the only explanation. No one could have bypassed their security. They'd received no alerts until it was too late, and the facility had been breached.

"Bowers and his men will take care of those guys. I'll

take care of you." King cupped his face, stroking his thumb over Leo's cheek. "Look at me."

Leo forced his eyes open. He wrapped his hands around King's wrists, needing to feel him, his strength. "King...."

King swallowed hard, his eyes intense. He dropped his gaze to Leo's lips before moving it back to Leo's eyes. "Stay with me."

Leo nodded at the soft plea. He couldn't give any more thought to the meaning behind those words outside of their current situation. King turned, peeked around the corner, and seeming to make eye contact with someone, motioned straight ahead and nodded.

"Bowers is going to cover us. Ready to run for it?"

"No, but surviving sounds really good to me, so let's do it."

King took Leo's hand in his, their fingers laced together, as he raised his free hand and the gun he held. They darted out from behind the wall to an uproar of deafening shouting and shooting, but Leo stayed by King's side and ran. He caught a string of shouting, stunned when he recognized it as... Russian? Armed men had taken cover behind the analysts' workstations while Bowers, his men, and military personnel took cover behind the remaining workstations opposite the intruders, as well as behind the server wall. As per his word, Bowers and his men covered them.

Two men jumped in their path, but before they could take aim, King had taken them down—one shot each to the head. He hadn't hesitated, just pulled the trigger. They rounded the corner of the command center toward the emergency exit that led to another gray corridor and a set of concrete stairs that would take them to street level.

"Holy shit!" Leo stumbled, nearly plowing into King from behind when he stopped abruptly.

A group of six men blocked their path. The larger of the men pointed his gun at King. "Hand him over," he snarled.

King subtly moved his body, and Leo recognized it for what it was. He was taking a fighting stance. "Come and get him."

"What? Are you crazy?" Surely King could see they were outnumbered. Before Leo knew what the hell was going on, King had shoved the gun at him.

"Shoot anyone who tries to touch you."

Leo's protest died on his lips as the men charged King. He took several steps back, and tried to take aim, but he was too scared of hitting King, seeing as Captain America decided he was going to fend off six guys at once. Leo had grown up around soldiers all his life. He'd seen them train but never seen any of them in action. He'd certainly never seen a Green Beret fight. It was incredible and frightening at the same time. There was no holding back, each move made to cause as much pain as possible, each move designed to take out his enemy—a punch to the solar plexus, a jab to the throat, a kick to the side of a knee. King clapped his hands hard against one guy's head over his ears, and the man screamed before falling over. The sound of bones breaking, snapping, bodies hitting the ground in a bloodied heap had Leo's stomach churning.

With four on the ground, King ducked under one guy's punch, and when he came up brought his palm up with him, striking the guy under his chin. The blows reverberated through the room, and Leo stood frozen as the last guy hit the floor in a lifeless heap. Wiping blood from his nose like it was nothing, King marched over to Leo, took the gun out of his hand, grabbed his wrist, and hauled him toward the exit.

"We'll talk about it later," King said, not even sounding

breathless.

What was Leo supposed to say to that? "Sure, how about we find the nearest Starbucks, you buy me a Strawberry Acai Lemonade Refresher and then tell me about all the dead guys."

"If you have a better way of dealing with trained mercenaries sent to kidnap you, by all means please share."

"Sarcasm? Really?" Leo asked, throwing King's words back at him.

"Come on, smart guy." King pulled Leo in front of him and gave him a gentle push when they reached the stairs.

With a grumble, Leo climbed until they reached the top. King squeezed in next to him and entered his security code into the panel, then opened it up so the system could scan his retina and finger. The door clicked, and King carefully opened it, keeping Leo behind him. It was chilly out, but not enough for them to look out of place due to their lack of outerwear.

"Where are we?" Leo asked, looking around and seeing nothing but trees and water. The door they'd come out of was several feet away from the rest of the building, in the ground, and concealed by grass and shrubbery.

"According to the evac plan, that street there should be Memorial Parkway, so if we make a right at the end of it onto South 3rd Street, then Laurel Street and a left onto River Street, the Boathouse Marina won't be far. We're looking at roughly a five-minute walk."

"What's at the Boathouse Marina?"

King's expression was oh so serious when he answered, "Boats."

"Has anyone informed you, you're a sarcastic ass sometimes?"

"Me? I'm a fluffy bunny, remember?"

"The words *fluffy* and *bunny* should never be used in reference to you. I've certainly never said the words *fluffy* nor *bunny*."

"What words would you use to describe me, then?" King led him down Memorial Parkway toward the side of the street lined with trees. "Keep in mind I killed nine guys for you."

"Wow. You just threw that out there, huh? What do you do for your second date? Take down a small dictatorship?"

"Date? Is that what that was?" King moved Leo to his left, so he was protected by the trees and King. "I was thinking along the lines of dinner and a movie, but if taking down a small dictatorship is what does it for you, I can oblige. Not sure what I can do for our third date to top that."

Leo stopped in his tracks and turned to poke King in the chest. "You know, you're not cute."

King's smug smile shouldn't have given Leo butterflies in his stomach, but it did. "Told you."

With a frustrated grunt, Leo stormed off, ignoring King's amused chuckle.

"You shouldn't tease like that," Leo grumbled when King ran in front of him and stopped him, his brows drawn together in concern.

"Wait a second. You're upset."

Leo crossed his arms over his chest, grunting petulantly. "No."

"Why are you mad? Is it because of what I said about killing those guys? I'm sorry, I guess my sense of humor can be a little dark, though most people would argue I don't actually have a sense of humor."

"I don't know what it says about me, but that's not why I'm mad."

King's frown deepened. Realization seemed to dawn on

him, and his expression grew dark. "You're mad about the whole date thing."

Leo shrugged, his gaze off to the side. "It's not so easy for some of us, you know? We can't bench-press ponies or put together an explosive device with a paper clip and gum wrapper."

"I can't do that. That would be Red and Jack."

Leo arched an eyebrow at him. It was good to know King wasn't perfect, especially with his urge to strangle the man. If he could even wrap his hands around the man's thick neck.

"I'm sorry." King cupped Leo's cheek. "What makes you think I was teasing you?"

"Um, have you seen you?"

"I have," King replied, turning and starting to walk away. He stopped, and with a sigh, Leo caught up to him. "I'm not the catch you seem to think I am, and before you argue with me, I'll once again remind you I just killed nine men, and I won't lose sleep over it either."

They headed down Laurel Street, sticking close to the trees on the brick path. It was quiet, not a soul around at this time of night. Leo would have jumped at every shadow that moved were King not with him.

"That doesn't make you a bad person."

"You're right. It makes me a fucked-up person. That's fine. I made peace with my demons long ago."

"What?" Leo grabbed King's arm and stopped him. "You're not fucked-up. Those guys were going to kidnap me and send me who the fuck knows where, and then torture me, or who knows. You didn't just risk your life for me; you saved me. Those weren't good men. I'm not the morality police here, and I'm not about to judge a guy, but when they accepted money to destroy another human being, they have no one to blame but themselves when the consequences come to bite them on the ass."

"Some of those men could have been desperate, families to take care of."

"So mercenary and kidnapper are the only options? Bullshit." Leo cupped King's face and met his gaze. "You're not like them, so stop it."

King turned away from him and started walking again. "You know what I was doing before your father approached me about coming here to help?"

"What?"

"I was in London. Hunting a man. I spent weeks doing surveillance and reconnaissance on this guy. Finally I followed him home, tortured him, and forced him to come back with me to the US, then handed him over to the FBI. Your dad was waiting for me on the tarmac."

Leo glanced at King as they walked. "There's way more to that story than you're telling me. Who was the guy? I'm guessing you didn't turn him over to the FBI for jaywalking. He did something to you." *No, that wasn't King.* "He did something to someone you care about."

"He hurt someone I've come to consider family."

"And?"

"He hurt a lot of other young men."

Leo didn't need King to explain what that meant. "So he got away with it, was in London, and you convinced him to turn himself in."

"By torturing him."

"I'm sorry, am I supposed to feel bad for him? Sounds to me like the guy was a fucking rapist and should have had his dick ripped off and fed to the sharks."

King stopped walking and stared at him. "That was... surprising."

"Why? The man was a monster, and if you hadn't stopped him, who knows when it would have ended. Am I supposed to see you as some kind of psychopath vigilante, because as far as I'm concerned, you're a hero."

"No," King snapped, thrusting a finger at him. "You get that idea out of your head right fucking now. I've killed and hurt people. I am *not* a hero."

Leo could be just as stubborn. "You are to me, so you're out of luck there, soldier."

King looked like he had a few choice words for Leo but smartly decided to keep them to himself. They were almost to the boathouse when King's phone rang. He quickly picked up.

"Yeah? And you expect me to believe that?"

Leo stayed where he was as King walked off to growl quietly at whoever was on the other end of the phone. It was most likely Bowers. Leo couldn't hear what King was saying, but whatever it was, was not pretty. A couple of minutes passed before King hung up and headed back to him.

"Come on."

"We're going back?"

"The bunker has been secured."

"Are you kidding me?" Leo stopped in his tracks. "I'm not going back there. What? They just expect me to sit at my bullet-ridden workstation and pretend none of that happened? I can't work there, King. Even if the situation is contained, that place was supposed to be a top-secret location. Whoever sent those men knows I'm there. You think they won't try again? What about the innocent people working in the building? The ones who have no idea they're sitting on a landmine? If something happens to them because of me, I won't be able to live with myself."

"Okay, okay," King soothed, taking hold of his arms and running his hands over them until Leo let out the breath he hadn't realized he'd been holding. "Do you need to be in the same room with the analysts to work on the project?"

"No. Anything pertinent shows up on my system. It's just for security." He scrunched up his nose. "So much for that."

"What about the computer you're creating the project on. Does it have to be the one in the bunker?"

Leo shook his head. "I use a system I created called Jarvis. It's also installed on my laptop and computer at home. I installed it on the computer at the bunker. I'm the only one who can access it."

King seemed to consider his words. "Do you live in a house or an apartment?"

Leo's brows shot up. "I'm sorry?"

"Your home, Leo. Tell me about where you live."

"Um, I live in a condo on the west coast of Florida."

"Where?"

"Indian Shores. On the beach."

"What floor is your apartment on?"

"The fifth and sixth floors. There's only six floors and eight apartments in the whole building."

"So you're at the top. Private beach?"

"Yes."

King handed Leo the black phone he'd been given. "Show me."

"Sure." Leo first checked the phone's connection was secure—because fuck Bowers—and brought up his condo, then handed the phone back to King, who inspected the double screen containing the map of Leo's condo and the floor plans.

"Perfect. Let's go."

"I thought we weren't heading back in?"

"We're not." King put the phone to his ear. "Meet us outside the evac exit." He hung up, and when they arrived at the door that led to the bunker, Bowers was there waiting for them.

"Wait here," King said, leaving him a few feet away to meet Bowers, not that Leo wouldn't be able to hear them from here. Well, unless they whispered.

What was going on? Baffled, he stood back, tapping his fingers against his leg as he waited. Their muffled voices soon turned into angry growls. Unable to keep his curiosity at bay, Leo silently moved a little closer. Bowers hissed furiously at King, whose stoic expression gave nothing away.

"Are you out of your fucking mind?"

"Do you want this project done or not?"

"You really think I'm going to let that kid out of my sight? Do you realize what would happen if anyone got wind of what he was working on or what he's capable of?"

"Which is why we'll take every precaution necessary to keep him safe. That's why you're here, right? Leo isn't comfortable in this environment, especially now."

"Not comfortable?" Bowers's face went up in flames. "Do you have any idea how much this project is costing? What we're in the middle of here?" King opened his mouth, only to be cut off by Bowers. "Of course you don't, and do you know why? Because you're nothing but a glorified nanny. You were brought in to make the de Loughreys happy and cooperative. You're here to make him chocolate milk and tuck him in so he can do his fucking job. So why don't you go back downstairs, continue your little slumber party, and stop pretending you're anything more than what you are." Bowers leaned in to King and poked him in the shoulder, his growl menacing. "Dispensable."

Leo balled his hands into fists at his sides. *That no-good son of a bitch! How dare he talk to King like that!*

King's eyes narrowed. "Yes, Washington made that very clear when what was left of my unit and I returned home."

"Maybe you should have done a better job leading."

"Fuck you," Leo spat out as he marched over to stand beside King, aware of King's stunned expression. "How dare you be so disrespectful! You should be ashamed of yourself." He was so angry he was practically bouncing. "This man sacrificed for our country, for *you*, and you're going to treat him like shit?" Leo stepped up to Bowers, his eyes narrowed and his voice a low growl. "You say one more disparaging remark against him, and I'm done. Good luck telling your superiors that you screwed up their top-secret project. Now pack up my shit, because I'm going home."

Bowers stared at him before letting out a harsh laugh. "Are you fucking kidding me? You really think I'm going to let you go anywhere?"

Leo crossed his arms over his chest and arched an eyebrow. "That's fine. I'll wait while you call up your boss and explain why I refuse to work. Don't forget to mention that little detail regarding your super-secret squirrel bunker being breached."

"You think I won't find someone else?' Bowers took a step toward Leo, but King placed himself between them, shielding Leo. Bowers leaned around him, thrusting a finger at Leo. "When I do, I'll throw your ass in a hole where no one will find you."

Leo smirked at him. "Go ahead." He motioned to the bunker around them. "Because I'm sure all this is for a guy you could easily replace." He folded his arms over his chest again and grinned smugly. "You're screwed, and you know it. Now if you want your program, you're going to put together a team, move me back into my apartment, and behave like a good little suit."

Bowers was a volcano ready to blow. One more prod from Leo, and the guy would erupt black smoke and lava. What was wrong with Leo? He'd never been so bold. Provoking the schoolyard bully was never a good idea, but damn if he didn't feel invincible. Was it because he knew King would protect him, keep him safe? Or because he was getting tired of being pushed around. At the same time, he didn't want to do anything that would put King in harm's way more than he'd already done. Leo let out a sigh and addressed Bowers.

"Look, we both want the same thing. You want your project, and I want my life back. I can't work here. I've been telling you that from the beginning, and it's not because I'm trying to be a pain in your ass. I can't, especially now. You've read my file. I'm not trying to be difficult. It's the way I'm wired. Get me home, and I'll get it done."

Bowers seemed to be mulling over Leo's words, when King cleared his throat.

"I also want to bring my team in on this." Before Bowers could protest, King held up a hand to stop him. "I want to keep Leo safe as much as you do, and quite frankly, I don't trust you or your organization. Your black site was breached. You have a traitor in your midst."

"Excuse me?" Bowers fumed.

"Cut the bullshit, Bowers. How else do you think they got in there? My men are all former Special Forces, which might mean shit to you, but security is our business, and had we been in charge, you bet your ass that clusterfuck would never have happened. I want my guys in the building."

"Anything else I can do for you?" Bowers asked sweetly.

"Would you like me to serve you breakfast in bed? Make you an ice cream sundae? Rub your feet?"

Leo narrowed his eyes. "How would you feel about sucking—"

King slapped a hand over Leo's mouth and crushed Leo against his side. "Just do it, Bowers."

With a low growl and several curses, Bowers reached into his pocket, pulled out a set of keys, and tossed them at King. "Behind the church across the street. Get in the back and wait. I'll send a driver." With that he stalked off and disappeared through the bunker door.

King looked down at Leo. "You going to behave yourself?"

Leo narrowed his eyes, and King gave him a pointed look. *Fine.* He nodded, and King removed his hand.

"That guy's an asshole," Leo growled. "Don't think I'm going to forget what he said to you. Let's see how he likes it when he wakes up in the morning and finds himself with several gay porn site subscriptions. His inbox will be flooded with so many wieners he'll have to change his name to Oscar Mayer."

King blinked at him before throwing his head back and laughing, the sound was booming and made Leo smile. He threw an arm around Leo's shoulder and led him across the street to the vehicle behind the church. "Looks like you're going home."

The words sank in, and a wave of happiness washed over Leo. Before he knew what he was doing, he threw his arms around King and hugged him.

"Thank you."

A heartbeat later, King returned the embrace, somewhat awkwardly—like he wasn't accustomed to hugging or something—but that just made Leo's heart swell all the more because this wasn't the first time King had held him.

"No. Thank *you*."

Leo knew he shouldn't get too close to King. Once the project was done, King would be returning to his life, and Leo would… still be Leo. Maybe King meant it when he said they were friends. It would be more than Leo could have hoped for.

FIVE

A RUSTLING SOUND caught King's attention, and he chuckled as Leo opened a giant yellow bag of red Swedish Fish. So that's what Leo made the driver stop for.

Leo held the packet out to King. "Swedish Fish?"

"Why not." King reached into the bag and grabbed a couple of the jelly sweets and popped them into his mouth. "Is it the shape or the taste?"

"Both. Who doesn't love Swedish Fish? It even has a TV series of sorts." Leo removed his phone from his pocket, tapped away at the screen, then leaned over to show King. It was some kind of online show with canned laughter. It was very short with the next one starting right after.

"What... what did I just watch?"

"The Swedish Fish is their new roommate."

"Yeah, I gathered that from the episode title. My question, I suppose, is more of a why? As in why does that exist?"

Leo shrugged. "Why does anything exist? I suppose you mean what purpose does it serve, and the logical answer would be that it serves no purpose, but in truth, it's just fun, so I guess it does have a purpose. You might not understand it, but for those who do, it does something for them, no matter how small, and that's what matters, right? Taking joy in the little things."

King couldn't argue with that.

They were still in the back of one of Bowers's black Suburbans, the windows tinted pitch-black. Leo hadn't stopped smiling since they left. He was happy, which in turn made King happy, and he wasn't about to delve any deeper into his thoughts than that. Considering what had happened back at the bunker, Leo seemed surprisingly calm. King supposed knowing he was going home was contributing to Leo's current cheerful state.

Once Bowers had resigned himself to the fact they'd be moving Leo, an entirely new security plan was put in place—one that included the four Kings, Jack, and Joker. King had meant what he'd said. He didn't trust Bowers, the NSA, and anyone else involved with this op, especially now. He had no intention of leaving Leo's side, which meant he needed his brothers-in-arms to keep an eye on the building and surrounding area, as well as any chatter that might pertain to Leo. Several of the men in the bunker had spoken Russian, but until Bowers looked into it, there was no telling who'd sent them after Leo.

As if reading his thoughts, Leo spoke up. "Do you think he'll tell us?"

King highly doubted it. "He'll tell us a load of information that will essentially give away nothing."

Leo snorted. "Sounds about right."

"Can you access the bunker's security feed from your computer without alerting Bowers?"

Judging by Leo's uninspired expression, King would hazard a guess that he'd asked a stupid question.

"Right. I want you to play the footage for Jack. He was our communications sergeant. If anyone can get us some intel on who those guys were, he can."

"Sure. You all really are like brothers, huh?"

King nodded, returning Leo's smile. What was it about Leo that made King feel so... light? He never smiled this much, but when Leo looked at him, those pink lips pulled into a soft expression, King couldn't *not* do the same. Well damn. Ace was going to give him so much shit.

"Pains in the asses, but I wouldn't trade them in for anything. Ace is a smartass who rarely shuts up. He was our weapons sergeant. Lucky, his cousin, was also a weapons sergeant. Together they're a force to be reckoned with. Red was our medical sergeant. He's the sweetest guy you'll ever know, so don't let his size intimidate you. Jack, like I mentioned earlier, was our communications sergeant. You guys will probably have a lot to geek out about. Joker was our engineer sergeant. His temper is as explosive as the bombs he deals with. Just don't mention his height. He's very touchy about it. He'll be bringing his partner, Chip."

"Is Chip a Green Beret as well?"

King chuckled. "He could have been. He's Joker's furry companion."

"A bomb-sniffing dog? That's amazing."

"Chip is pretty special."

"So what's with the playing card nicknames?"

King chuckled. "One of our youngest brothers-in-arms, Pip, nicknamed everyone. We were always playing cards, and he'd accuse us of being cardsharps. Ace, Lucky, Red, and I were nicknamed after the king cards in a deck because we'd formed a special bond since the beginning. Even when we first met, it felt like I'd known them my whole life. We balance each other out."

Leo worried his bottom lip, his expressive eyes filling with sorrow. "Pip. He's one of the guys who didn't make it home?"

Shifting uncomfortably, King moved his gaze out the window. "Yeah. We lost half our ODA." He felt a gentle hand on his arm.

"I'm so sorry."

King couldn't bring himself to speak, simply patted Leo's hand where it rested on his arm. If Leo knew the truth of what had happened to King's unit, the guilt would eat away at him. Another reason Leo could never find out. If the General hadn't told his son, then it wasn't King's place to do it. He moved his hand and held up his personal phone to signal he had to make a call. Leo nodded and turned his attention back out his window.

Putting in a call to Ace's number, King placed his phone to his ear and waited for his best friend to pick up. Two rings in, and Ace answered, his voice filled with concern.

"Hey, everything okay?"

"Yeah, listen. I need you, Red, Lucky, Jack, and Joker to rearrange your schedules. I'm going to text you an address, and I need you all there as soon as possible." With Ace's phone not being secure, King made sure to give the address to a café in St. Petersburg. "A man named Bowers is coming to meet you. Listen to what he says and follow his instructions. I'll see you all soon."

Ace didn't ask questions. He was well-versed in government matters, as were the rest of their brothers-in-arms. The drive from the black site in Palatka to Leo's condo on the beach took a little under three hours. At this time of night, there wasn't much traffic on I-75 or the many back roads they took. King had remained vigilant, not liking the driver's choice in taking country back roads with little to no lighting, but Bowers had reached his limit. Rather than spending any more time arguing with the man, King had gotten them moving.

When they finally arrived at Leo's building, King got out first, telling Leo to wait while he did a quick sweep of the area. With the coast clear, he went around to Leo's door and opened it for him, keeping Leo close as they made their way into the building. Bowers and his team were already in place, showing how desperate the guy was to get this project completed.

The new security plan included taking over Leo's building. Since they were dealing with the NSA and the government, the building was declared to have structural problems requiring the occupants to leave. The condo owners were being compensated handsomely for however long it took to "fix the damage." Bowers's team would take up residence until Leo finished the project.

The entire building was filled with government agents going undercover as contractors. The condo just below Leo's would be occupied by the Kings, Jack, and Joker, and between the five of them, they'd work in shifts with one of them staying in Leo's apartment at all times with King and Leo. The ground floor apartment would hold the majority of the armed agents, the first line of defense should someone get past the hidden security around the building and make it inside. With all the hidden cameras installed in the building and around the property, if anyone decided to do something stupid, the Kings would see it coming.

Inside, the lobby was decorated in a classy beach theme, as he imagined most of the buildings in the area were. To the south of Indian Shores was Redington Shores, consisting of more residential areas, where Indian Shores tended to be more vacation rentals, but Leo's building was close enough to Redington that it was mostly residential. This time of year, folks from up north migrated south. Although Florida was somewhat cooler in the winter— seventy-degree weather instead of ninety-degree weather— with the exception of a week here and there of actual steep temperature drops, they had mostly warm weather. For those escaping the ice and snow, the beach was still inviting at seventy degrees. It was also perfect weather for theme parks. With two weeks until Christmas, no matter where you went, there was a flurry of people, traffic, and activity.

Leo inserted a keycard into the slot on the elevator panel, then pressed a sequence of buttons rather than simply pressing for the fifth floor. He smirked at King's raised brow. "I added a little extra security when I moved in. I'll give you and your guys the code."

"What if someone just presses for the fifth floor?"

"Then I get buzzed, and I can talk with whoever's in the elevator." He motioned up to the corner of the stainless-steel wall. "Camera. There's a security office in the building, which I imagine Bowers has already taken over. Though if they make it to the elevator, it means they'd been cleared by security and buzzed in at the front doors."

The elevator opened up into a hallway outside a set of steel doors. Looked like Leo had made quite a few changes when he'd moved in. The security panel outside Leo's front door was impressive. King couldn't imagine there were many homes with a security system that required handprint and retina scan identification.

King had studied the floor plan of Leo's penthouse condo. It was bigger than he'd expected at over seven and a half thousand square feet, with two floors, the second of which Leo used as his office. It was easily a second apartment, due to its nearly three-thousand-square-foot size and the fact it had its own small kitchen, bathroom, and balcony. The lower floor was expansive with a master suite and bathroom, three additional bedrooms, two and a half bathrooms, a media room, living room, dining room, breakfast area, several balconies, plenty of windows, a beachfront view, and laundry room.

The condo itself had stone floor tile, crown molding, and solid wood cabinets. It was decorated in rich browns, creams, and pops of black and gold, and was very tidy and uncluttered. King hadn't known what to expect from Leo's home, but he found himself frowning. The condo was gorgeous. It also resembled a showroom. Untouched. No framed photos, no art on the walls, no throw blankets or pillows. Nothing that so much as gave a hint to who lived there, which was at odds with Leo's homebody nature. How could someone who rarely left his home live somewhere that looked like no one had stepped foot in it in years. It was clean, which led King to believe someone came regularly to maintain the place.

"Very nice," King said, offering Leo a smile.

Leo surveyed the apartment and shrugged. "It came like this. My dad picked it out for me." He shifted uncomfortably. "I wanted to live somewhere quiet, but I'm not good with things like apartment hunting or decorating. It's a bit much, but my dad felt I needed space since I don't go out that often, but it's not the space, it's what's in it, you know?"

King nodded. He lifted his arm and Leo's bags. "Should I put these in your room?" The huge master suite was on this floor ahead of them to the left of the living room.

"Actually, I spend most of my time upstairs." He tapped his fingers against his leg. "I sorta... sleep there more than down here. Um, pretty much... always."

Puzzled, King followed Leo up the winding staircase to

the second floor. He froze at the top of the stairs. It was like entering a whole other world, a world that was all Leo. The space was warm and inviting, the colors, textures, and feel of it a perfect match for the vibrant young man. It was as if Leo had taken this space and created a nest for himself. A safe haven. It made sense, but at the same time left King completely baffled. Why not make the rest of the apartment his own? He'd essentially created a studio apartment for himself on the second floor. Why?

The floor was faux wood and the walls were painted a dynamic blue. Lighting ran along the left and right sides of the ceiling, giving the room a soft atmospheric glow. A huge flat-screen TV hung on the right wall, in front of it sat an extra-long black-and-white couch with blue throw pillows, and kitty-corner to that was a trendy black futon with white-and-blue throw pillows. A matching black-and-white coffee table was positioned in the center.

Against the wall opposite the trendy yet cozy living room area was Leo's computer station. A long, sleek, black desk held multiple monitors with a larger one mounted on the wall. Several gadgets lay in neat, tidy rows across the desk, along with a unique-looking keyboard, drawing tablet, and trackball mouse. Leo's chair was unlike anything King had ever seen, and it was clear why he'd had trouble working with the one they'd given him at the command center. This one resembled a slim recliner, and was currently reclined back with the footrest up, a cozy pillow on the headrest, and a fleece blanket draped across it.

Speakers were strategically positioned on the walls, and at the end of the expansive room was a set of sliding glass doors that pretty much took up the length of the wall. Outside, a balcony nearly as big as the upstairs area faced the beach. The balcony was the same length as the second floor and much wider, taking the shape of the rest of the building. You could easily fit a pool out there or land a small chopper. Unlike the downstairs area, this floor was filled with energy and life. Photographs of Leo and his family in elegant black frames had been painstakingly hung around the room. White bookcases on either side of the TV housed rows of books, comic books, and movie and comic book collectibles, including a statue of a giant gray Hulk being shot in the face with webbing by a tiny-by-comparison Spider-Man perched atop a lamppost.

King placed Leo's bag on the couch as the doorbell rang. He swiped his gun from the belt holster he'd gotten from one of the soldiers before he'd left.

"You really think the bad guys are going to ring the doorbell?" Leo asked, heading for the stairs. King quickly cut him off.

"Probably not, but I'm not taking any chances. Stay here."

"Okay." Leo headed for the kitchen, and King hurried downstairs. He checked the little screen by the door, relieved when he saw the guys outside. Holstering his gun, he opened the door for them.

"Wow. Real charmer that Bowers," Ace muttered as he walked past King into the apartment, followed by the others. King closed the door, then turned to Ace, whose scowl melted away, a grin appearing on his face as he approached King and brought him into a tight hug. "Missed your grumpy ass."

King grunted, but he returned Ace's hug. His chest swelled with pride as he greeted each of his brothers.

"What's going on?" Joker asked, looking around the apartment, his sharp blue-gray eyes taking in everything.

Chip sat obediently at his heels, tail wagging at King who scratched him behind the ears.

"Come with me." King led them upstairs. The bathroom door was closed, so he'd wait until Leo was done to explain.

"Nice setup," Jack pitched in, his gaze on Leo's desk. "Whose place is this? Bowers didn't say much."

Joker snorted. "Mostly a lot of bitching about how he didn't want us here, and something about pain in his ass?"

A soft clearing of the throat caught everyone's attention, and they all turned to Leo, standing by the kitchen counter. He waved bashfully. "Um, hi. That would be me. The pain in his ass."

"Everyone," King said, smiling as he held an arm out to Leo who, without skipping a beat, hurried over to King's side. King ignored his friends' wide eyes as they looked from Leo to King and back. "This is Leo. General de Loughrey's son."

The gasps were loud, and Ace's startled gaze flew to King's. "The General?"

King nodded. He turned to Leo, ready to introduce the guys, but Leo stopped him.

"Wait, don't tell me." He cocked his head to one side, studying the five men in front of him. They looked bemused but went along with it. "I'm going to say you're Red," Leo said with a chuckle, pointing to Red and his bright red hair.

Red smiled. "That's right. Though that's not why I got the nickname."

"You're right. It's because you're the King of Hearts."

Red blinked at him. "How'd you know?"

"You give off that gentle-giant kind of vibe."

Ace laughed, patting Red's shoulder. "That's Red all right. The jolly red giant."

Red elbowed Ace in the ribs, making him laugh.

"And you must be Ace. King of Spades."

"That's right. I see my reputation precedes me."

"I would not be so quick to think that is a good thing," Lucky teased.

"You're Lucky, the King of Clubs." Leo turned to the remaining two men. "You're Jack, and you must be Joker."

"He's good," Jack said, nodding his approval.

A bark made Leo jump, and he lowered his gaze to Chip, his smile going huge. "I'm sorry. I didn't mean to leave you out. You must be Chip."

Chip barked, and waved a paw at him in greeting, making Leo laugh. He turned to King, his smile reaching his big brown eyes. "And you're the King of Diamonds. Makes total sense."

"Oh yeah? How's that?" King asked.

"The whole diamond-in-the-rough thing." Leo didn't shy away this time, despite his flushed face. "Personally, I think you're great just the way you are, without all the polish."

The room fell silent, and King was aware of his brothers staring at him, jaws hanging open. He crossed his arms over his chest and glared at them. "You guys want me to throw you back in the ocean so you can join the rest of the fish?"

Leo laughed loudly, oblivious to everyone's stunned gazes on him. He snickered as he turned to King. "Oh my God, I just thought of the Swedish Fish video but with the guys there instead. Can you imagine?"

King barked out a laugh at the thought of Ace seeing a giant red Swedish Fish at the door. The guys visibly jumped, and Ace took hold of Red's arm before leaning in.

"What's happening right now? Red, I'm scared."

King rolled his eyes. "Ass."

Leo looked from King to Ace. "What?"

Ace shrugged. "Nothing. Seeing King laugh is like winter in Florida. Blink and you miss it."

Leo frowned. "What do you mean? He laughs all the time."

Oh God. King groaned and put a hand to his face. He was *never* going to hear the end of this.

Ace choked on air. "I'm sorry," he wheezed. "What?"

Leo shrugged. "Yeah. I've seen him laugh and smile a bunch of times."

Everyone's head snapped to King.

"What?" he growled. Thankfully, his friends were not stupid men, nor did they have a death wish, so they kept their mouths shut. King turned his attention to Leo. "Leo, these goofballs are my brothers, and I trust them with my life. I trust them with you. Do you know what that means?"

Leo nodded. "You trust them. That's all I need to know." He waved cheerfully at the guys. "It's so great to meet you. Thank you for your service."

The guys nodded their thanks, all of them clearly still reeling from that little truth bomb Leo had dropped on them. It wasn't like King *never* smiled or laughed. He pursed his lips in thought. Maybe it wasn't all the time, but he wasn't always a miserable grump. Was he? It was different with them. They were like family. He didn't have to pretend around them. Not that he pretended around Leo.

Ace stepped forward, addressing King. "Can I talk to you in private?"

Taking the hint, Jack jumped in, smiling widely at Leo. "Hey, you have a sweet setup. Mind showing me?" Jack followed Leo to his desk while King headed for the balcony. They stepped outside, and Ace slid the glass door closed behind him. It was a little chillier out here, what with it being almost three in the morning and the cool breeze coming in off the ocean.

King knew what Ace was going to say before he said it, so he put a hand up to stop him before the words were out. "My job is to look out for him and help him in any way I can."

"I don't even know where to start," Ace muttered, still stupefied.

"Don't hurt yourself."

"Fuck off. This is serious."

King sighed. "Usually it is when the NSA and the military are involved."

"Tell me how this happened." Ace took a seat in one of the comfortable-looking lounge chairs, and King dragged another chair closer to him.

"When I returned from London, the General was waiting for me at the airport. We took a ride, and he told me about a top-secret op involving an asset that wasn't cooperating. At first, he was asking me questions, seeking my advice on how to handle the situation, so I gave my input. That's when I discovered the asset was his son." King met his best friend's eyes. "He's scared for Leo, Ace. You know how these things go. Hell, we've lived it. The General needed to have someone on the inside looking out for Leo. None of these guys have his best interest at heart. Leo's nothing but a human computer to them. How could I say no?" King sighed. "They're forcing the General to retire."

"What?"

"Leo said it was punishment for keeping him hidden from them."

Ace cursed under his breath and sat back. He rubbed a hand over his face. "Shit. Makes sense. One thing you could never doubt when he talked to us was how much he loved his kids." He shook his head before meeting King's gaze. "And this thing between you and Leo?"

"There is no thing between me and Leo."

Ace tilted his head toward the glass doors. "Does he know that?"

"All I'm doing is what the General asked. Leo is a sweet guy. He's very smart but very vulnerable. He needs me."

"For how long?"

"I have no idea how long this op will take."

"That's not what I meant, and you know it." Ace also knew King wasn't going to discuss it, so he moved on to something else. It wasn't what King expected to hear. "How could the General ask you to do this after what happened? I know you, King. This is going to eat away at you."

King's heart felt heavy. "I'll have to deal with it. Leo's well-being is my priority."

"And if he finds out? What happens to his well-being then? What happens to *your* well-being?"

"He won't find out." King wouldn't let that happen.

"Really? Because from what I remember, the kid's a fucking genius. I mean, that's why he's in this mess, right?"

"He has no reason to go poking around, and I have no intention of broaching the subject with him. He's been through enough, and the last thing I want is to hurt him. Jesus, they came after him, Ace." King leaned forward. "The black site that was supposed to be secure was breached. That means they have a traitor among them."

"Shit, what happened? Did you guys get hurt?"

"No. I got him out of there."

Ace eyed him. "How?"

"Took them out."

Ace blinked at him. "Holy shit. You care about him."

"Of course I do. He's General de Loughrey's son."

Ace pressed his lips together in a thin line, his expression unimpressed. "You're really going to play this game with *me*?"

Shit. If there was one person who could see right through him, it was Ace. King cleared his throat. "It doesn't matter. I'm here to do a job, and when it's done, Leo goes back to his life, and I go back to mine." Ace opened his mouth, but King shook his head. "This conversation is over."

"Why, because you say it's over?"

"Yes."

"That's not how adult conversations work."

"And you're suddenly the expert on adult conversations?"

"First of all, fuck you. Second of all, that's not how this brotherhood works. You don't get to push us out. You're always there for us, but you never let us be there for you."

"What are you talking about?"

"You don't have to be the fierce protector all the time, shouldering the weight of the world all on your own."

"Yes, I do." King stood, feeling Ace's heavy sigh deep down in his soul. He'd lost enough people in his life that he cared about. He wasn't about to lose any more. Whatever it took to protect his family, he would do it, had done it. If that meant always being on his guard, keeping a certain distance, so be it. It was the price he paid for their safety.

Ace stood, blocking King's path to the door, his gold-green eyes filled with concern and heartache. His voice was quiet when he spoke, but the words hit King as if he'd shouted them. "It wasn't your fault."

"It was my decision."

"*Our* decision. We knew the risks, and we voted to do it anyway. You have to stop blaming yourself."

King pushed past Ace. They'd had this argument countless times, and in the end, it changed nothing. King had still failed, Red still had PTSD, and their brothers were still dead.

"Ward."

King stilled. He closed his eyes when Ace's hand came to rest on his shoulder.

"You're not alone. You have a family who loves you and wants nothing more than to see you happy. Please. You can't keep living like this, filling your life with nothing but work and guilt." Another heavy sigh before Ace dropped his hand, leaving King cold and empty. "Just... think about it."

The door opened, and Ace returned to the guys, all of whom stood around Jack and Leo as they argued over who was the bigger cyber nerd. The guys teased, laughed, and judged who "won that particular round of geek," as Joker put it. Ace said something about Jack, earning him a playful punch from their friend and a boisterous laugh from Leo. As if sensing King, Leo searched the room for him before his eyes landed on King. His smile widened, and for the first time in his life, King was uncertain. Was that how he'd been living his life? Was Ace right? Had guilt been the only thing driving him since his return?

It was true his time in the service had made him the man he was now, but outside of his demons, he had a good life. He was grateful for what he had and the people he shared his life with. It was probably all this talk about the General and his past that had him feeling so off-kilter. He'd just closed the door behind him when Leo appeared in front of him, his smile dazzling. He really was something special. Whoever ended up winning Leo's heart would be one lucky guy. He hoped they'd take good care of him, make him happy. Leo deserved to be happy. To be loved, and fiercely.

"Your friends are amazing. How do you guys get any work done?"

"What do you mean?"

"They're a freaking riot."

A riot. He supposed they were a screwy bunch. Certainly never a dull moment.

"Listen, I'm going to go over the plan with the guys. It's really late. Why don't you get to bed? It's been a long night. I can take the guys downstairs if you're sleeping up here."

Leo nodded. He looked like he wanted to ask something, but glanced at the guys, who were all standing around waiting for King. "Sure. Feel free to take any of the spare bedrooms. Good night."

"Good night. If you need anything, you come get me."

Leo nodded before waving at the guys. "It was great meeting you. Have a good night."

The guys wished him good night, and Leo was about to leave when he spun back around and caught King's arm, then pulled him to one side. King noticed Leo was using him to shield him from the others. Looking over his shoulders, he motioned for the fellas to head for the stairs.

"Why don't you guys head to the living room. I'll meet you down there in a minute." King waited for the guys to be out of the room before turning his attention back to Leo. "Everything okay?"

"Yeah, um, could you thank the guys for me? They're risking a lot being here, and I really appreciate it."

"Of course."

"Also, um...." Leo's face went red, and he cleared his throat. "If, um, you don't feel comfortable in any of the rooms downstairs, there's, um, plenty of space up here."

King placed his hand on Leo's shoulder. "We'll keep you safe, Leo. I promise."

Leo nodded, his bottom lip between his teeth as he ruffled his hair. "I know. Thank you. For everything." He shuffled awkwardly from one foot to the other, and King tried to decipher what it was Leo needed. What had changed in the last few hours? He had a group of strange men in his apartment. Granted, they were King's brothers, but that didn't change the fact Leo didn't know them and this was his safe place. King needed to reassure Leo he was safe.

"You're welcome." King pulled Leo in for a hug, and the sigh Leo released made King smile. He knew he shouldn't get used to this, shouldn't encourage Leo, but the frightful truth was that King had no idea who was comforting whom here. Leo pulled back, and with a soft expression, he turned and headed over to his bag on the couch.

King headed downstairs and found his friends all huddled together on the same couch, murmuring quietly, Chip on the floor by Joker's feet gazing up as if he were part of the conversation. They looked like a bunch of mischievous schoolboys who were clearly up to no-good. Lucky for them the couch was big and wide enough for all five of them, including poor Red who was stuck in the middle.

"What's going on?" King asked, sitting in the loveseat opposite them.

They all sat back at the same time, including Chip, and King slowly leaned away. "That had to be the single creepiest thing I have ever seen. Don't *ever* do it again."

Ace snorted out a laugh, the rest of them joining him. Something was going on, but King decided what he usually did—that he wanted no part of whatever plot they were scheming.

"Let's get to it, shall we? Ace, you're down here in this section of the apartment. The rest of you will be in the apartment just below. The entire building has been taken over by the NSA. Bowers is on the ground floor level with his men. Jack, bring in whatever equipment you need and get set up. Leo will get you into the security system. I also want you to review the footage from the attack at the bunker."

Lucky looked surprised. "Bowers is giving us access?"

Ace snorted. "Please. That guy wouldn't piss on us if we were on fire. Tony Stark up there is going to get us what we need."

"Peter Parker," King corrected.

Ace squinted at him. "I'm sorry, what?"

King cleared his throat. "Peter Parker. He's more like Peter Parker. Anyway, that's his code name for unsecured communications. Actually, it's, uh, Spider-Man." He sighed. "The op is called Avengers."

"And what's *your* code name?" Joker asked, a smile splitting his face.

King cursed under his breath. *Christ. Here we go.* "Captain America."

The roars of laughter that filled the room could have woken the dead, and King pierced them all with a glare.

"Would you ass-hats shut up? Leo's trying to sleep."

They sobered up in a heartbeat.

"Did you just use the word *ass-hat*?" Red murmured, eyes wide.

The silence didn't last.

With a heavy sigh, King sat back, arms crossed over his chest. "Get it out of your systems. Ass*holes*. How's that? Like that better?"

"I can see why he'd go with Captain America," Ace said thoughtfully, "but that's more Red. You're a bit too scary to be the Cap. I'm guessing he picked your code name before he actually got to know you."

"I'll show you scary," King warned, and Ace threw up his hands in surrender.

"Dios mío. I know this op is all serious and shit," Lucky said, wiping a tear from his eye, "but this is fucking amazing."

King lifted a brow. "Are you done now? May we proceed, or do you all need another moment?"

"You may proceed," Ace replied, his lips twitching.

"Thank you," King said dryly. "That's real kind of you."

"We're magnanimous that way."

"Still trying to impress your billionaire boyfriend with your word of the day app?"

Ace flipped him off.

"Anyway," King said, sitting forward again, "like I was saying before you all decided to be dicks, or what is otherwise known as every other day of the week." Ace opened his mouth, and King narrowed his eyes. "If the next words out of your mouth aren't something helpful, you're going to be rooming with Bowers."

Ace promptly shut his trap.

A snicker reached King's ear, and he let his head hang. "Leo, you're supposed to be sleeping."

Leo rounded the corner in his pajamas, looking all soft and comfortable, his feet bare. "I'm sorry. I wasn't eavesdropping, I swear. Okay, maybe I was a little, but I can't sleep."

"Did you even try? I've been gone for, like, two minutes."

Leo's expression said he was not impressed. "I did try, Mr. I'm a Tough Green Beret Therefore I'm Always Right."

Someone snickered to his left, and King cast them a

sideways glance. Whoever it was, they were about to be dead.

"Besides, if you're discussing my protection, I should be a part of this conversation, don't you think?"

King was about to say no, no he didn't think, but Leo was already dropping down onto the couch cushion next to him. He pulled his legs up, laced his fingers over one drawn-up knee, and propped his chin on his hand, his eyes on King and his smile wide.

"Go on."

What was happening to his life right now? Looking at the faces around the room, King resigned himself to the fact he was outnumbered. His backup wasn't backing him up, so he'd just have to get on with it.

"Fine," he grunted.

By the time they'd finished going over everything, the sun was rising, so everyone ended up crashing in Leo's apartment, with the guys taking the bedrooms downstairs, Leo sleeping on the futon upstairs, and King on the long couch beside him. Despite the late hour, King wasn't one to sleep in. He didn't get up at his usual time of five thirty, but he was up by seven, which he supposed was sleeping in for him. Careful not to wake Leo, King stood silently and stretched. The couch was actually very comfortable, the cushions extremely plush. He glanced over at Leo, who was curled up on his side, hair a mess, no glasses, lips parted softly in sleep. King resisted the urge to run his fingers through Leo's hair, but only because he didn't want to wake him.

Going downstairs, he noticed the bedroom doors were all closed, so the guys were still asleep. None of them really slept in much, so they'd be up any minute. In the meantime, he'd make them all breakfast. He should have thought of checking the fridge first, considering how long Leo had been away from his apartment.

When he opened the pantry, King found the usual kitchen essentials, like trash bags, sandwich bags, Tupperware, and so on. As for food—if it could be called food—the shelves were packed with huge boxes of Goldfish crackers and boxes of Starbucks coffee pods.

Nothing else.

Hopefully the refrigerator would yield better results. King opened the huge double doors and came face-to-face with an empty freezer and an entire fridge full of peppermint mocha creamer. And nothing else. It would have made sense, what with Leo spending all his time upstairs, except the kitchen upstairs was empty. He turned and bumped into Leo.

"Shit, I'm sorry." King grabbed Leo's shoulders, bringing him close to steady him.

"My fault," Leo murmured, his cheeks slashed with red and his fingers curled around King's arms. As if noticing, he dropped his eyes to King's right bicep and gave it a squeeze. "How does that even happen? I mean...." He poked King's pec with a finger. "It's like a wall of muscle. You must work out a lot. That's dumb, of course you do." He moved his finger around, gently prodding King's chest. "I bet you can probably bench-press me like I'm nothing. I almost pulled my back moving the couch when I dropped the remote under it." At King's snicker, Leo's eyes widened, and he snapped his gaze up. "I'm totally feeling you up right now. Oh my God. I'm so sorry. I can't believe I did that. Like, who does that? Because what comes out of my mouth isn't weird enough, now I'm randomly feeling you up? Though technically, not really feeling you up, I mean, I'm not trying to touch your, um, I mean...."

King didn't think it was possible for Leo's face to get any redder.

"But that doesn't mean it's okay. I don't like people touching me. Except you. I don't mind that. Shit. That's not —that sounded kind of like I'm saying I *want* you to touch me, but that's not what I meant. I mean I wouldn't mind you touching me, and holy shit, I should shut up now." Leo closed his eyes, letting his head fall against King's chest as he muttered under his breath. "I am so not good at this."

"It's okay," King assured him softly, aware Leo hadn't made to move out of his embrace, and King hadn't released him. He should really let go.

Leo shook his head. "No, it's not. I'm an adult. Why am I so weird?"

"Hey, look at me."

Leo shook his head again.

"Leo," King urged softly, placing his fingers under Leo's chin and lifting his face. When Leo refused to open his eyes, King brushed his fingers down Leo's jaw. His skin was soft, and he smelled of mint and something else. "Open your eyes."

Leo slowly opened just one eye, making King chuckle.

"It's okay. I promise. And you're not weird. We all have our quirks."

"Is that what we're calling it?" Leo asked with a huff.

"Aw, now who's grumpy? How about I make you some coffee with that peppermint mocha creamer of yours? In the meantime, you can put together a grocery list."

"For what?" Leo asked, leaning on the island counter when King moved away to get their coffee started.

"You only have creamer in your fridge."

"I have to stock up during the holidays because it's the only time they have that flavor. It's my favorite."

"Makes sense. So how about a shopping list?"

"For what?"

Didn't he just answer that? "Food, Leo. You have no food in your fridge. Or your pantry."

Leo opened his mouth, but King held up a hand to stop him. "Your fishy snacks are not food."

"I, um, don't grocery shop."

"What do you eat?"

Leo walked over to one of the drawers and opened it. King stared in horror at the collection of take-out menus. There were dozens of them, all neatly folded with tabbed dividers in alphabetical order.

"I can't cook," Leo murmured, rubbing his arm as he stared down at his feet, his cheeks burning with obvious embarrassment.

"That's nothing to be ashamed of. Jack can't cook either, but I've shared a few recipes that have worked for him. I can show you too."

"I, um, I appreciate that, but, uh, it's not that I'm not good at cooking. I *can't*. Too many uncertainties and variances. I have trouble focusing, which is not a good thing where heating and cooking things is concerned." He shrugged. "Fire hazard and all that."

"Don't apologize. How about you make me a list of what you like to eat. I'll put together a shopping list and handle meals."

"I can't let you do that. You've done enough for me as it is. It's fine. I can just order takeout."

"I enjoy cooking. So do the rest of the guys. When we lived together, the guys and I used to take turns cooking. It was good for us. If we're cooking for ourselves, why wouldn't we make enough for you?"

Leo peered at him. "Are you sure?"

"I don't offer unless I mean it."

"Okay. Thank you."

"You're welcome. Now, do I need to buy any kitchen-ware? Pots or pans?"

"The kitchen is fully stocked. My sister set this whole apartment up for me. Like I said, I'm not... normal."

King walked back to Leo and took hold of his shoulders, smiling at the way Leo automatically stepped into his arms and laid his head on King's chest. "What you're trying to say is that something is wrong with you, and there is nothing wrong with you, Leo."

"My brain doesn't work like most people's."

"No, it doesn't. But that doesn't mean it's wrong or that you're somehow less than. It's okay to need help, to lean on others who care about you and want to help you. Don't for a moment think that you're anything other than wonderful. Besides, there's nothing wrong with weird. I think we're all a little weird in our own way."

Leo wrapped his arms around King's waist and let out a soft sigh. Instead of fighting it, King just went with it. He knew he was doing wrong. Leo was growing attached to him, and if he were honest with himself, he'd admit that he was also getting attached, and that wasn't going to do them any good. Yet having Leo in his arms felt right.

The air shifted around him, and he silently cursed himself. The problem with family was their inability to stay out of your business. He peered over his shoulder and glared at the five men standing there grinning like idiots. Ace's smile grew wider, all gleaming white teeth as he put both thumbs up. Good God, when had his life turned into an episode of some teen drama?

As if sensing something was off, Leo pulled back, his eyes huge when he saw the guys.

"Morning," Ace said cheerfully, waving.

King groaned. Time to restore order. "It's just like I was telling you, Leo. Here we have five perfect examples of weird. Chip is the most well-adjusted of the bunch." Five smiles turned to scowls, and King felt better already. "Good morning, fellas. I hope you all slept well." Jesus, he hoped that's not what he looked like when he supposedly pouted. "There's coffee."

Instant smiles.

"Sorry, there's only peppermint mocha creamer," Leo said, clearly embarrassed.

The guys shifted their gazes from Leo to King and back before they all spoke up at once about their love for all things peppermint mocha. Dorks. Man, he loved them.

While Ace and Lucky got to making them all coffee, one pod at a time, King got the ball rolling. They all had a lot of work to do.

"Lucky, can you and Ace run out and grab us all some breakfast?"

"Sure," Lucky said. "There is a great little café down the road. It had very good reviews. Something about frogs, but great food."

"Don't get anything with tomatoes for Leo."

"No problem."

"After breakfast, Red, would you mind picking up some groceries for me? I'll make a list, and you guys can add to it.

Red gave him a little one-fingered salute. "You got it."

"Meal rotation sound good to everyone?"

Unanimous yes.

"Jack, you and Joker can take first watch. Make whatever arrangements you need for equipment."

"Roger that," Jack pitched in.

"Everyone, watch your six."

After coffee, they all dispersed, and King turned to find Leo grinning widely at him. He appeared a little starstruck, if King were honest.

"Wow. I used to watch my dad give orders, but it was never like this."

"I wasn't giving them orders."

"No, I know that, but you still have that commanding officer voice, like it's an order but it's not. What I mean is, the way they look at you, it's like they're happy to do whatever you ask them to do. Like making you happy makes them happy."

"Really?"

"Yeah. You never noticed?"

"No. They've always been that way."

"They admire you."

"I suppose they do. I was their warrant officer, and I'm older than them."

Leo rolled his eyes. "You're older than Ace by, like, a year. You're missing the point completely."

"No, I get what you're saying. I just don't see it. This is how we've always been." He never really thought about what people saw when he and the guys were together. It had always been that way. If he was there, he was the guy with the plan, and everyone was happy to follow. Any one of the guys could lead if they wanted, and King would happily let them, offer his guidance if they wanted it, but they always turned to him first. King always assumed they did so out of instinct, not because they wanted to.

"Must be really nice," Leo said absently, nudging his empty coffee cup.

"What's that?"

"Having such a big family. Knowing there are people you can count on who will be there for you without question. I mean, you didn't even tell them why you needed them, just that you did, and they showed up, ready to do whatever you asked. That's pretty amazing."

"You have that too, Leo."

Leo's gaze shot up to meet King's. "What do you mean?"

"You have us. Whatever happens, you can always count on us. Always."

"But I'm not family."

"Yeah, you are."

Leo's eyes filled, but he quickly blinked the wetness away. "I should go get dressed. Thanks again. For everything."

Before King could ask what was wrong, Leo was disappearing upstairs. Had he said something wrong? It was a statement he never made lightly, and he meant it. Whatever happened, King and the rest of the guys would be here for Leo. It was obvious Leo had been let down a lot in his life, and he had little faith in the longevity of any kind of relationship. Worst of all was that he clearly blamed himself for people not sticking around. King would show him what true friendship meant. If only King could stop his heart from warring with his head and trying to convince him there was more going on between them than friendship.

SIX

KNOWING King and the guys would keep him safe—plus the fact the entire building was occupied by Bowers and his men—Leo immersed himself in his algorithms and codes, surrendering to the power of his mind and letting it go. Routine helped him, and he continued his, despite the Kings.

Family.

King's family.

What was Leo supposed to have said to that? Other than how much he wanted it to be true. Leo didn't dare hope. He'd had "friends" before. People who said they cared about him, but the moment they began feeling he was a burden to them, they vanished from his life like they'd never been there. He'd learned quickly to move on, to not let it hurt him. It wasn't their fault he was too much to deal with. He'd learned to keep his distance from people. It was easier than getting attached and watching them walk away from him. He didn't think he could stand the pain to see King do the same. What happened to keeping his distance?

Kinda late for that now, don't you think?

No, he could still turn this around. All he had to do was focus on his work. He could do that. Lose himself in the program he was creating. With King in the same room with him day in and day out, Leo had no choice.

Every morning when he got up, one of the Kings was already downstairs in the kitchen cheerfully cooking breakfast, with the exception of Jack and Joker. Jack wasn't allowed near the stove, and Joker avoided it at all costs. Lunch and dinner went the same, with King bringing Leo's meals up to him after Leo decided it was safer to eat at his desk. Eating meals with King and the guys gave him a false sense of belonging. He wasn't one of them, no matter how many times King told him he was. When this was over, they'd go back to their lives, and Leo would be left behind. And why wouldn't they? Leo felt guilty enough for keeping some of the guys away from their significant others. They tried to assure him it was part of the job and they talked to their guys every day. Ace apparently had a billionaire boyfriend, Colton, who ran a huge shipping company. They'd been living together in Colton's mansion in Ponte Vedra. The story of how they got together had enthralled Leo.

Ace's cousin, Lucky, lived with his boyfriend, Mason, in St. Augustine Beach. Mason had been a cop, then a detective before being hired by King. Now he was a team leader for King's department at Four Kings Security. Red's boyfriend, Laz, was a freelance fashion photographer, and together they lived in Red's beachfront condo in St. Augustine Beach, where the rest of the guys lived. Jack and Joker seemed to be enjoying their bachelorhood.

Hours turned into days, and days turned into weeks.

Leo managed to keep his distance from King as much as possible, using work as an excuse. He'd completed one section of the six sections of code needed, and a week later he'd finished the second. Four more to go, then testing. He typed away at his computer every day, stopping only when King made him. Leo was man enough to admit he growled a bit when King brought him out of his zone, but that only lasted as long as it took him to realize King had "woken" him up by brushing his fingers down Leo's cheek and calling him *sweetheart*. Man, he was such a sucker. The only other time Leo seemed to snap out of it was when he was really thirsty or hungry. Like now.

The loud growl of his stomach broke Leo out of his zone. How was he starving? Hadn't King just made him a sandwich? Dropping his gaze to his watch, he cursed under his breath. Holy shit, six hours had passed since lunchtime? He turned his head and found a giant bowl of the most delicious-looking pasta he'd ever seen. It smelled so good he was in danger of drooling all over himself.

"Chicken Alfredo, lots of mushrooms and Parmesan."

Leo blinked up at King. "How'd you know I love mushrooms?"

King chuckled, amusement lighting up his blue eyes. "You told me so."

"I did?"

"Yep. A little over two hours ago when I asked you. Has that always been a thing with you?"

"What's that?"

King motioned to the pasta. "Eat. You're getting so absorbed you lose track of the world around you. It's like you're in a trance."

Leo nodded as he stuffed his face, letting out a moan. God, this was so good. Way better than any of the take-out stuff he ordered. He swallowed his mouthful and took a sip of what he discovered was Red's sweet tea. It was the most amazing sweet tea ever. "Yeah, once I'm in, I get lost in there until something pulls me back."

"Isn't that dangerous?" King asked, concerned.

"Oh, definitely. That's why I have a program that stops my progress every four hours so I can hydrate."

King peered at him. "Except you haven't been using it."

Leo cleared his throat, averting his gaze. "I disabled it."

"Leo, why would you do that? And why wouldn't you tell me something so vitally important?" King took hold of Leo's chin and turned his face, the genuine fear in his eyes stunning Leo.

"You put your neck on the line for me, and in return I promised I would get this thing done." Not to mention the longer he spent around King, the harder it would be when King was gone. They were already a month into this mess together, and Leo was getting too used to having King around.

"Have you thought about how that would work out if you ended up dropping dead in the middle of it?" King's brows drew together, anger flaring. "Did you think about what that would do to me to see something happen to you when it could have easily been prevented? What exactly did you expect me to say to your dad?"

"I'm sorry," Leo muttered. "I wasn't thinking. I... I didn't want to let you down." Man, he sounded so pathetic. He knew better, but he was so behind he'd just wanted to catch up a bit.

"Hey," King said softly, grabbing Leo's attention. "Don't do it again, okay? Now eat up, then set your program for every four hours. You'll get it done, but not to the detriment of your health."

Leo nodded. He picked up his bowl of pasta again as King headed for the bathroom.

"I'm going to take a shower."

"Okay," Leo said through a mouthful of pasta. King chuckled, and Leo chastised himself. What was he, twelve? He finished eating, then washed up his bowl and cutlery before returning to his desk. Did he need to take a shower yet? Shit, when had he last taken a shower? The days were all blurring together. He sniffed at his armpit and wrinkled his nose. Okay, he was smelling a little ripe.

"Sorry, forgot my clothes on the couch."

Leo almost swallowed his tongue. *Are you kidding me?* Nothing could have prepared him for a naked, freshly showered King with only a short bath towel wrapped around his tapered waist. Wasn't this how most porn videos started? *Are you high right now? Don't think of porn!* Oh God, he was thinking of porn. Leo wanted to look away, but his body was a dirty traitor. Not only could he *not* look away, but his eyes were glued to King's body. The man's physique was obscene. He had no right to be that hot. King picked up his duffel bag, and Leo jumped from his chair.

Eight-pack! "I was right!"

"I'm sorry?"

"Um, I, uh, was right about that, uh, code I was thinking about earlier. I just remembered that I was right."

"Okay." King didn't sound convinced, but he didn't ask, thankfully.

You know what would be great right about now—other than you not acting like a total basket case? A strong breeze. A conveniently placed hook or doorknob where that towel might get caught. Please, Jesus, make his towel fall off.

Leo blinked and jolted to find King standing in front of him.

"Are you okay?"

No. Why would he be okay? He was definitely not okay

with King standing so close all naked and.... Leo reached out and poked King's flat stomach. His eyes went huge, and he gaped up at King.

"I'm sorry. I just poked you. That was inappropriate. You have an eight-pack. You're forty-one, and you have an eight-pack."

King arched an eyebrow at him. "Are you saying I'm old?"

Now would be a great time for a meteor to land on him. "No." He shook his head fiercely. "You are not old. Nope. What I meant to say and failed miserably at, yet again, is that it's impressive. I mean, some guys struggle to get any kind of pack, much less six, and in your case, eight. What do you bench? A couple of those tiny Fiats?"

King blinked at him before barking out a laugh. He turned to head for the bathroom again, shaking his head in amusement.

"I'm serious," Leo called out after him. "You know what I can bench-press? The replacement spare. On the Fiat."

King's laughter echoed from inside the bathroom.

"Wait, come back here!"

King turned around, and Leo could have kicked himself. He'd been so focused on the man's abs, he'd completely disregarded the fact King was covered in tattoos.

"Oh my God, you have tattoos!"

King looked bemused. "You only just noticed? This is not the first time I've been shirtless around you."

"What the what?" When had King been shirtless? What was wrong with him? Judging by King's flying eyebrows, Leo would hazard a guess that King had been shirtless often. *Stupid brain. How could you betray me like this?*

"Those are incredible." Leo stood and took a step

toward King to inspect the artwork on his chest. The tattoo was a massive and stunning piece that went from his left shoulder, across his chest to his right shoulder. A regal lion's head took up his left pec, a crown nestled in its majestic mane. On his right pec was the Special Forces insignia with the word *Brotherhood* beautifully written inside a ribbon. Behind the crest and lion were detailed flowers, and on his right shoulder above the flowers running across his collarbones to the lion were the words *Flectere si nequeo superos, Acheronta movebo, which pretty much translated to "If I cannot move heaven, I will raise hell." Or literally, "If I cannot deflect the superior powers, then I shall move the River Acheron."* On his left arm, he had two black bands, and in between each band, three black stars. Six stars. "Is this for them?"

King nodded. "I always carry them with me."

"And the lion?" Leo asked, running his fingers over the proud lion.

"Our commander used to say we fought like lions. No matter how exhausted or injured we were, we fought with everything we had in us. The guys and I all got lion tattoos in his honor, and in honor of our ODA."

"And the flowers?"

"Chrysanthemums were my mom's favorite."

Leo nodded. He took King's hand in his and squinted at it. "Wait, was that always there?" Between King's right thumb and forefinger was a small black diamond-shaped tattoo. "Wow, epic fail, Leo. Geez. Like that would be the first thing someone notices on a hot guy, right? Okay, well maybe not the first, but it would certainly jump out at you, especially considering how long we've been around each other now, and I just called you hot out loud, so now would be a good time to hit the showers and maybe the water will wash away my mortification. Excuse me." Leo headed for the bathroom, ignoring King's deep rumbling laugh.

Showering felt amazing, and although it didn't completely wash away his mortification, it certainly helped. He changed into his pajamas because the next time he came out of the zone would be to pass out for the night. Though he might be sneaky and try to wake up late in the night and get more work done. Who the hell was he kidding? Sneaking? With King sleeping in the same room? The guy didn't just have eyes in the back of his head; his hearing and Spidey-sense were on par with Chip's. Seriously.

Leo set his alarm, knowing if he didn't, he'd get another scowly lecture on his health from King. He didn't set it for four hours, though, since he was done with his meals for the day. Instead he set it for six hours. Then he headed over to his computer and began his work for the evening.

When the alarm went off, Leo stood and stretched, turning and freezing at the sight of King stretched out on the couch fast asleep. He looked so peaceful. His boots were off, his socked feet crossed at the ankles, long legs stretched out. One hand rested on his flat stomach, the other lay on the pillow above his head, pulling the snug black henley he seemed to favor over his firm muscles, his body taking up the length of the long couch. Knowing all the delicious tattoos that lay under that shirt sent a shiver through Leo.

Mesmerized by King's slightly parted lips, Leo inched a little closer. His beard had grown out some, and Leo was certain he'd never known anyone more rugged and handsome. What kind of man did King go for? Probably someone equally fit and handsome, who wore a suit to work and had a gym membership, made protein smoothies, and watched the news for fun. Certainly not a scrawny nerd sixteen years younger than him, who came with an airport's worth of baggage. What could Leo possibly offer a man like King? He couldn't even give him good sex, if Leo's past partners were any indication of his sexual prowess.

Unable to help himself, Leo inched even closer, silently moving around the couch. He was just checking that King wasn't cold and in need of a blanket. It was the least he could do, seeing as how King insisted on sleeping on the couch rather than one of the big beds downstairs. Not that Leo was complaining. He'd been stupidly gleeful when King had made the decision.

"What are you doing?"

"Not watching you sleep," Leo blurted. "Because that would be weird." He took a quick step back, forgetting about the coffee table. The back of his legs hit the edge of the sleek black surface, and he flailed, throwing an arm out to King, who snatched hold of his wrist and yanked him forward, saving him from landing painfully on the coffee table. Instead he landed on King.

"I'm such a dork," Leo groaned, his face making a pretty good show of attempting to set itself on fire. At King's chuckle, Leo buried his face against King's shoulder. Oh, that was a mistake. Not good at all. Not that King wasn't good. He was freaking amazing. Not good because Leo was sprawled on King, feeling him, smelling him.... His pulse went through the roof when he realized King had one arm wrapped around his waist, his free hand around Leo's on his chest. Leo pulled back enough to meet King's gaze. "You're so hard."

King's eyes went wide, and Leo gasped, mortified.

"Oh shit, that's not—what I meant is your body. Muscles. Your hard muscles, not—I should shut up, but apparently my mouth has other ideas where you're concerned." King's eyes dropped to Leo's lips at the mention of his mouth, and Leo swallowed hard. "I swear I'm not trying to make everything sound like an innuendo; it just happens. Not that it happens all the time. You make me nervous, and when I'm nervous, I ramble. You're probably thinking I must live in a constant state of nervousness then, which is probably accurate since I tend to ramble most of the time, and I want to stop, oh man, do I want to stop, but I—"

Why weren't his words working? It took Leo a moment to figure out that he couldn't hear himself talking because King's lips were against his own. Leo gasped. King was kissing him. At his gasp, King pulled back, uncertainty filling his bright blue eyes. Panicked King would freak out and never kiss him again—as he most likely would come to the realization that he'd made a terrible mistake—Leo grabbed King's face and kissed him.

King's arm tightened around Leo's waist, and his lips parted, inviting Leo to deepen the kiss. If this was going to be their one and only kiss, Leo was going to make the most of it. He slipped his tongue inside King's mouth, and heat exploded through Leo unlike anything he'd ever experienced. King's sexy groan reverberated through his chest, making Leo shiver from head to toe. He savored King's taste, the warmth of his mouth, the softness of his lips. Leo had no idea kissing could be like this—like Popsicles at the beach in the summer. Okay, so maybe King didn't taste like his favorite Rocket Popsicle, but it filled Leo with joy nonetheless. Leo shifted up, slipping his fingers into King's short hair as his tongue tangled with King's.

"Wait," King mumbled against Leo's lips, and Leo pulled back, their breaths coming out labored. "Leo, I'm so sorry."

Shit. King hadn't wanted to kiss him. But it hadn't felt

that way. God, he was so stupid. Embarrassment slammed into him, and he scrambled to get off King.

"Leo, wait."

"You don't need to apologize." Thankfully, King didn't try to keep him there. Leo made to get up, flailed, and ended up on the floor between the couch and the coffee table. He lay on his back, his hands covering his face. How was he ever supposed to look King in the eye?

"Leo, please hear me out."

Leo didn't budge, his hands still on his face as King wrapped his hands around Leo's wrists, the touch searing. "It's okay," Leo mumbled. "Just give me a minute. Maybe you can go downstairs. I'm sorry I attacked you."

"Attacked me?" King cursed under his breath, moved his hands to Leo's waist, and hauled him up like he didn't weigh a thing.

A squeak escaped him when, instead of being placed on the couch, Leo found himself sitting across King's lap.

"Leo," King urged softly, running a hand up Leo's back, soothing him until Leo finally lowered his hands. "You didn't attack me. If you'll recall, *I* kissed *you*."

"You made a mistake. It's okay. I'm sorry I took advantage. You've been nothing but amazing. I violated your trust—"

"Stop," King snapped, making Leo jump.

"I won't have you using those words to describe what just happened. I wanted to kiss you. What's more, I *really* enjoyed it."

Leo's heart skipped a beat. "You did?"

"Yes." King cupped Leo's cheek, brushing his thumb over Leo's skin.

"Then why did you stop and apologize?" Leo asked softly, leaning into the touch.

"Because I care about you, and I'm afraid of hurting you." King carefully moved Leo onto the couch and stood. He ran a hand through his hair. "I have *never* had a problem with control. My whole life is about control. I don't second guess myself. I don't hesitate. I think things through, and I get the job done, not that you're a job. Jesus, listen to me. With you...."

"With me...?" Leo had to admit this was the first time he'd seen King like this. He was usually so unflappable. Not that he was flustered exactly. He doubted that word even entered into King's vocabulary, but he was definitely... off-balance.

King closed his eyes and let out a deep breath before meeting Leo's gaze, the heat and need in his blue eyes slamming into Leo. *Oh my God.* King *did* want him. *Him.*

"With you, I have to fight with myself for control. That's never happened to me before."

"You want me?" Leo asked, the words so foreign to him. How was it possible?

King folded his arms over his chest, his lips pressed together in a thin line as he nodded, his gaze elsewhere.

Fuck, he was so cute.

"You really want *me?*"

King turned his narrowed gaze on Leo. "Why wouldn't I?"

Leo looked down at himself. "Um, where do you want me to start?"

"How about I start instead?" King counted off Leo's qualities on his fingers, and Leo was not only charmed by how adorable the man was, but that King meant every word. "You're funny, so smart, kind, sweet—"

"Your scowl is adorable," Leo said.

"Pay attention. I'm telling you how amazing you are."

"Right." Leo gave a curt nod, oh so serious. "Continue."

King peered at him but did as Leo asked. "You have an amazing smile. I love the way you laugh, how your mind works."

Leo's heart was doing a little jig. This gorgeous, powerful, intelligent man wanted him. Leo stifled a gasp. What if they had sex and Leo was so awful King changed his mind?

"No. Don't do that. Rewind."

Leo blinked up at him. "Huh?"

"You thought something not good about yourself, and now you're doubting yourself again. You're doubting me."

How did he do that? No wonder the guys were always grumping about not getting away with anything.

As if reading his thoughts, *again*, King smiled softly at him. "You have the most expressive eyes of anyone I've ever met."

"What if the sex is terrible?"

King's impression of a deer in headlights was spectacular. It truly was. "What?"

"Not that we're going to have sex right away, or at all. I mean this whole you telling me how awesome I am is supposed to be a gentle, yet very flattering, let down, right? So it doesn't matter, and your eyes are doing that angry death-glare thing that makes the guys downstairs run away like someone's lit their asses on fire, so I'm going to shut up now."

King sighed and took a seat on the couch beside him. "I'm not angry with you, Leo. I'm angry at whoever or whatever caused you to see yourself as anything but the beautiful person you are. I'm not trying to let you down gently. I'm telling you that I'm afraid of the hold you have on me. I'm afraid of letting you down, of hurting you, because you deserve so much more." He cupped Leo's cheek again, his thumb brushing over Leo's bottom lip. "This is all uncharted territory for me, and for the first time in my life, I feel lost. If I don't know what to do, how am I supposed to keep you safe? And I don't mean from danger; I mean from me."

Leo's pulse sped up, and he did something he'd never done before.

He took the lead.

"Then let me guide you." Leo sucked King's thumb into his mouth, an explosive heat raging through him at King's visceral reaction, the black of his pupils spreading into the now-darkened blue, like a feral predator about to pounce. Feeling bold for the first time ever, Leo stood and stepped in between King's knees, smiling knowingly when King took hold of Leo's hips, his fingers digging gently. Leo could see it. The very tremulous restraint King had on himself. Leo had never known anyone who wielded that kind of control over himself and others.

This won't do at all.

Leo straddled King's lap, rubbing his groin against King's. He was so damned hard. The groan that rose up from King's chest had Leo wrapping his arms around King's neck and undulating his hips. He smiled wickedly against King's lips, his tongue poking out to lick along King's bottom lip. Where the boldness was coming from, he had no idea, but hearing King's groans, seeing how desperately he was clawing at his restraint, was driving Leo insane.

"I don't want to hurt you," King whispered, his fingers digging into Leo.

"You won't," Leo promised. And if he did get hurt, it would have been worth it to have had King for however long he could. Leo undulated his hips, rubbing himself against King's hard erection as he nipped at King's stubbled jaw.

He pressed his cheek to King's, his words quiet by King's ear. "I need you, King."

With a growl, King grabbed Leo and hauled him underneath him, his mouth taking Leo's in a breathless, scorching kiss. Leo gasped at King's all-consuming need. He moaned at the feel of King's hard body pushing him down into the couch cushions. The way King kissed him, as if he would lose his mind if he didn't have all of Leo, had Leo desperate for more. King's kisses turned sloppy, urgent, one hand in Leo's hair, the other slipping under Leo's shirt, his fingers blazing a fiery trail across his skin. Leo was doing this. *He* was shattering this man's control. Leo scrambled to grab hold of King's shirt, fisting the black material and pulling, their lips pausing their ravenous assault only long enough for Leo to pull King's shirt off and drop it to the floor.

If he'd been able to stand not touching King's skin, he would have wanted to look his fill, to study every muscle of King's delicious chest, run his fingers over every line of his tattoos, but right now, all he wanted was to touch, feel, kiss, and taste. King pulled back just enough to get Leo's shirt off him, and Leo did his best not to fold his arms over his chest, especially when King sat back on his heels to look at him.

"You're so damned beautiful."

Leo's cheeks heated, but before he could say a word, King's lips were back on him, only this time they were on his neck, his shoulder, his chest. Leo arched his back, sucking in a sharp breath as King trailed kisses, licked, and nipped his way down Leo's torso. His body was doing a pretty good job of making him feel like he was going to go up in flames any minute. Needing to touch King, Leo slipped his fingers into King's short hair, his head thrown back and a low moan escaping through his parted lips when King started lavishing attention on Leo's nipples. Leo was so damned hard he was in serious danger of coming in his pants. He needed release, but he didn't want this to be over. Being the object of King's desire was a heady experience.

"King," Leo breathed, arching up into him. "Please."

King nipped at Leo's side, making him bark out a laugh. King chuckled. "Ticklish, are we?"

Leo shook his head. "I don't know what you're talking about."

"Of course you don't. We'll have to explore that a bit more next time."

Next time.

Please let there be a next time.

King unzipped Leo's pants, a groan rumbling out of him as he swiped his thumb over Leo's leaking cock. "Fuck, look at you. Your lips are all pink and swollen, your face flushed, your breath panting. Beautiful. You're a very dangerous man, Leo."

"Me?" Leo gasped as King unzipped his own pants. "How... how am I dangerous?"

King slicked up both their cocks with their precome, his lips brushing over Leo's before he started the slow, torturous movement of getting them off.

"You have the power to bring a man like me to his knees." King moved his hand faster, jerking them together.

"You would do that?" Leo breathed, wrapping his legs around King and digging his fingers into the muscles of King's back. "You would get on your knees for me?"

King met Leo's gaze, their lips inches apart. "I crossed an ocean to hunt down a man who hurt someone I care about. I'm terrified of what I would do to protect you."

"Like keeping me?"

"I wouldn't keep you just to protect you, Leo. I'd keep you because I wouldn't be able to stand the thought of not having you with me. Of someone else touching you, kissing you." King's strokes became harder, faster, and Leo trembled beneath him. "Being inside you."

God, Leo wanted all those things *so. Damn. Bad.* He wanted King to keep him, to always want him, protect him, lose himself in Leo. Before he could respond, King brought their lips together, tongues tangling, panting breaths mingled. Leo was so close, his muscles tight as pleasure unlike anything he'd experienced flooded through him, setting him alight until his orgasm slammed into him and he cried out, King's roar muffled against Leo's neck. Ribbons of come hit Leo's stomach and chest. Holy mother of dragons! Had he just...? Had they...?

King lay against his side, his chuckle reverberating through Leo. "I can almost hear your brain working furiously. Hold on. Let me get us cleaned up before we end up glued together." He carefully got up and disappeared toward the little kitchen.

Leo didn't budge. He barely breathed. Too afraid if he did, he might wake up from whatever work-induced dream this was, because that was the only explanation he could come up with for why Ward Kingston, ex-Special Forces soldier, had confessed to wanting him, and had jerked them off together. Leo promptly shut his eyes tight. Everything was okay. If he didn't open his eyes, nothing would change, everything would remain magical and he could stay in this blissed-out moment forever.

"Leo, open your eyes."

"Nope." Leo swallowed hard at the damp cloth against his skin. A heartbeat later, he felt King looming over him.

"Get up."

"I'm good. But thanks anyway." Leo's eyes flew open when King picked him up. "Dude, you can't do that!"

"Do what?" King asked innocently as he sat on the couch, then lay down with Leo sprawled on top of him.

"You can't just pick me up like a stray kitten because you have ginormous biceps and an eight-pack."

"I can't?"

"You're not cute."

"Actually, I believe you said I was adorable."

"You know what's not adorable?"

"My being right?"

Leo sighed. "I'm not going to win this, am I?"

"No. Now do you want to talk about what happened?"

Leo laid his head over King's heart and traced the lines of King's tattoo with his fingers. "Could we maybe close our eyes and stay like this for a while."

King kissed the top of his head. "Sure. Remember everything I said, okay? None of that has changed."

But everything else *had* changed. Leo wasn't sure how to feel about it. On the one hand, he was ridiculously happy. On the other, he was afraid he was in too deep. Afraid King would wake up in the morning and think it was all a big mistake, or worse, would do so weeks from now, months from now, when Leo's heart was wrapped up in the amazing man holding him. Who the hell was he kidding? Leo's heart was already wrapped up in King.

Not wrapped up in King, falling for him.

Oh God. He was falling in love.

SEVEN

KING WOKE up the next morning like he never had before—with a smile on his face.

Leo lay sprawled over him, his head on King's chest and arms holding him tight, as if he were afraid King would leave. What would it take for Leo to trust in him? Leo trusted him with his life, no doubt on that, but when it came to his heart, Leo had been pulling away more and more. King couldn't blame him. Not when King couldn't come right out and say what he wanted. Mostly because he didn't know what he wanted. He knew *who* he wanted. He'd told Leo as much last night. The problem was what came next? That's where Leo's past heartaches came into play. Even if whatever was going on between them didn't go anywhere, King still wanted Leo to be a part of his life. Now if he could just get Leo to believe that.

King ran his fingers through Leo's soft hair, closing his eyes and inhaling Leo's sweet scent—a mixture of peppermint, citrus, and Leo. What would the General think if he saw them? Would he be happy for his son? The General had never mentioned anything about his son's relationships or the type of person he wanted for Leo. He'd only ever mentioned wanting him to be happy. Could Leo be happy with someone like King?

"What are you thinking?" Leo murmured sleepily. "And you say I think loudly."

King chuckled. "I was just wondering what your dad would think of this."

Leo took a few breaths. "Of what?"

The hesitant way he had asked the question wasn't lost on King. "Us. You being with me."

"That's easy. He'd be thrilled."

"You think so, huh?" King continued to absently stroke Leo's hair. "How do you figure?"

"He's only ever wanted me to be happy, and yeah, he worries a lot. Way more about me than my sister, but it's you. He trusts you."

"Pretty sure that trust wasn't an invitation for me to get into your pants."

Leo trailed kisses up his jaw. "No, that was *my* invitation."

Knowing where this was heading since Leo's hands had started roaming, and King couldn't trust himself not to make a mess out of Leo, he sat up, laughing softly at Leo's very loud groan of displeasure.

"Come on. We need to get some breakfast in you."

"I can think of something else I'd rather have in me," Leo mumbled, getting up.

King laughed again and swatted Leo's perky round ass, making him jump. He was about to get up when Leo straddled him, pushed him down, and kissed King until they were both forced to come up for air. King stared at him, his chest rising and falling with rapid breaths. *Holy hell.* He reached for Leo, but Leo was too quick, jumping off him and stepping away from the couch.

"Where do you think you're going?"

"To get some breakfast." Leo's crooked grin was wicked. He was gorgeous. Hair sticking up in all directions, lips thoroughly kissed, pajama pants hanging low on his hips, his chest bare, that sinewy, slender frame on display. King stood and slowly stalked toward him.

"Is that right?"

Leo edged toward the stairs. He nodded, his bottom lip pulled seductively between his teeth. Then he turned and bolted downstairs, King running after him. He caught Leo at the bottom of the stairs and wrapped his arms around Leo's waist as he lifted him off his feet. Leo laughed loudly.

"Oh my God, put me down!"

King hoisted Leo over his shoulder and walked with him into the kitchen. The conversation stopped abruptly, the only sound came from Lucky's Spanish curses as he flailed and fell off the kitchen counter, where he'd been sitting as he talked to Ace, who'd been cooking.

"Dude," Leo said with a grunt. "We talked about this!"

"Did we?" King asked, pretending to recall the incident. "I don't remember having that conversation."

"You can't just go around slinging people over your shoulder—hey guys—like a towel. Oh God, is that what I weigh to you? Why don't you throw Red over your shoulder? Let's see how that feels."

Red huffed. "I'm not *that* heavy."

"Buddy, your bicep is the size of my head, nice try."

"Also," King said, pouring himself a cup of coffee, "I can lift Red."

"Of course you can," Leo replied with a disgusted snort. "Seriously, guys? No one's going to help me out here?"

Joker scoffed. "Better you than me, pal."

"Wow. Thanks. I feel the love. Ooh, are those breakfast burritos? Ace, you make *the* best burritos."

"Thanks. To go?"

Leo grunted, and King turned to Ace with a grin. "Yep. Leo's got work to do." King placed Leo on his feet, laughing when Leo poked him in his side.

"Thanks, Ace." Leo took the Tupperware containing two breakfast burritos along with a huge coffee tumbler filled with Leo's favorite coffee and peppermint mocha creamer. "See you guys later. Thanks for not rescuing me. I hope you all do better if the Russians come."

Joker let out a bark of laughter as Leo disappeared upstairs. "He's awesome."

"Agreed," Jack said, slipping Chip a piece of bacon and laughing when Joker punched him in the arm.

"I think you should keep him," Lucky told King.

Turning, King came face-to-face with Ace, who looked about ready to burst.

"Just get it out of your system."

Ace pumped his fists through the air before thrusting a finger in his face. "Ha!"

"I'm not sure what your 'ha' is referring to."

"Oh, how the mighty have fallen."

King stared at his best friend. "Surely you're not implying what I think you're implying."

"Oh, I imply, brother. I imply. All the implying." Ace waved his hands at King and his general person. "There is so much implying going on, I can barely stand it."

"You're ridiculous." King took another sip of coffee and leaned against the counter. Was he really having this conversation? Who was he kidding? He was talking to Ace. Of course he was having this ridiculous conversation.

"I am, and I don't even care, because Ward Kingston is falling in love!"

"Would you keep it down?" King hissed, putting his coffee down and shoving Ace toward the bedroom. He closed the door behind them and spun around, sighing at Ace bouncing around, a stupid smile stretching from ear to ear. "You're worse than a child."

"Still don't care." Ace put a hand to his heart. "You should have seen you two. So fucking sweet."

"You know what's not sweet? Me breaking your fingers."

"You can be as grumpy as you want, but I know that deep down, inside that steel box where you locked your heart away, a certain cute little nerd didn't just pick the lock, he blew it up with C-4."

"That analogy was terrible."

"You're not listening. *I. Don't. Care.* What matters is that here—" Ace poked King's chest over his heart, and King snatched hold of his hand, twisting his arm until Ace doubled over. "Ow, ow, ow."

"Are you done?"

"Never! You'll have to break my hand, because I will *never* not be fucking thrilled about this."

With a heavy sigh, King released him. "You're exhausting."

"And you're in love."

"I'm not in love."

"You're right. You're in denial. Don't worry, the epiphany will come. Always does. Believe me."

King dropped down onto the mattress at the foot of the bed. "It's been, like, a month, Ace. You can't fall in love with someone in a month. *I* can't fall in love with someone in that time." Shit, it took him longer to pick out a new microwave after Joker blew up his last one.

"Says who? It was meant to be."

"That doesn't exist. That whole soul mates thing is bullshit."

"Wow. Did you ever believe in Santa, or did you come out of the womb asking your parents for power tools and flannel shirts?"

"I don't know. Do you ever listen to yourself when you speak?" King asked, squinting at him. "Because half the shit that comes out of your mouth makes no sense."

"Growl at me all you want. It's my measuring tool for gauging how right I am when you argue with me."

There was no winning with Ace. So why was he even bothering? He sighed heavily, and Ace joined him, sitting beside him on the bed, both of them going silent. It wasn't possible. Even if he felt like he'd known Leo for years, they'd only really met not long ago. It took King twice as long to arrange a date after meeting a guy he was interested in. None of this made any damned sense.

"Do you think it could work between us?"

"King, I love you, but I don't *love* you. Besides, I have Colton, and you have Leo."

"I'm going to seriously hurt you."

Ace cackled before his expression softened. "Why wouldn't it? He's a great guy. A little... eccentric, but sweet, funny, and he's clearly crazy about you."

"But we're so different. So, so different."

"Really? Because what I saw out there wasn't your differences. Besides, maybe that's what you need. You've always gone for guys who took themselves too seriously. Remember Monochromatic Mitch?"

King snorted. "How could I forget? We went over to his place for dinner, and when he asked you what you thought of the new apartment, you said it was "like walking into a Hollywood movie—before they were filmed in color. Wonder why he never invited us back?"

"I seriously thought we'd just stepped into a Hitchcock movie. I was expecting Norman Bates to pop out in a granny wig, wielding a knife. You could practically hear the violins screeching whenever that guy walked into the room. Who the hell wears nothing but varying shades of gray other than a ghost?"

"I'm not even going to address all the things wrong with that sentence."

"My point is, those guys didn't work out because they weren't Leo. He's bright and colorful, keeps you on your toes, and holy shit, King, he makes you laugh. You've laughed more times since he's been around than... ever." Ace's smile faded, and he dropped his gaze to his fingers. "It was like looking through a mirror back to before we lost them. I love you, but, man, I've missed your laugh."

King blinked back his tears, smiling when Ace wrapped an arm around his shoulders and brought him in for a hug. Ace was right. He remembered a time when he used to laugh, and often. It seemed like a lifetime ago. Then everything changed. *He* changed.

"There's no guarantees," Ace said gently. "We know that better than anyone, but you have a chance at something special. Take it and run as fast and far away with it as you can. Don't let anyone take it from you."

King had a lot to think about. He cared about Leo, deeply. Was it love? He couldn't say for sure, because he'd never been in love before. He'd had relationships, cared for the men he'd been with, some more than others. But love? No. Love meant surrendering your heart, allowing in the fear, uncertainties, and insecurities. It meant allowing yourself to be vulnerable, to place your trust, your heart into someone else's hands. Falling in love meant giving up control, and that was something King didn't think he could give up completely.

"Speaking of something special," Ace said, interrupting his thoughts. "It's Christmas Eve in a couple of days."

"Shit." With everything going on with Leo, King had completely forgotten. After missing one too many Christmases, and never knowing if it would be their last, they made it a point to always spend Christmas with their families. King hadn't missed one since his return. He supposed it was bound to happen. He couldn't leave Leo alone on Christmas. He'd just have to apologize to his family and make it up to them somehow. His sister would understand.

"I know what you're thinking, and don't be an idiot. Bring Leo."

King stared at him. "You want me to tell Bowers I'm risking Leo's life and the government's top-secret project so Leo can celebrate Christmas?"

"You're not risking Leo's life. Colton's house is stupidly secure. You know this because we made it that way after that jackass tried to kidnap him. If it'll make Bowers feel better, he can have his guys patrolling the property. Leo's been working damn hard on this project. His dad's in another country who knows where, and his sister still isn't back from Europe and wherever the hell she went with her husband. Leo needs to be surrounded by family."

King swallowed hard. *Family.* King had no trouble seeing Leo as part of his family, but that didn't mean Leo felt the same.

"Before you argue against it, think about it. Ask him, see what he says. Lucky and I are taking Colton and Mason down to Miami to spend Christmas Eve with our families, and we'll be back at Colton's later that evening." Ace stood and patted King's shoulder. "We'll take care of presents."

With that, Ace left.

The idea of having Leo with him for Christmas made King's heart swell. His family would love Leo. Most of them already did. The guys didn't just think he was great—they truly believed he was great for King, and he was. He wasn't going to fight that part anymore. Leo made him... happy. Groaning, he let his head fall into his hands. One day at a time. He'd take it one day at a time. For now, he'd focus on helping Leo get through this.

When he left the bedroom, the guys were gone, leaving only Ace in the living room working on his laptop. He didn't bother looking up but blew King a kiss. Shaking his head in amusement at his best friend, King headed upstairs, where Leo was furiously typing away at his keyboard, weird numbers, letters, and symbols flying across the screen. He'd check on Leo again in a couple of hours, since Leo kept trying to be sneaky, insisting he "forgot" to turn on his alarm.

In the meantime, King checked in with Jack and Joker, who were in the apartment downstairs. With Leo in the zone, he wasn't aware of anything but the program he was working on. He wouldn't even hear them. "Hey, any word on those guys from the bunker?"

Jack shook his head, the secure video feed showing him and Joker in the background practicing commands with Chip.

"As soon as Leo gave me access, I reviewed footage and started running these guys through several databases. I got a whole lot of nothing. No criminal records, no connections to anyone within the US, no known syndicates, gangs, or extremist group affiliations.

It's like these guys don't exist. You know what that means."

"Someone's gone through a lot of trouble to make it seem like they don't exist." The awful truth being it was most likely someone within their government. "What about your contact with Interpol?"

"He's working on it, but it'll take a little time. I've been digging into one of the analysts. His behavior is suspect and stood out, but I would wait until we have more information before mentioning it to Leo. No sense in upsetting him."

King sat up, his muscles tensing. If one of the analysts had something to do with the attempt to kidnap Leo, Leo was going to be furious. "Who?" One particular name came to mind.

"Harold Carr."

Damn it! He should have known the guy was up to something. "Tell me."

"I don't know if he's guilty, but the guy's a total creep. He spent more time spying on Leo than he did working. In the two weeks before you arrived, he was either arguing with Leo, watching him, or following him around. His browser history shows he's been looking into Leo and the General. I've reviewed the footage several times, and in those two weeks, Harold kept sneaking off to talk to Bowers. There's no audio feed, but it's obvious he was complaining about Leo. Bowers seems to humor him at first, but after, like, the fifth time the guy ends up in his office, Bowers gets pissed, growls something at him, and tells him to get lost, which clearly makes Harold even angrier. So far nothing in his profile shows any connection to the kidnappers. I'm checking Harold's finances. On the surface, he seems clean, but something feels off."

"Okay. Keep me posted. Thanks."

"Sure thing." Jack hung up, and King closed his laptop. If Harold was hiding something, Jack would find it. Could Harold be a spy? Whatever was happening, they'd have to find out on their own because Bowers wasn't about to share any intel with them. Not that King would stop trying to get *something* out of the man. While Jack did his thing, King would pay Bowers a visit downstairs. He might not get any new information, but he'd have the satisfaction of annoying the hell out of Bowers for a while.

KING CHECKED his watch and stood. Leo had been at it for hours. If he left Leo to his own devices, he'd keep going until he passed out. He was so determined to get this thing done. If it weren't for King bringing him his meals, Leo would probably work straight through the day. After checking in with Ace downstairs, King grabbed a light lunch for himself and Leo before returning upstairs. He set the plate with Leo's sandwich and Goldfish crackers on the desk then stepped up beside Leo.

It was as if Leo wasn't even there. Usually, it took a few minutes of King stroking his cheek or running his fingers down Leo's jaw to snap him out of it. Curious, King bent down and kissed Leo's cheek.

Leo froze, fingers hovering over the keyboard, eyes going huge and round as saucers. He slowly moved his eyes to King, the rest of him unmoving.

"Hi," King said, smiling warmly.

"Um, hi." Leo gingerly lowered his hands to his lap. "Well, that was... weird."

"What? My kissing you?"

"Yeah. No. I mean I started working, and you were

nowhere around, and then I felt you kiss me, and suddenly there you were."

"Guess that's what happens when you get sucked into that vortex of yours. I was curious if that would get you out of it quicker." He couldn't help his smugness. "I'd say it worked very well."

Leo narrowed his gaze at him. "So you kissed me just to get my attention?"

"I did. Yes."

"Well, you have it. Now what?"

King chuckled and straightened. "Now, we take a break for lunch."

With a small huff, Leo picked up his sandwich. Every meal went the same, with Leo never realizing how hungry he was until he took the first bite. Then King would blink, and then Leo's food was gone.

"Tell me how much you know about self-defense." King started moving the furniture to make room for them, his eyes darting to Leo as he stretched, his baseball tee rising and revealing a patch of what King knew to be very soft skin and the faintest happy trail going from his navel to disappear beneath his loose lounge pants, pants that left nothing to the imagination as far as Leo's pert backside and tantalizing package.

"I know nothing. Zip. Zilch. Nada. Not because I didn't try to learn, but my instructor said, and I quote, 'I would have better luck training a plank of wood.' And then he went on to say a bunch of stuff after that, but I wasn't listening."

King nodded. "Okay. What happened?"

"Other than him being a total d-bag? Whenever he'd give a command, I'd think of something else."

"Word association."

A smile spread across Leo's face. "Yes! Exactly. He expected me to remember all these words for each command, but that didn't make sense to me."

"So, let's say someone's about to shoot at you, and I want you to drop to the floor. What word would make you think of dropping down?"

"Penny."

"Like the coin?"

"Yeah. You know, drop a penny, pick it up."

"Okay." King nodded, walking around the empty space he'd created. Leo stood watching him, his expression puzzled but fascinated. "*Penny*," King shouted, pleased when Leo dove to the floor, his hands over his head and eyes wide. "Good."

"Oh my God, what the hell? You scared the crap out of me!" Leo jumped to his feet, marched over to King and punched him in the arm.

"Ouch! What?" King chuckled and moved away to avoid Leo's pummeling. "How else would I know if it worked?"

"You... you're... a jerk." Leo crossed his arms over his chest, glaring at King.

"Aw, are you mad?" King circled Leo, making the circle tighter with every turn until he was behind Leo, his chest pressed up to Leo's back, and his hands slipping around to Leo's chest. He murmured in Leo's ear. "Good. Get mad, Leo." King walked over to the futon, unzipped his gym bag, and removed two black-and-white boxing mitts. He tossed one onto the couch and slipped the other one on before he walked back to Leo. He held the mitt up, pointing to the white circle in the middle. "See this circle?"

Leo nodded.

"Good. I want you to punch it."

Leo shifted from one foot to the other. "King, I don't think...."

"Punch it!"

"Don't yell at me!" Leo growled, punching the mitt hard.

King smiled. "Nice job."

"You're kind of a sadist."

"I've been called worse."

Leo huffed, but his lips twitched at the corners. "I know what you're doing."

"I know you do," King said. "You're one of the smartest guys I know." He leaned in to whisper. "Don't tell Jack."

Leo chuckled. "Okay, just tell me what you want me to do. And no more yelling."

"No more yelling," King promised. He'd only done it because he knew he'd get a reaction out of Leo. King had learned early on that Leo hated being yelled at. It would upset him at first, but then he'd get pissed until it built and built, then *snap*. "That was good, but you're going to hurt your arm if you don't stop locking your elbow. Let's practice jabbing. Maybe we should practice your stance first." King removed the glove and held it under his arm. "You're right-handed, so stand straight, legs together."

Leo did as instructed, and King stood next to him. "Turn your body slightly to the right, and move your right leg back like this. Good. Bend your knees, not too much. Yeah, just like that. This will help you keep your balance. Now, fists up, elbows in. Always keep your elbows tucked in, protect your ribs. Turn your arm as you extend it, like this. Keep your wrist straight, and don't lock your elbows." King demonstrated slowly, and Leo mimicked the move exactly. "Then jab." He did it quicker, and Leo did the same. "Perfect. Well done."

Grabbing the mitt, he slipped it on again, took a stance, and faced Leo. "Hit the circle. Snap and jab."

Leo took his stance, focused on the circle and punched.

"Great! Again."

The more Leo hit the white circle, and the more King encouraged him, the harder Leo's punches became, his confidence rising. They practiced for a while with the right and then the left, and before too long King had Leo alternating, left, right, left, right. From there they moved onto hooks and uppercuts.

They spent the next few hours going through defense moves. Leo was a natural; he simply struggled with confidence. He needed to be pushed, but he wouldn't respond to anyone pushing. If he didn't have complete trust in the person, Leo would shrink away, his anxiety and fear getting the better of him, but with King? With King, Leo pushed back. Hard. The more King pushed, the more determined Leo became to show he could do it. Because he trusted King, felt safe with him. Could be himself with King.

After an intense session of sparring, they went through more commands, going through them several times, and once King was sure Leo would remember their word association, King got them both dinner, and Leo went back to work. He'd been making great progress and was close to finishing the third section of code for the program.

THE FOLLOWING DAY, King tested Leo, and although he'd pissed Leo off for scaring him, Leo would do as commanded. Tomorrow was Christmas Eve, and King still hadn't asked Leo to join him and his family. He wasn't sure why. They'd fooled around a few more times since that first night, and after waking up in the middle of the night with

Leo sprawled on him, he decided to start sleeping on the futon, since there was more room. As much as he loved having Leo on him, not being able to move all night wasn't good for either of them. Also, Leo had kneed him in the balls by mistake last night. Well, at least he'd said it was a mistake. It was suspect, since King had scared Leo so badly with one of his commands earlier that evening that his Goldfish crackers had gone flying.

Walking into the living room, King frowned. "Leo?" Seeing as how the only place Leo could hide was the bathroom and he'd just come from there, King headed downstairs. "Ace, is Leo down here?"

Ace lifted his gaze from his laptop. "What? I thought he was upstairs."

"He hasn't come down?"

"Nope. I would have noticed." Ace jumped from the couch and joined King in searching the whole of the apartment.

"Fuck, he's done it again!" King started to pace. "Shit. Why? Leo only disappears when he's anxious. Why is he anxious? He's been fine for weeks."

"What is it? What's he done?"

"He's pulled his Houdini act again. Why do you think Bowers and his men haven't stormed the place?"

Ace gaped at him. "Are you saying Leo walked out like he did in the bunker? Where the hell did he go?"

"I don't know." King started to pace when it occurred to him. "No, wait. I do know. He's looking for something to eat. Every time he disappears, it's because he's anxious and goes searching for a snack."

"But the closet is full of his Goldfish crackers, and the drawers are stuffed with bags of those Swedish Fish."

"It must be something else." King ran for the door and

took hold of the handle. "Shit. The door's unlocked. Damn it, Leo."

"Should I get Bowers?"

"No. Stay here in case he comes back. I'll call you if I need backup. If we both go running, Bowers is going to sound the alarm, and Leo doesn't need that kind of stress."

As much as King wanted to run, if he did, he'd alert Bowers. Not even Jack had caught Leo walking out. How in the hell did he do it? King reached the street, his heart pounding in his ears. He refused to let his judgment be clouded by worst-case scenarios. Leo had to be somewhere close by. The majority of the food places on this side of the beach were to the left, so he'd start there. Taking off down the sidewalk, he brought up the map of the area in his mind and tried to think like Leo. If he wanted a snack, where would he go? At this time of night, not many places were open, and the bars or restaurants that were open weren't likely to carry the kind of snack Leo would go for. Donuts. There was a donut shop a few minutes' walk down the road. But it was closed. Leo would know that, wouldn't he?

Movement caught his attention up ahead, and he saw Leo crossing the street several feet away, unaware of the traffic heading his way. The speed limit on this street was reduced, but at this time of night, with the low visibility, it would be too easy for someone to miss seeing Leo. King bolted for Leo, racing across the street as cars approached, and tackled Leo as a car screeched by, horn blaring. They hit the short row of bushes, rolled over them, and landed on the grass on the other side. After quickly getting up, King helped Leo to his feet, brushed the dirt off him, and checked him over.

"Are you okay? Are you hurt?"

Leo blinked at him as if coming out of a daze. "King?"

"Jesus, Leo, you can't do that!" King's bellow made Leo flinch, and King kicked himself. "I'm sorry. You ...." How could he make Leo understand what he'd put him through? He grabbed Leo's hand and placed it over his heart. "Do you feel that?"

Leo's eyes went huge, and his head shot up.

"You did that, Leo." King's heartbeat was pounding, his chest rising and falling with his rapid breaths from the scare Leo had given him. "If something had happened to you—"

Leo threw himself into King's arms, smashing their lips together, and for the first time since he'd discovered Leo was missing, King could breathe. He returned Leo's hungry kiss, his arms wrapped around him, holding him tight against him. A blaring car horn had King pulling back, but only long enough to let his chin rest on the top of Leo's head.

"Please don't do that again. If you need something, anything, tell me."

"I'm sorry. I was lost in my head like I tend to be when I'm working, and I suddenly had a really bad craving for donuts."

"Why didn't you say something?" King asked, holding him out at arm's length. "I would have sent someone. The donut shop isn't even open. It's been closed for hours, Leo."

"I know that, but it's kind of like I'm day-walking or something. I'm still in my head, and I don't realize what I'm doing until I've done it."

"We'll finish talking about this back at your apartment, okay?" King knew there was more to this than Leo was telling him. His "day-walking" was linked to anxiety. Leo was fretting about something, and King needed to know what it was, needed to assure Leo everything was going to be fine.

King kept Leo close as they walked briskly back to the

apartment. As expected, the door to the first-floor condo was thrown open, and Bowers stormed out, nostrils flaring, face red. King threw a hand up to stop him.

"It's fine. He's fine. I'll take care of it."

Bowers gritted his teeth, hands balled into fists at his sides before he marched back into the condo and slammed the door. When they got upstairs, all the guys were waiting for them in the living room. They all stood, their eyes filled with concern.

"Thank fuck," Ace said, running over. He put his hands on Leo's shoulders. "Are you okay?"

Leo nodded. "Um, yeah."

"Are you sure?" Lucky asked, looking him over.

Another nod.

Red stepped in front of Leo. "You're not hurt anywhere?"

Leo shook his head, his brows drawn together like he didn't understand what was happening. King leaned in, whispering in his ear. "They were worried about you."

A sharp intake of breath was quickly followed by a hard swallow. "I'm sorry I worried you guys."

"It's getting late," King said, motioning for Leo to go upstairs. "Why don't you go ahead and take a shower. I'll be up in a minute."

"Okay." Leo headed upstairs, looking like he was lost in thought. Hopefully nothing that would have him disappearing again. Maybe now that he knew King wasn't the only one who'd worry, his instincts might fight him on going for a midnight stroll.

"How do we stop him from doing that?" Lucky asked, concern etched into his face. "I mean, we didn't even see him leave. It makes no sense how he got past all those cameras."

"We reviewed the footage from the bunker," Jack said, "and Lucky's right. It makes no sense."

"There's something that keeps bothering me about that. There is no way it happens to work out every time. That would mean a hell of a lot of coincidences." Something was going on.

"What do you mean?" Ace asked.

"Bring me your laptop. Jack, bring up the footage from now when Leo disappeared." King handed Jack Ace's laptop, and they all gathered around him when he took a seat on the floor, laptop on the coffee table so they could all see. It was there, clear as day, Leo coming downstairs and walking right out the front door. From the outside security cameras, they stared in disbelief as the cameras captured every other part of the building except where Leo was.

"How?" Red asked, stunned. "Aren't the cameras sensitive to motion?"

Jack nodded. "Hm, we should work backward." He looked up at King. "Where were you when Leo disappeared?"

"I was in the bathroom."

"Why?"

King arched an eyebrow at Jack. "I had to take a piss."

"Why at that exact moment?"

Other than the fact he had to go? Jack's line of questioning was odd, but if he knew Jack, there was a good explanation for it, so he went along with it. "I don't know. Leo started playing this spa music with a trickling stream or something, and suddenly I had to go."

Jack played the footage from the cameras downstairs. "There he is walking out of the apartment." He pressed a key, and the camera changed to Ace, who was out on the small balcony.

"What were you doing out there?" King asked. How could Ace not have seen Leo?

"I heard a noise come from there. Like a hard *thump,* so I went to investigate."

"Wait, what is that?" King asked, pointing to something black on the floor under the dining room table. "It looks like a... handball. Leo had one of those back at the bunker."

"I'm pretty sure it wasn't there before," Ace muttered.

Jack reviewed the footage of Leo coming down the stairs, rounding the wall, and heading out the door while Ace investigated the noise he'd heard at the balcony. Rewinding, Jack gasped. "Holy shit, that's it. Why the hell hadn't I seen it before? The guy really is a genius."

"What?" King frowned at the screen. "What did you see?"

Jack tapped away at the screen, bringing up two simultaneous feeds. "You were right, King. They're not coincidences. Whether Leo realizes it or not, he's creating the circumstances for him to make a clean getaway. He found a way to distract you, get you out of his way. This time he played the music that made you feel like you had to piss, and as soon as you were in the bathroom, my guess is he lobbed this ball down the stairs, his brain easily calculating the numbers, how hard and where the ball had to hit the wall to make it down the stairs and hit the balcony door, which had Ace getting up to investigate. Ace opened the doors and leaned out, and Leo walked right out the front door. Ten bucks says any footage we see from Bowers has similar instances happening, and if we go out there, ten bucks says we'll find more of these little black balls. It's like Mouse Trap!"

King stared at him. "What?"

"That kid's game. You know, you turn the crank and the

shoe hits the bucket, the little ball rolls down the incline, down the slide, then hits another ball that falls into the tub, the dude flips into the barrel pool thing and down comes the cage that traps the mice."

"You remember way too much about that game," Ace muttered.

"It fascinated me as a kid."

"Of course it did."

King could hardly believe it, and yet it made perfect sense. "So, every time he disappeared, it's because he set off a chain reaction."

Jack nodded. "Meaning, by the time he got to the door, no one would be guarding it. Do you really think he doesn't know what he's doing?"

"Let's find out." King straightened and called out for Leo. Within seconds, Leo appeared downstairs. He slowed down when he saw everyone huddled together, all eyes on him.

"Um, yeah?"

"Come here a minute. We want to show you something." King motioned him over, and Lucky shifted so Leo could step up beside King. He leaned into King, as if seeking his warmth. Needing to reassure him, King wrapped an arm around him, pulling him close against him. "Jack, play the footage."

They replayed everything for Leo, and then King explained what they'd realized. Leo's jaw dropped, and he moved his stunned gaze to King. "I did that?"

"You didn't know?"

Leo shook his head. "I had no idea. Like I said, it's kind of like sleepwalking but awake. Sort of."

"And what wakes you up from this sleepwalking?" Ace asked, taking a seat on the couch across from them.

"I generally don't snap out of it until I have what I want or something grabs my attention or takes me by surprise."

Jack closed the laptop and stood. "The problem is we can't snap you out of it if you find a way to distract us so we don't even know you're getting up to go."

Leo's cheeks flushed, and he shifted from one foot to the other. "I don't think we have to worry about that anymore."

"What do you mean?"

Leo's gaze flicked to King before moving his attention back to Ace. "I only do that when I'm worried about something. I usually end up making myself so anxious about it that I get cravings and then need to go off and get what I'm craving in the hopes it will help me feel better."

"Like donuts?"

Leo nodded.

"So what's got you worried?" King asked gently, holding Leo as he turned in King's arms to face him.

"Could we talk about it in private?"

"Of course." King patted Jack's shoulder. "Thanks, guys."

Everyone left except for Ace, who resumed his seat on the couch while King ushered Leo upstairs. When they reached the living room, Leo started to pace.

"What's wrong?"

"I just realized that it's Christmas Eve tomorrow. You shouldn't be here babysitting me when you could be with your family. It's not right." Leo tapped his hands against his legs.

That's what had Leo so anxious. King should have known. He kicked himself for not asking earlier.

"First of all," King said as he approached Leo and brought him into his arms. "I'm not babysitting anyone. I'm here to look out for you. Second, I should have asked sooner, but I was afraid you'd say no. I'd really like it if you came with me."

Leo stared at him. "You... you want me to come with you? For Christmas? To be with you and your family?"

"Yes. I will warn you. It'll be loud. With Ace and Lucky alone, you know there's bound to be shenanigans, but I would love to have you there with me."

Leo searched King's gaze, as if trying to see if King meant it. "You really do want me there."

"Yeah. Everyone's going to want to meet you and talk to you. Will you be okay with that?"

"Why would they want to talk to me?"

"Because you're wonderful. And...." It was King's turn to feel a little embarrassed. "I've never brought anyone home for Christmas."

Leo stared at him, and King was about to apologize, when Leo was on his toes, arms wrapped around King's neck, kissing him.

Desire and need exploded through King, setting him on fire, a fierce desperation the likes of which he'd never felt before threatening to consume him. With a growl, he grabbed Leo's ass and hauled him up against him. Leo's soft gasp sent a shiver through King. He'd never wanted anyone so damned badly. How had this happened so fast? This wasn't him. He didn't do this sort of thing. Didn't lose himself at all, much less so quickly. It's as if every defense he'd ever put up was useless against Leo.

Leo pulled back enough to suck in a breath, his lips swollen from their kiss. "King...."

"Tell me," King whispered. "Whatever you want, it's yours."

"You. I want you."

King didn't think about his next course of action.

Instead he carried Leo downstairs, thankful Ace had taken himself off to bed. Not that he would have stopped even if Ace *had* been in the living room. If King was going to have Leo for the first time, it wouldn't be upstairs, where anyone could walk in on them, or on a futon with barely enough room to maneuver.

Inside the master bedroom, King kicked the door closed and dropped Leo onto the bed, their lips briefly parting with the movement before King was on him again and they were mauling each other's mouths. Leo pulled King's shirt off and threw it somewhere to the side. Their mouths found each other again, and they continued to kiss as they stripped each other of their clothes until it was his heated skin against Leo's. King couldn't get enough of Leo—his scent, the feel of his soft skin, the taste of his mouth…. King was on the verge of losing his mind if he didn't have all of him.

Leo scraped his nails down King's back, and King growled against Leo's lips before grabbing Leo's thigh and wrapping his leg around his waist. He slid his hand down from Leo's knee to his inner thigh, slipping his hand between them to take hold of Leo's hard cock, loving the whimper Leo let out. *Gorgeous. Vulnerable.* Leo writhed beneath him, arching his back to press himself against King. He had no idea the hold he already had on King.

King used the precome from the tip of Leo's leaking erection to ease the friction and pulled back just enough to take in the stunning sight of Leo's face as he moaned and begged King. His plump lips were parted in pleasure, his face flushed, hair a mess, and his brows drawn together in ecstasy. King had never seen anything so beautiful. Something wild and frightening edged out from the shadows inside King as he released Leo and smeared precome over Leo's stomach before putting his finger to Leo's lips.

"Get it wet."

Leo's eyes were so dark they were almost black as he sucked King's finger into his mouth, his tongue swirling around it. Every soft gasp, every moan, every sharp intake of breath Leo took chipped away at King's resolve. He pulled back and placed his finger to Leo's hole just as he swallowed Leo's cock down to the root, moaning at the taste of Leo and the way he cried out King's name. Leo fisted handfuls of the duvet, quiet curses leaving his sinful lips as he watched King sucking, licking, and nipping, King's finger buried deep in Leo's ass. He slid his free hand up Leo's stomach to his chest, tweaking a nipple and groaning around Leo's hard length when Leo bucked beneath him. Leo's muscles were softly defined, his skin flawless, his body sleek and slender with tiny moles sprinkled lightly here and there.

Leo slipped his fingers into King's hair, and King popped off to add a second finger to Leo's entrance, his hand soothing Leo's flank as he readied him, his brow beaded with sweat as he fought for control. The more Leo writhed beneath him, the more desperate King was to be inside him, to feel his cock gripped in Leo's tight heat.

"King," Leo gasped, arching his back, his head thrown back. "Please."

"Lube and condoms?"

Leo threw a hand out in the direction of the nightstand to King's left. After removing his fingers from Leo, he moved quickly, kissing the breath out of Leo before heading to the drawer and removing what he needed. He tore through the foil packet and rolled the condom down his painfully hard length. Then he poured a generous amount of lube on his hand, slicked himself up, and used the remaining lube on Leo. King positioned himself between Leo's legs, needing to see his face as he placed the tip of his cock to Leo's hole. He gingerly pushed in little by little, ignoring Leo's pleas for more. King was thick and long, and much as he needed to be inside Leo, he wouldn't hurt him. Sucking in a sharp breath, King slowly sank deeper, the tight heat making him shiver from head to toe.

"King, now. Please."

Control.

"Ward!"

Fuck control.

King folded himself over Leo and thrust the rest of the way in. Leo cried out, his fingers digging into King's shoulders, making him groan. He was finally buried balls-deep inside Leo, and he paused a moment in an attempt to gather himself, but Leo was having none of it.

"Let go," Leo demanded, undulating his hips and taking hold of King's face, their gazes locked on each other. "You don't need to hide from me. I want to feel *all* of you. Let. Go."

King searched Leo's gaze, seeing nothing but truth, trust, and desire. With a feral growl, he pulled out and shoved back in, shivering at Leo's cry, the way his body trembled beneath King's.

"Faster," Leo ordered. "Do it, Ward."

"Fuck." King snapped his hips, and Leo cried out again, the sound working its magic on King. He should have told Leo not to call him that. No one had called him that since his parents—the only people who'd known him as the man he'd been before. "Say it again," King demanded, his voice low and rough.

Leo met his gaze and cupped his face. "Make me yours, Ward. Leave your mark on me."

King pulled almost all the way out and slammed back inside Leo, moving as deep as he could go, the bed shifted beneath them as Leo clung to him, needing him, wanting him in every way. Terrified of the words that might find their way out of his mouth, King crushed their lips together, his tongue diving deep into Leo's mouth claiming every inch of it just as he was doing with his cock inside Leo.

No one would ever hurt Leo again. Not if he had anything to do with it. Whatever happened between them, however this ended, Leo would be safe. King would make sure of it. The thought of someone else's hands on Leo's soft skin had a quiet rage burning through him, and it scared the hell out of him. He didn't want Leo with anyone. Didn't want them to know the taste of his lips, the softness of his skin, the sounds he made when feeling pleasure. He wanted Leo for himself.

King pulled Leo with him as he sat back on his heels, Leo impaling himself down on King's rock-hard length.

"Fuck! Ward, please. *Please.*" Leo cupped King's face and brought their mouths together, his fervent kisses matching his pace as he fucked himself on King's cock. King gripped Leo's waist, fingers digging into his flesh, as he guided Leo up and down, meeting the movement with his own thrusts, the room filled with the sounds of their panting breaths, soft curses, and Leo's body hitting King's.

Leo threw his head back, his eyes shut, and King couldn't resist nipping at Leo's neck and sucking on his skin. They moved furiously, both holding on tight to each other, their bodies slick with sweat, faces flushed. King drove himself up into Leo over and over, already wanting to feel himself inside Leo without the condom, wanting to come inside him and mark him, leave a part of himself inside Leo.

"Oh God." Leo dug his fingers into King's hair, his hips bucking and losing their rhythm as he chased his release. A heartbeat later, Leo shouted King's name, and his entire body shook from the force of his orgasm.

"Say it," King demanded, his orgasm tearing through him. "Say it!"

"Ward. I need you so bad."

King dropped Leo onto the bed under him and thrust in hard and deep, pumping himself inside Leo as come filled the condom, his muscles tensed and his teeth gritted at the intense wave of pleasure that exploded through him. His arms shook, and he carefully pulled out of Leo. He tossed the condom into the trash beside the bed before collapsing beside Leo. *Holy shit.* He stared at the ceiling as he tried to catch his breath. Leo left for the bathroom, returning soon after with a damp cloth to clean the come off King's chest. Tossing the little towel in the trash, Leo climbed into bed then rolled against King's side, his hand going to King's chest, the only sound in the room coming from their panting breaths. He took Leo's hand in his and placed it to his lips for a kiss.

"So, uh, when's round two?" Leo asked, breathless.

King laughed. "Some of us aren't in our twenties, remember?"

"Really?" Leo propped himself on his elbow and ran a finger over King's abs. "'Cause moves like that make a guy wonder." He straddled King's hips, and leaned in to kiss King, drawing a moan from somewhere deep inside him. Fuck, if King could go again right now, he would. "How about you just relax and let me do a little exploring."

King hummed. He wasn't about to say no to that. "Explore away."

Leo started his little adventure by trailing kisses down King's jaw, down his neck, and over his Adam's apple, his hands wandering. He kissed his way down King's chest, over his pecs, stopping to flick his tongue over one nipple, making King hiss. "You did say explore right, and not torture?"

Leo's smile was wicked. "Is that what I said?" He flicked his tongue again, and King moved his hands only to have Leo grab his wrists and pin them to the bed on either side of King's head. "Did I give you the order to move, soldier?"

King cursed under his breath, and Leo's answering chuckle was decadent. "I should have known you were going to be trouble."

"You could use a little trouble, if you ask me."

"Oh yeah?"

Leo nodded. "Now don't move those hands."

King did as ordered and kept his hands to the sides of his head as Leo continued to torture him with kisses, licks, and flicks of his tongue to every dip and curve of King's torso. Leo was already half-hard, and King wondered when he'd lost his grip on his control. Definitely after Leo. He'd never had that problem before Leo, especially in the bedroom.

True to his word, Leo took every opportunity to torture him, gliding his hands up King's legs to his inner thighs, making sure to avoid his groin. He sat on King's stomach and palmed his now hard cock. King moved his arms, and Leo stopped. *Little shit.*

"Are you disobeying orders, soldier?"

King breathed in deep through his nose and released the breath slowly through his mouth. "No, sir."

"Good. Now, I'm going to jerk off and come on your stomach. If you move, I stop."

"I was wrong. You're not trouble." King narrowed his eyes at Leo. "You're evil."

Leo released a villain-worthy laugh before he started

pumping his cock, slowly at first, his hand twisting, using his come to ease the friction. His skin was flushed, his lips swollen, his entire body showed evidence of being completely wrecked by King.

"You're so fucking beautiful," King said, drawing his legs up, bending his knees, and forcing Leo closer. Leo's knowing smile had King's skin feeling too tight. He could do this. He'd been through real torture. This was a walk in the park.

Leo undulated his hips, rocking into his hand, the rosy tip of his cock leaking over his fingers. He put two fingers to his mouth, parting his lips, and working his tongue around them, his eyes half lidded and filled with lust. King had never seen anything so mouthwatering.

"Feed me your cock," King said, barely recognizing his own voice. It was gravelly and deep, strained. "Leo." Was he begging? Fuck this. He didn't beg.

"You want to suck my dick?" Leo asked boldly, holding his cock just out of King's reach.

King narrowed his gaze. "You're two seconds away from being very sorry."

"Show me," Leo challenged.

EIGHT

LEO WAS PLAYING A DANGEROUS GAME. He knew that.

Baiting a man like King, purposefully poking and prodding, challenging, trying to get him to lose his control was foolish. It was also the most exciting experience of his life. Gauntlet thrown, Leo sprang out of bed, but a steel grip suddenly held him around the waist. King spun him around, hoisted him up, and pushed him against the wall, pinning Leo there with his body, his rock-hard cock pressing against Leo's.

King smashed their mouths together, his fingers curled into Leo's hair, his hold tight. Leo wrapped his legs around King's waist, thrusting his hips, their leaking cocks rubbing against each other.

"Yes," Leo hissed. Fuck, he loved how strong King was. How he could lift Leo without any strain. Had anyone else shown that kind of strength around him, Leo would have been wary, but he knew no matter the circumstance, even if King's control were to snap, King would never hurt him.

Knowing Leo had that much of a hold over a man like King, a man with so much power, made him feel giddy, almost high. "Fuck me, King. I want to feel you for days."

King lined his cock up with Leo's hole, and Leo gasped. Their eyes met, and he nodded. "I trust you."

"I get tested every quarter. I can show you the results."

Leo swallowed hard. "They ran tests before taking me to the bunker."

King didn't bother with more words. He drove himself inside Leo, and Leo banged his fist against the wall, the burn yielding to incredible pleasure.

"Fuck!"

"You asked for it, baby," King growled, scraping his teeth down the side of Leo's neck. "We're in for a world of trouble, you know that?"

"How do you figure?" Leo was breathless, the feel of King bare inside him, filling him, made him tremble. He nipped at King's ear and scraped his nails over King's shoulders, drawing a hiss from him. Leo bit at his jaw, not hard, but enough to make King curse. Loudly.

"Saying no to you is going to be fucking impossible."

Leo tweaked one of King's nipples, his grin wicked. "I'm glad you've realized that early on."

"You're a smart-mouthed little shit sometimes, you know that?"

"Guess you better find a way to shut me up."

King thrust his hips hard, and Leo cursed. "You love to push my buttons."

"Hell yes. I love watching you lose control. Love knowing I'm the one doing it. Me. No one else."

"Leo," King warned, snapping his hips again. "You're playing a very dangerous game."

"Don't I know it," Leo said with a moan, running his fingers over King's bottom lip as King drove himself in deep and hard, pumping himself against Leo, his back hitting the wall over and over. Fuck, it felt amazing. King didn't treat him like he was fragile. Like he might break if he was held too tightly. "Play with me, King. Lose yourself to me."

King found a way to shut Leo up all right. He dropped Leo onto the bed, rolled him onto his stomach, and plastered his chest to Leo's back before lacing their fingers together. He moved Leo's arms up above his head, kicked Leo's legs wider, and drove himself in deep and hard.

"Oh fuck!"

King jerked Leo toward him as he thrust up, the sound of King's groin smacking against Leo's ass joining King's animalistic growls and Leo's screams. King's heavy weight on Leo was delicious, and fuck, he was so full. His body shivered, skin slicked with sweat, every part of him burning with need.

"Oh God, Ward." Leo was going to come, every muscle pulled tight as King slammed into him repeatedly, hitting that magical little bundle of nerves inside his ass. The bed moved beneath them, the headboard knocking into the wall, and Leo worried the place was going to crumble around them.

"Leo," King roared, burning heat filling Leo, the knowledge it was King filling him with his come had Leo screaming King's name, his body shaking as he came with his cock trapped between him and the mattress. King continued to pump himself inside Leo until he collapsed on top of him, his ragged breaths warm by Leo's ear. They lay together, King's heavy weight on him while their breathing steadied.

"King?" Leo inquired softly when King didn't show any signs of life. "Shit, did I kill you?"

"Fuck you," King grumbled against Leo's hair. "I'm not that fucking old."

God, he loved the grump.

Leo's eyes went wide. *Love.* Oh fuck, he'd fallen in love. With King.

"I guess I should move," King murmured, his breath ruffling the back of Leo's neck.

"I'm good," Leo said, worried King would see the truth in his eyes and make tracks. Because things weren't complicated enough, that's just what King needed right now. King slipped out of him, groaning, no doubt at the way his come slipped out of Leo's ass. At least that's what made Leo groan. He stayed where he was, a chill going through him when King moved away. The toilet from the en suite bathroom flushed, and Leo sighed when he felt the damp cloth cleaning him up.

"Roll over."

Leo did as he was told, his cheeks burning when King cleaned up his stomach, then the wet patch on the bed. While King went to get rid of the cloth in the bathroom, Leo scrambled up and got under the duvet. When he didn't hear anything, he chanced a peak and found King standing by the bathroom door looking uncertain.

"I hope you're not thinking about sleeping anywhere other than right here," Leo said, eyes narrowed. Where the hell all the boldness came from, he had no idea, but he was running with it. He wanted King here beside him. The guy didn't get to fuck him and then disappear. If King meant what he'd said, then he'd join Leo.

King arched a blond brow at him. "You're kind of bossy."

"Bossy bottom, that's me. Get that fine butt over here. I'm cold." He could see King was trying not to smile as he rounded the bed and climbed in beside Leo. Without hesitation, Leo snuggled up close. "Now this is more like it."

"I'm glad I could be of service."

Leo hummed. "You servicing me. I like the sound of that."

"Easy, tiger. Round three will have to wait. And I swear if you say anything about my age, I will take you over my knee and...."

Leo snickered. "Just realized that wasn't much of a threat, didn't you?"

"Shut up."

Leo burst into laughter at King's put-out tone. He rolled onto his back, and held his stomach, tears in his eyes from how hard he was laughing. It certainly didn't help him when he looked over to see King glowering at him.

"Yeah, yeah. Smartass."

When Leo was done, he rolled toward King, smiling at the contented look on his face. He snuggled close, and King wrapped an arm around him, holding Leo against him. He closed his eyes.

"Go to sleep, sweetheart."

Leo placed a kiss to King's skin before closing his eyes. He couldn't think about what would happen next. One day at a time. That's how he had to take this. It was all so very new to him, and from what King had said, to him too. They were both navigating uncharted waters, and Leo hoped wherever it led them, it didn't end with Leo sinking into the darkness below with a broken heart.

LIVID WASN'T a strong enough word to describe the various shades of red and numerous levels of anger Bowers experienced when King told him he was taking Leo to Ponte Vedra for Christmas Eve and Christmas Day. Two days of not working on the program. The dude was a total Grinch, without the cute dog. If Leo hadn't promised he'd work nonstop on the remaining three sections of code the moment he got back, who knew what Bowers would have done. The truth was, Leo was very close. He'd have to really push himself, but he could get it done. Then it just needed testing. He was almost free. Before, Leo had been trying to get the project finished so he could go back to his life, but now he was finishing with the hope that once he got back to his life, it might include King. He wanted to see where things went between them more than anything.

Once Bowers accepted, informing them he'd send a small army with them to keep watch on Ace and Colton's property, Leo started feeling nervous for other reasons.

King squeezed his hand as he drove them north on I-75. "It's going to be fine."

"What if your sister hates me?" Surely she wanted the very best for her brother, and Leo wasn't sure he was it.

"First of all, my sister's not like that. Unless someone's an asshole to her or her family, she loves everyone. Her husband, Nash, is a great guy, and so are Mason, Colton, and Laz. You've already met the rest of the guys, and they love you, but I know it can be a bit much when everyone's together, so if you need to escape at any point, you just let me know. No one's going to be offended. Red sometimes needs a little quiet time, so you'll see him go off on his own for a bit and come back later."

Leo nodded. He knew King was right, but that didn't

stop him from feeling nervous. As they got closer to Ace and Colton's mansion—because seriously, of course Ace snagged himself a billionaire who lived in a mansion on the beach— Leo tried to push down his nerves. He reminded himself this was King's family, and like King said, he'd already met the most important men in King's life, and they seemed to like Leo, so maybe the rest would feel the same.

Bowers's men were already on the property, and Ace had promised Leo that he and Colton were okay with all the added security. Colton sounded like a great guy, and if he was with Ace, Leo figured the man had to have some major patience. Ace was awesome, but he was kind of like Leo in some ways. A big ball of energy, though Leo was more rambling-nervous energy and Ace was more "always seems high on espresso" energy.

They pulled into Colton's drive, and Leo smiled so wide his face hurt. "Oh my God." The multistory mansion was gorgeous, decorated in what had to be thousands of twinkling white lights, making it look like an ice palace in the middle of a winter wonderland.

"Ace loves Christmas, and Colton loves spoiling Ace. Can you tell?"

"And Ace doesn't mind it?" Leo asked, getting out of the car. He waited for King, who came around the front and took hold of his hand. People tended to get a little funny where money was concerned, especially in relationships when one person had a lot more than the other.

King led Leo toward the front door. "Nope. Everyone has a different way of expressing their love. Colton is an only child from a very wealthy family. I think the way he grew up has something to do with it, but that's how he shows Ace his love. Don't get me wrong, he shows it in other ways too, but he's got plenty of wealth, so if he wants to spoil the man he loves, why shouldn't he? Ace isn't going to stop him. Colton's also very responsible. He doesn't buy things on a whim. It needs to mean something to Ace."

The door opened, and a very tall, handsome man in an expensive-looking suit greeted them, his genuinely warm smile reaching his bright blue-gray eyes. "King. How wonderful to see you again." He moved his friendly gaze to Leo. "You must be Leo. I'm so excited to meet you."

Leo returned Colton's smile. "You are?"

"I've heard all about you." Colton jumped when Ace appeared, poking him in his side.

"Honestly, Anston. Stop skulking around corners."

"And so it begins," King muttered, shaking his head, but Leo could tell he was amused by the way his lips twitched.

Leo chuckled at Ace's teasing and Colton's fussing as if he was put out, but the adoration in Colton's eyes for Ace shone unmistakably bright.

"Leo, this is Colton, who for some strange reason has allowed Ace to live in his house."

Ace threw an arm around Colton's shoulders. "Um, because he loves me and can't bear to be parted from me. Isn't that right, snookums?"

Colton let out a mock gasp. "Wait, you're living in my house?"

"Funny," Ace drawled.

With a rumble of a chuckle, Colton held out his hand to Leo. "Colton Connolly. Lovely to meet you. Welcome to our home."

"Leopold de Loughrey, but I prefer Leo." Leo shook Colton's hand. "Thank you for having me."

Colton turned to King and hugged him tight before

giving Ace a playful shove out of the way and stepping to one side so they could come in. Inside the hall, Leo froze. He'd never seen anything so beautiful. The inside of the house was just as lavishly decorated as the outside, with intricate wreaths, lush garland, twinkling lights everywhere, white poinsettias, candles, and all manner of Christmas decor.

"This is amazing," Leo murmured, allowing King to lead him farther into the house.

"Thank you." Colton beamed.

Leo paused to admire a stunning white-and-gold reindeer almost as big as him, standing regally near the end of the hall. "After my mom died, we kind of stopped decorating. I think my dad only celebrated because my sister and I were still little. It didn't feel the same, though. Every Christmas morning, my mom would help us decorate sugar cookies. She even made me a cookie cutter in the shape of a fish in honor of my favorite crackers," Leo said with a soft laugh. He noticed the way Colton's expression softened and how Ace exchanged a look with King. Leo had no idea what it meant, but he was too enchanted by the extravagant beauty around him to worry about it.

Judging by the noise coming from the living room—including a couple of barks—Leo would hazard a guess that's where the others were gathered. Boisterous laughter filled the air, everyone talking at once. Normally the noise level would bother him, but for some reason, it didn't. He felt... safe.

"All right you heathens. Quiet down," Ace shouted, getting everyone's attention.

Suddenly Leo had twelve pairs of eyes on him, including Chip's, and he took a tentative step back, but

King wrapped an arm around him and tucked him in close. Leo relaxed into King, allowing his warmth to wash over him. He hoped his smile wasn't as awkward as it felt. Everyone remained silent, and it took Leo a moment to realize they were waiting on King to take the lead.

Clearing his throat, King motioned to a big guy with fair hair and blue eyes. He was handsome, with hair falling over his brow and a crooked grin. "Cowboy here is Lucky's boyfriend, Mason Cooper. He supervises the department I head at Four Kings and does a very fine job of it. Mason, this is Leo."

Mason tipped his head. "Nice to meet you, Leo."

Leo smiled at the thick Texas drawl. It made total sense now. He could easily see Mason wearing a cowboy hat and sitting on a horse as he rode off into the sunset.

King turned to a young man more Leo's build but taller, with kind blue eyes and his black curls cut in a trendy haircut. By his slim-fitting button-down shirt and slacks, Leo figured he was looking at Red's boyfriend, the fashion photographer.

"This is Lazarus Galanos. Red's boyfriend."

"You can call me, Laz," he said with a wave. "It's so nice to meet you, Leo."

A beautiful blond woman with King's blue eyes approached, her smile warm, and instantly Leo knew she was King's sister.

"This brat is my sister, Bibiana Kingston, but everyone calls her Bibi."

"Brat? Who are you calling a brat? I'm the older sibling," Bibi teased, holding her arms open to Leo, who didn't hesitate. He walked straight into her embrace and returned her hug. She gave off a quiet, gentle sort of strength, one that reminded him of King. It also made him miss his own sister.

He pulled away and stepped back into King's waiting arms. "It's so nice to meet you."

"This is my husband, Nash," Bibi said, gazing lovingly up at the tall, handsome black man who wrapped her up close and kissed the top of her head. He smiled brightly at Leo and held out his hand.

"It's nice to meet you, Leo. Welcome to the madhouse."

Leo laughed and shook Nash's hand. He liked him already.

With a huff, Bibi poked her husband's side, making him squirm and laugh. "What? The poor man should be prepared. God knows I wasn't."

"Don't listen to him," Bibi said, then put a finger to her lips. "Actually, most of the crazy is over there." She motioned to Ace and Lucky, who were each trying to push the other off the armrest of the couch where Colton, Mason, Red, and Laz were seated. Didn't matter there was plenty of empty couch space elsewhere.

"Hey," Lucky and Ace protested at the same time.

"Totally legit," Nash murmured, laughing when the cousins flipped him off.

"It's great to meet you all. Thanks for having me here."

Chip trotted over, tongue lolling and tail wagging. He lifted his paw, and Leo laughed as he took the paw in greeting. "Well, hello, sir. It's nice to see you again."

Having greeted Leo, Chip returned to his person's side, nudging Joker in the leg with his nose to get his attention, earning himself a scratch behind the ear as Joker continued talking to Jack. Rarely was one seen without the other. They were thick as thieves. Leo envied them a little. He'd never had a best friend. Someone who kept all your secrets and got angry on your behalf, who defended you and told you when it was time to get your head out of your butt. Then again, most of the friendships in this room had been forged under fire. A brotherhood that could never be broken. Leo had grown up around soldiers and weapons, but his father had tried his best to raise Leo outside of it all. Many of the military dads Leo had met in his lifetime had been proud their children followed in their footsteps. His dad hadn't wanted that for Leo. Not because he thought Leo couldn't hack it—even if Leo himself had believed that—but because he was afraid of losing Leo.

Leo should have been nervous, and under normal circumstances he would have been anxious meeting so many new people at once, but he wasn't. It couldn't just be because of King, could it? Leo's sister had introduced him to friends of hers and her husband's, but Leo never felt at ease with those people the way he did here. Maybe it was because of how open and friendly King's family was. It was clear they were very close and loved one another. They teased, cursed, and hugged one another.

Ace grabbed Nash and planted a sloppy kiss on his cheek, making the big man laugh loudly. His wife huffed and placed a hand on her hip, rolling her eyes when Ace hugged Nash close.

"We have to be careful, or she'll suspect something. We can't let her find out about us," Ace said in a loud stage whisper.

Bibi grinned wickedly. "You want to steal my husband? Go for it. You get to keep his gross collection of unwashed college football jerseys. I'll keep your hot billionaire boyfriend and his mansion."

Ace released Nash. "Wait a second."

Nash looked Ace over. "Dang, what was I thinking? If

I'd gone for Colton, I could have had my own private plane."

"Oh, I see how it is," Ace said, flipping Nash off. He scrambled over Mason, ignoring the cowboy's grumbling protest, and crawled onto Colton, somehow managing to wrap himself around the taller man. "He's my billionaire. You all get your own."

"My money feels very loved," Colton muttered, his face squished against Ace's.

Everyone laughed, and Leo joined King on the long couch across from the guys, his heart doing a little flip when King sat near the armrest and tugged Leo close, his arm coming to wrap around him, keeping their bodies pressed together. Had someone said something to the group ahead of time? Because according to King, this was the first time he'd ever brought anyone home for Christmas, yet no one questioned who Leo was or why he was there.

While Colton detached himself from Ace to join Bibi and Laz, who were headed for the kitchen to get snacks for everyone, Leo leaned in to King, speaking quietly.

"No one seems surprised to see me."

"That would be because Ace talked to everyone the moment he knew we'd be joining them. I mentioned wanting to save you from being interrogated, and he made it happen. He might act like an ass at times, but he'll always come through for you."

"Thank you." Leo tapped his fingers against his leg until he felt King's breath ruffling his hair, his voice quiet.

"I also might have told them I was bringing someone special and not to make a big deal about it, even if it is a big deal."

Inside, Leo did a happy dance. Outside, he was calm

and collected, until King brushed his lips over Leo's temple, followed by a kiss in the same spot.

King had kissed Leo.

In front of everyone.

Leo pretended he didn't notice everyone else pretending not to notice King's affectionate gestures. Mostly Leo was too stunned to do anything else. He didn't take King for a PDA kind of guy. Not that he expected King to play tonsil hockey with him in front of his family, but Leo hadn't known what to expect, considering they hadn't really given a name to whatever was between them.

Sinking a little more into King, Leo took a moment to admire the gorgeous living room and the huge Christmas tree in the corner, the top of which almost reached the high ceiling. It was candy-themed, playful yet elegant, a perfect combination of Ace and Colton. Beautifully wrapped gifts were piled high beneath the tree and several layers deep, all matching the tree's candy colors. From what Leo could tell, some of the candy on the tree looked real, undoubtedly Ace's idea, though if that were the case, Leo was surprised there was any candy left on it. The guy always seemed to be eating.

Colton, Bibi, and Laz returned with bowls and plates filled with all kinds of deliciousness, from cookies and a cheese platter, to chips and dips. Leo's mouth watered as everything was placed on the huge coffee table in the middle of the room.

"Ace, Nash, Lucky, you guys are in charge of drinks." Bibi motioned toward the kitchen, and the three men didn't so much as question the order. They jumped to it. Clearly King wasn't the only Kingston with a commanding presence.

Once the living room was overflowing with food and

drink, a good deal of it alcohol, since everyone was spending the night, it was apparently time for games.

"First up, Scattergories," Bibi announced. "You all know the drill. Divide into two teams."

Leo gave a start when everyone bolted from their seats to the couch he and King sat on. They all scrambled to fit, and Leo laughed as he was forced onto King's lap. What the heck was happening?

Bibi placed a hand to her head as if she were summoning patience. "You can't all be on the same team as Leo."

Wait, they all wanted to be on *his* team? Leo lifted his questioning gaze to King, who shrugged, his eyes filled with laughter.

"Have you ever played this game?" King asked, a *thump* momentarily distracting Leo, and he cringed as Joker groaned from the floor. Chip was immediately all over him, licking his face and pulling at his shirt to help him up. Leo turned his attention back to King and shook his head in response to his question.

Growing up, he never really played board games. They weren't challenging enough, and the other kids stopped wanting to play with him, stating that playing with him was no fun and not fair because he always knew all the answers.

"When the dice is rolled, whatever letter comes up is the letter your words have to start with. You get the most points by coming up with words that no one else has come up with."

"Sounds pretty straightforward. But why does everyone want to be on my team?"

"Because they want to win. You're a genius, remember?"

Ace, having been displaced, narrowed his eyes at everyone piled on the couch.

"Whatever you are thinking, forget it," Lucky warned from Mason's lap. "You don't fit."

"Challenge accepted." Ace dove across them, making everyone shout, curse, and groan. He lay on his back, stretched out, his head on Nash's lap, and his hands behind his head. "I'm ready to play. For my winnings, I'll accept cash, credit, or gift certificates."

Bibi marched over, her glare fierce. "Jack, Joker, Ace, Lucky, and Nash, get your butts on that couch over there right now. King, Red, Laz, Mason, and Colton are on Leo's team."

There was a collection of groans, but the guys got up and did as they were told. Bibi could easily give Leo's dad a run for his money. Leo slipped back onto the couch next to King, smiling when Chip jumped up and curled in next to him before letting out a bark.

Bibi rolled her eyes. "Fine, you can stay with Leo."

Joker gasped and thrust a finger at Chip. "You traitor!"

Everyone laughed as Chip dropped his furry head onto Leo's lap and covered his face with his paws.

"Is it okay to pet him?" Leo asked Joker, who waved a hand in dismissal.

"Go for it. He's an attention whore. And a traitor. You think you know a guy and then *bam*, right in the back. After all the bacon."

Chip lifted his head and cocked it to one side.

"Oh, now you acknowledge my existence?" Joker folded his arms over his chest and sniffed. "I'll think about it."

Chip lowered his head back onto Leo's lap, big dark eyes aimed at Joker and tail thumping against Red's leg. How could anyone resist those eyes? Leo pet his head, amazed by how soft and sleek Chip's fur was. It had a beautiful shine, and his ears were huge! Leo had never seen a dog with pointy ears that big. King leaned in to murmur in his ear.

"See? Even Chip loves you."

As Bibi set up the game, a thought occurred to Leo.

"What if we win?"

"*If*? You doubt us?"

"No, I mean, what if we win and they get upset." Leo motioned to the guys sitting opposite them.

"They won't get upset, I promise. I can't, however, promise they won't try to bribe you in order to get you on their team next time. It's a pretty good way to get free stuff."

Leo blinked at him. "Are you serious?"

"Oh yeah." He lifted a leg. "Where do you think I got these boots?"

Leo gaped at him. "Someone gave you those boots so you would be on their team?"

King nodded. "My family is *very* competitive. They're not sore losers, but they will do everything they can to win. Ace and I wear the same size shoes, so that was my price for being on his football team. Nash actually played college football, so he made out like a bandit that game."

"So... Ace gave you his brand-new boots, just like that."

"Yep."

"Wow. No one's ever *wanted* me on their team, much less enough to bribe me."

"That makes no sense."

Leo shrugged. "I guess my knowing all the answers made them feel bad." He never wanted to make anyone feel bad about not knowing something. Leo would never get upset with someone for informing him of something he didn't know. He found it a perfect learning opportunity. He never lorded his smarts over anyone. Everyone had smarts; they were just different. Leo's street smarts were pretty much nonexistent. He'd been sheltered all his life by his family, and anytime they were together, there were usually guards with them because of his father.

King had gone thoughtful, and Leo frowned.

"You okay?"

"How about this," King said with a smile. "If you don't feel comfortable answering at any point, you can always tell one of us, and we'll answer for you."

Leo hadn't thought of that. "Okay."

King hadn't been kidding about how competitive his family was, and Leo loved that he wasn't the only one with unique words. Everyone had different skills and knowledge the others didn't, all of which they drew from for their words—Laz his photography, Red with his medical knowledge, Bibi and Nash the culinary arts, Mason his former ranching and police experience, Ace his general Ace-ness, and so on. Leo's team still won, and it was just as King said. No one was pissed they lost. They teased one another, joked about their choice of words, but not a hint of maliciousness or anger.

With King excusing himself to go to the restroom, Leo took the opportunity to admire the view of the beach from the wall of glass that stretched from the living room down past the dining room and kitchen. A set of glass doors led out onto a wraparound balcony, the end of which had stairs leading down to the pool and the private walkway to the beach. Bowers's men occasionally came into view as they patrolled the property.

Leo shifted his focus to the glass and the reflection of King's family in the living room as they argued over which Christmas movie to watch first. He smiled, his heart squeezing when King stepped up behind him and wrapped Leo in his arms, his cheek coming to rest against Leo's.

"Your family is amazing."

"They're a pretty good bunch, aren't they? You okay? Do you need a breather?"

Leo shook his head. "I'm good. Just reflecting."

Jack stepped up to them, clearing his throat. "Sorry to interrupt, but can I borrow Leo for a few minutes?"

King released Leo, and Leo turned to Jack, curious.

"Sure, what's up?" Leo asked.

"I wanted you to have a look at my security system. See what you think."

Leo blinked at him. "You want my opinion on your security system?"

Jack shrugged, his boyish smile wide. "Well, yeah. I mean, I'm good—okay, damned good—but you work at a whole other level. I'd love for you to check it out, see if anything jumps out at you that can be improved."

Leo glanced at King. "Is he serious?"

King puffed his chest up a little. He almost appeared... proud. "Where cybersecurity is concerned, the buck stops with Jack. You're the first person he's ever asked to do this."

Leo turned back to Jack, the butterflies in his stomach going wild. "I'd be honored." He tried to tell himself not to make more out of it than it was. Jack said he wanted his opinion, but if Leo did find something, he'd probably just humor him and never ask him again. No one liked having their work corrected, especially when that work was part of who you were. King followed quietly along as Jack led Leo through the house, pointing out the various high-end cameras, where the panic room was, the various security measures put in place, and finally the system itself, which was located in the wall of Colton's office. It could also be

accessed via a panel near the kitchen, but after one particular incident where Ace decided to upload his music,
scaring the hell out of Colton, and not being able to fix the
volume, Jack had decided the main hub should be within
Colton's reach.

It was impressive, for sure, but something jumped out at
Leo, and he tapped his fingers against his leg. Not missing a
beat, King leaned in and placed a reassuring hand to his hip,
his words soft and encouraging. "Tell him. He wouldn't
have asked if he didn't want to know."

Swallowing hard, Leo turned to Jack. "It's a great
system, but what happens if someone manages to make it
into the house?"

"No one can hack this system. I built it myself from
scratch."

"I can," Leo said, hoping he wasn't overstepping.

Jack appeared thoughtful. "I'm listening."

"You'd have to be really *really* good to get past all these
security measures, but someone like me could. The chances
of that happening are super-slim. I mean, if you have my
level of skill and want to do some damage, you wouldn't be
going after Colton. You'd be going after something big. Let's
say someone like me does come after Colton for whatever
reason. Once he's in the system and you have hostiles in the
house, then what?"

"That's what the panic room is for."

"What if Colton can't make it there? Okay, worst-case
scenario. Colton is upstairs in his bedroom. Ace isn't here.
Our hacker gets into the system, locks Colton in the house
and everyone else out. Armed guys are on the ground floor.
Colton can't get to the panic room or outside. He's trapped."

Jack seemed to consider his words. "What would
you do?"

Leo was taken aback by Jack's genuine curiosity. His rapt attention was focused on Leo, like whatever Leo was about to say was probably going to be fascinating.

"Install OC aerosol devices that are connected to a secondary nonwired system, make sure it has an alarm, infrared detection, and face recognition—so it doesn't get triggered by anyone programmed into the system. Include a delay timer and failsafe code Colton and Ace can use so the cable guy doesn't accidentally get incapacitated, but you'll still know when someone's in their home. Four six-ounce cans per device should cover roughly four thousand square feet. I'm sure you can work out the logistics, but that way if someone does get into the system, the moment intruders step out into the hall, they're going down, giving Colton enough time to get to the panic room and call for help. I would also consider creating a passage that goes from some-where on this floor down to the panic room. It'll cost a pretty penny, but considering someone already tried to kidnap Colton once, I'd say it's worth the expense."

Jack blinked at him, and Leo took a small step toward King. Shit, he hoped he hadn't insulted the guy.

"Damn, you're absolutely right. That's a great idea!"

Leo gave a start at Jack's enthusiasm. "It is?"

"Yes! I mean, it's very unlikely someone could get into my system, but we need to consider that cyber criminals aren't simply multiplying but getting smarter. There are people out there like us who *could* get in if they wanted it hard enough, if they wanted to hurt Colton for some reason, or someone paid them enough. Who the hell knows, right? We should be prepared for all scenarios, no matter how unlikely. I could easily rig an internal system like the one you described. Thanks, man." Jack patted Leo's shoulder. "Hey, maybe when this is all over, if you've got some free time, we could meet up and talk? I'd love for you to consider maybe doing some freelance stuff for me. If you're interested."

Leo gawked at him. "Me? Freelance? For *you*?"

Jack's face turned pink, and Leo could have kicked himself. Jack hadn't been saying it to make Leo feel better. He really wanted Leo to consider working with him.

"Shit, I'm sorry," Jack replied, shaking his head. "I got carried away. You've probably got way more important things to work on. Pentagon-level shit and all that."

"I'd love to," Leo blurted.

Jack's expression brightened, and a big smile spread across his face. "Yeah?"

"Are you kidding? It would be awesome!"

"That's great! Thanks. Call me, okay? King will give you my number. If you'll excuse me, I'm going to make some notes on what we talked about. I love these guys, but they don't really get excited about this stuff like I do."

"Are you kidding? There's nothing more exciting than starting a new project. The possibilities are endless."

"Right? See, you get it. This is going to be amazing. Joker's gonna flip his shit when he finds out he's got to deal with two of us now. I can't wait." Jack cackled as he went off, and Leo stood stunned.

"Did that really just happen?"

"Fuck, that was hot."

Leo's eyes widened, and he turned, a little gasp escaping him when he found himself the focus of King's lust-filled gaze. King's eyes were dark, pupils blown, and a low groan rose up from his chest as he stepped closer to Leo. What was happening right now? King wrapped Leo in his arms, bringing him up hard against his body, his thick, hard length stabbing Leo in the stomach. Oh my God, he *was* turned on.

"The way your mind works is a thing of beauty. You see things the way no one else does. The rest of us, we go hunting for all the pieces, hoping to make them fit, but not you. For you, the pieces are already in place, leaving you to focus on finding what's missing." King brushed his fingers down Leo's jaw. "You're amazing."

Leo waited for the punchline, but there wasn't one. King truly believed Leo was someone special. Not only that, but he found it attractive, so much so that he was dragging Leo with him through the house.

"I need to get you alone before I end up bending you over Colton's desk. Pretty sure he wouldn't appreciate us having sex in his office."

Leo couldn't believe this was happening. He followed King toward the guest bedroom they would be sharing tonight. "You guys really do care about what I have to say." They didn't simply ask him his opinion; they valued it —valued *him*.

King stopped so abruptly, Leo almost ran into him. He turned, his blue eyes filled with... hurt.

"Why do you look so pained?" Leo asked, running a thumb over one of King's thick, blond eyebrows.

"I hate knowing how badly you've been hurt. It's why you can't see how truly remarkable you are." King cupped his cheek, and Leo leaned into the touch. "What can I do, sweetheart? How can I help?"

Leo stood on his toes and wrapped his arms around King's neck, brushing his lips over King's. "Don't you see? You're already helping, by being you. I know that sounds a little cheesy, but it's true. You coming into my life has been the best thing that's ever happened to me." There was a cheer from downstairs and loud Christmas greetings. Leo smiled against King's lips. "Merry Christmas, Ward."

"Merry Christmas, sweetheart."

As they kissed, Leo knew there was no going back. His life had changed—*he* was changing, and he liked the person he was becoming. He didn't feel so scared anymore, like he was insignificant. He wasn't. He meant something to his family, to King, to King's family. No longer was he on the outside looking in. He'd found somewhere he belonged, and he would fight with everything he had to keep it.

NINE

ONE DAY.

That's how long it took for his entire life to change, and it wasn't until this moment that King realized it. Had someone told him the turn his life would take by meeting one young man, King would have thought they were delusional. The instant Leo had stepped up to him in the bunker, he should have known. He'd laid his eyes on Leo, and something had begun to shift inside him.

King woke up on New Year's Eve wrapped around Leo, his heart light and his thoughts filled with possibilities for their future. They needed to talk at some point about what came next. They'd been going with the flow, trying to focus on the situation at hand, neither coming out and saying what they felt or what they wanted. King no longer questioned what—or rather *who*—he wanted. He wanted Leo, in his life, permanently. The problem he faced was a new one for him. He didn't know how to go about making that happen.

Leo moaned and turned in King's arms to face him, slipping an arm around King's waist and holding him close, their legs intertwined as Leo buried his face in King's neck with a hum.

"Good morning, sweetheart."

"Great morning," Leo murmured half-awake. "You slept in."

King tended to get up much earlier than Leo, as Leo was *not* a morning person. He tended to stay up later than King and wake up later, whereas King was usually up before the sun rose, but somehow that worked for them. It gave King time to go through his morning workout routine, check his email, sort a few work things out, and make breakfast, all by the time Leo shuffled into the kitchen, hair sticking up as he rubbed his sleepy eyes. At night it meant King woke up to Leo either snuggling in close or starting something that would end with them getting hot and sticky.

This morning, King woke up and decided to stay in bed. "Ace is making breakfast."

"That didn't answer my unasked question."

King chuckled. "It just felt too good being here with you. Decided to stay."

Those three little words lingered in the air between them, their true meaning enough to have Leo rolling King onto his back and straddling him. He gazed down at King, his eyes searching for the truth in those words. King was staying. The logistics of how things would work between Leo being on the west coast of Florida and King on the east coast would be looked into later.

King placed his hands on Leo's thighs, caressing his skin and the fine hairs on his legs. The question was there in Leo's big brown eyes. They'd find a way to work it out. "How about some breakfast?"

Leo nodded, planting a quick kiss on King's lips before

climbing off him. Was Leo disappointed? Was he expecting more? A declaration? Not knowing how to navigate this thing between them was frustrating. Communication was key in any relationship, and he'd learned the importance of opening up and talking things out, but this was different. Why was he having so much trouble articulating his feelings for Leo?

With a grunt, he got up and used the bathroom after Leo, who was a little too quiet for King's liking. When they joined the guys in the dining room for breakfast, it was obvious something was wrong, but King had no idea what. He was pouring himself some coffee when Ace nudged up next to him.

"What happened?"

King glanced over his shoulder at Leo, who was giving Chip a piece of bacon, the guys looking worried and uncertain of what to do. Lucky and Joker tried to get Leo to smile with their shenanigans while Jack tried to draw him out of his pensive thoughts by talking to him about some new gadget. When nothing seemed to work, Red put a hand to Leo's shoulder, murmuring something quietly. Leo excused himself and hurried upstairs. Four pairs of eyes glared at King from the table.

"What did you do?" Lucky asked.

"I didn't do anything," King hissed quietly as he joined them.

Red sighed. "Maybe that's the problem."

Ace sat down, his worried gaze on the stairs where Leo had disappeared. "King, it's obvious he's in love with you."

King blinked at him. "What?"

"Come on, bro." Lucky shook his head at him. "How can you not see it?"

"I knew he was attached, I just, I don't know. He hasn't said anything."

Jack stared at him like he was missing a few marbles. "Of course he hasn't. You have to put yourself in his shoes, King. You're the captain of the football team turned Green Beret, and he's the science nerd who got shoved into lockers. You really think he's going to stand in front of you and tell you he's in love with you?"

"Listen to Jack. He's speaking from experience," Joker said, receiving a punch in the arm from Jack. "What? It's the truth."

"This science nerd is going to shove his foot up your ass if you don't shut up," Jack growled.

King's frown was deep. "This isn't high school."

"That won't erase years of bad experiences," Ace said gently. "How long has it taken him to believe that you really are into him? That you care about him? Or that we like him and aren't just putting up with him for your sake?"

King nodded. Ace was right. Leo struggled with his confidence, though with every passing day he grew bolder, surer of himself. Except when it came to King keeping him. Did he think it was nothing but sex between them? Surely, King hadn't given him that impression.

"I thought he knew," King said, releasing a heavy sigh. "I figured he could feel it."

"Look," Lucky said, drawing King's attention. "Some of us? We are not so good at using words to express how we feel, and in the moment when you are, you know, together, it's okay, you both feel it, but then the doubts creep in and you worry that maybe it was just that—in the moment. He needs to know, King. Even if you are not ready to say those three little words, he needs to know he means something to you. That you won't walk away when this is over."

The room was quiet, a rare occurrence when they were all together, the severity of the situation evident to them all. If King wasn't careful, he could ruin this, and he couldn't stand the thought of pushing Leo away. How was it he could run into a war zone with explosives going off around him, ammunition gone, and not blink, yet put a slightly awkward young man with plump pink lips, glasses, and big brown eyes in front of him, and suddenly he had no idea what the fuck to do?

Thankfully, the silence didn't last long. Ace grinned brightly at King. "Look at us being all adult and shit, helping you with your love life."

King's lips quirked up at the corners. He silently thanked Ace for the reprieve and stood. Red took hold of his arm, his eyes filled with concern.

"What's this really about, King?"

King cleared his throat. "Nothing. I'm not ready to make any declarations."

Ace's eyes went wide, and he cursed under his breath. "Shit. I can't believe I didn't see it."

Jack frowned at Ace. "What are you talking about?"

King dropped back down into his chair and ran his hands over his face. He should have known he wouldn't be able to get anything past his brothers. There was nothing King wasn't afraid to face head-on. Except this. "Red's right. This isn't just about my not wanting to tell him how I feel. I'm—"

"Scared," Ace finished for him.

"Why would you be—" Jack's eyes widened, and he cursed. "Yeah, okay. This is way more complicated than we thought."

Lucky looked between his brothers. "I don't understand."

When Ace spoke, the word was barely a whisper. "Syria."

"Oh fuck." Lucky sat back, a hand going to his head. "I didn't think of that."

"You have to tell him," Ace said, leaning in, his gold-green eyes filled with concern. "He can't not know, King. Not if you two are going to have a real future together."

"It's not my place to tell. When this is over, I'll talk to the General, tell him I'm involved with his son and that I need to come clean." *And hope Leo will still want me.* The unspoken words hung in the air like a thick fog.

"What if the General doesn't want you to tell him?" Joker asked.

King stood. "Then I have to ask myself, does my loyalty lie with the General or with his son?"

"If you need us," Red pitched in softly, "you know where to find us."

King patted Red's shoulder in thanks, his heart in his throat at how very fortunate he was to have his brothers. He headed upstairs, ready to tell Leo *something*. What he walked into was unexpected, to say the least. Leo looked... pissed.

"Shit. No, no, no. Come on. Please don't, please don't, please—" Leo jumped from his chair, fingers curled around fistfuls of his hair. "Fuck! *Fuck!*" He kicked his chair, and King hurried over. It wasn't like Leo to lose his cool like this. Occasionally when something went wrong, he cursed under his breath, ranted a little, bit the head off one of his fish-shaped snacks, but nothing like this.

"Hey, take it easy. What's wrong? Talk to me."

Leo shook his head. "This stupid—" He let out a frustrated growl and tried to avoid King, but King wasn't about to let Leo retreat back into his shell. Not after everything they'd been through and how far Leo had come.

"Leo, talk to me," King demanded gently, tugging on Leo's sweater and carefully pulling Leo into his arms. He brushed his lips over Leo's temple, coaxing his infuriated little wildcat. "Please."

With a huff, Leo let his head fall against King's chest. He shook his head, but King would wait all day if he had to. Several deep breaths and exhales later, Leo lifted his gaze.

"I've completed four of the six pieces, but this damned fifth piece is driving me fucking crazy. I'm not implementing the right coding, so I keep getting kicked out, which means I need to start the damn thing all over again. What if I can't get it? What if I'm not as smart or as good as everyone thinks I am? I don't... I can't—" He sucked in a sharp breath, his face turning red, and his eyes filling. "I can't...."

"You can and you will."

"No, I can't," Leo replied through his teeth. "I keep screwing it up. Maybe it's a sign."

"What do you mean?"

"This program is dangerous. What if it falls into the wrong hands? What if turning it over to the government *is* putting it in the wrong hands? With the right coding, it isn't just capable of spying on terrorists, but on anyone, including our own people. If you knew the whole truth of what this thing is capable of, you'd be terrified. No, you'd be sick. And *I'm* the one creating it for them. Then there's the other side of it. The one that'll protect our operatives, soldiers like you, like the guys, my dad. It could stop an attack. I keep going back and forth, back and forth. I thought about making it so the code couldn't be altered, but what if they find out? I don't know what to do anymore." Leo shut his eyes tight and curled his fingers around fistfuls of his hair.

"Leo, look at me."

Swallowing hard, Leo opened his eyes and met King's gaze. King hated seeing the doubt in his eyes. No one was harder on Leo than Leo. He rubbed Leo's arms and breathed, waiting for Leo to breathe along with him. Leo had been driving himself crazy since they'd returned from Colton's, trying to get this fifth piece of coding done, and it wasn't happening. The growing desperation was finally getting to him.

"If you're worried about the program falling into the wrong hands, maybe you do what you were thinking. Make it so the code can't be altered and call it a necessary security measure."

Leo seemed to consider his words. "Add so-called security measures that wouldn't allow them to abuse the program. They asked me to build this program; they didn't tell me *how* to build it or secure it. Maybe... maybe I can do something to—I don't know. It's still so dangerous."

"You can do this. You're frustrated. You can see the finish line, and now you just want to cross it, but you need to focus on the now. Focus on what's in front of you and not what comes next. Let it take however long it's going to take."

"This needs to be done, King." Leo pushed away from him, and King let him go. "I need to be done with this. I want my life back. I want them gone. I need...."

"What do you need?" King asked softly.

Leo stopped pacing, his shoulders falling. "You."

"I'm right here."

"For how long?" Leo's anger caught King by surprise. It didn't last, though, and Leo's shoulders dropped as he deflated again. "Besides, you're only here because you have to be."

King frowned. "What's this about?"

"You're here because you have to be," Leo snapped, "because you're doing my father a favor. You have no choice."

King crossed his arms over his chest. "I always have a choice. You think I'm here for your father?"

Leo turned to him, fear in his eyes, yet he was pushing King or at least trying to. He was frustrated, angry, afraid, and lashing out. Whatever he thought he could achieve by this wasn't going to happen.

"The way I see it, your father brought us together."

Leo's eyebrows shot up near his hairline.

"Don't look so surprised. Your father may have brought me into this project, and yes, it started as a favor to him, but that quickly changed, and you know it. *You* became the reason I stayed, the reason I'm still here, and I'm not going anywhere. If lashing out at me makes you feel better, knock yourself out, but you're going to finish this project because you're a fucking genius, and I have every faith in you. Also, I need a date for the wedding."

Leo opened his mouth, then closed it. "Wait, what? What wedding?"

"Ace and Lucky's cousin Quinn is getting married on Valentine's Day to his boyfriend, Spencer. No one expects me to bring a plus one, but I think this new year might surprise us all."

Leo squinted at him. "You want me to be your date to a wedding on Valentine's Day?"

"Isn't that what I said?"

"Yeah, okay, smart guy. I heard you." Leo crossed his arms over his chest, his pose mimicking King's. After seeming to mull it over, Leo cast him a sideways glance. "Why?"

King frowned at him as if it was obvious. "Who else would I bring?"

"Not good enough." Leo kept his arms crossed over his chest, his chin lifted and his stance wide. Well now. Someone was feeling *very* bold. King stalked over to him, loving the way Leo swallowed hard but didn't budge. "You're going to have to do better than that."

King stopped in front of Leo, their bodies barely touching. He grinned down at Leo. "Is that so?"

"Yeah. Time to grow a pair, Kingston."

King let out a bark of laughter and threw his arms around Leo, squeezing him close. "Fuck, you're amazing. Okay, how about this. I want you to go as my date because when you're seeing someone, they become your plus one to things like this. If I have to face Ace's family and be interrogated about everything from the last meal I ate to who the cute guy with the glasses who came with me is, it's only right that my boyfriend suffer along with me. That's how it works."

Leo's jaw went slack. "I'm sorry, I think I might be hallucinating. Did you say you want me to go as your... boyfriend?"

King chuckled and brushed his lips over Leo's cheek. "Yes, Leo. When this is over, I want to keep seeing you. I care about you, a lot, more than I've ever cared for someone who isn't family. I know they're probably not the words you want to hear, but I hope knowing that you, and only you, have my heart, along with the rest of me, will be enough for now."

Leo held his gaze, his eyes searching King's for the truth in his words. He cocked his head to one side, appearing to mull it over. A mischievous little smile spread across his face. "It's enough. For now."

Leo kissed him, and King surrendered to the love and affection pouring out of Leo, his arms wrapping around King's neck to keep him close. King had no intention of going anywhere. He wasn't going to mess this up. Leo was a gift, one he never thought he would receive. Once this was over, he'd make things right between them. Whatever the General's answer, King would come clean to Leo, and whether they had a future or not would be in Leo's hands.

"Okay, time to get back to it," Leo said with a sigh as he pulled away. "Just two more pieces and then testing."

"You can do it. I'll bring you something to eat."

Leo nodded and returned to his desk. It was close to noon now, so King whipped Leo up a sandwich and some chips, and the rest of the day went on like it usually did, with Leo typing away at his computer and King making sure he had everything he needed—water, food, and snacks. They all had dinner together, despite Leo wanting to keep working, but King played dirty, and with a few strategically placed kisses managed to convince Leo to come downstairs and eat a proper meal with them.

IT WAS late and around the time Leo would start craving a snack. Instead of heading into the kitchen to grab Leo a bag of his favorite Goldfish crackers, an idea popped into King's head.

The guys would be working in shifts tomorrow to spend some time with their men since they were all spending New Year's Eve at Leo's apartment. King stepped up to Ace, who was in the kitchen making some coffee, and although King was probably going to get teased mercilessly for it, he asked his best friend for a favor. Ace blinked at him before his smile spread wide, and King braced himself. When Ace didn't say anything, King sighed.

"Say whatever you're thinking."

"I was thinking what a sweet gesture that is."

King eyed him warily. "That's it?"

"That's it. I'll be back in no time. Red can help you with the other stuff in the meantime. The ingredients you need to get started are all here." Ace headed out, and King stared after him.

"You okay?" Red asked, stepping up beside him.

"He didn't crack a joke, tease me, or make a smartass comment."

Red stared at the door Ace had disappeared through. "Did you break him?"

King told Red his idea for surprising Leo, and Red smiled.

"That's really sweet."

King opened his mouth to reply, but his phone went off. "Hello?"

"Did you want me to get a little fishing pole-shaped one to signify his reeling you in?"

And there it is. "You're an ass," King grunted, hanging up on Ace and his cackling. He turned to Red. "Thanks for helping me."

"No problem. Leo's going to love it."

King sure hoped so. He wasn't entirely sure, but he wanted to do something to encourage Leo, and the idea just popped into his head. By the time he and Red had finished making the dough, Ace had returned with the cookie cutter and sprinkles. Once everything was done, King thanked the guys, headed upstairs, and placed the plate of fish-shaped sugar cookies with colorful sprinkles on Leo's desk for when Leo came out of his zone. It was sooner than he expected—as in the moment King moved his hand away from the plate.

Leo blinked several times as he stared down at the plate of cookies. Snapping himself out of it, he looked up at King.

"You made these for me?"

"I had help," King said, hoping he hadn't overstepped. "I know you said your mom made these for you, so I imagine they were pretty special. Since you didn't get them at Christmas, I thought you might like them now as a sort of reminder that I'm here for you and cheering you on. I hope I didn't overstep."

Leo's eyes welled, and King cursed under his breath, ready to apologize, when Leo flew out of his chair and threw himself at King.

"You're amazing," Leo said, breathless, before kissing King within an inch of his life. King held him close, returning the heated kiss, loving the feel of Leo's soft lips, eager tongue, and warm mouth. Leo's body shivered against King's, and if Leo wasn't in the middle of work, King might have been tempted to carry him over to the futon and have his way with him, but that would have to wait. King ran his fingers through Leo's hair before reluctantly moving away.

"You can do it."

"Actually," Leo said sheepishly. "I already did."

"What?"

"I got number five."

King whooped and grabbed Leo, spinning him around and kissing him hard, loving the sound of Leo's laugh. They were so close. He put Leo on his feet, King's smile matching Leo's.

"I'm so proud of you."

Fireworks exploded outside the glass doors, and King

checked his watch. Five minutes until midnight. He pulled Leo with him, slid the glass door open, and stepped out onto the balcony with Leo. Fireworks lit up the cloudless sky, the display put on by beachgoers and the community, an impressive spectacle of colorful bursts. King pulled Leo in front of him, his arms wrapped around him, and hands on his chest, their fingers laced together as they watched the show, the water's surface reflecting the shimmering sparkles raining down from the heavens.

Down on the beach, people counted down, and King turned Leo to face him. "I couldn't think of anywhere I'd rather be right now than here with you."

Cheers floated up, and Leo slipped his arms around King's waist. "Happy New Year, Ward."

"Happy New Year, sweetheart." King kissed him, losing himself in this magical moment, the fireworks in the sky feeling like the ones going off in his heart at the knowledge that after all this time, he'd found his person, the one man who understood him, who loved him just the way he was. Leo might not have said as much, but King knew. He could feel it in Leo's kiss, in the way he clung to King like he was everything.

King lost track of how long they stood in each other's arms kissing until Leo shivered. "We should get back inside," King said, rubbing Leo's arms. The temperature had dropped this week, with the late nights falling into the high thirties. The breeze coming in from the water added to the winter chill in the air. Inside, Leo turned to King.

"Thank you. I couldn't have done any of this without you, or the guys. The last one's going to be a bitch, and then we have testing, but I know I can get it done."

"I'll leave you to it, then." Another quick kiss, and King

left Leo with his fish-shaped sugar cookies, which were quickly added to the list of Leo's favorite fish-shaped snacks.

UNFORTUNATELY, Leo hadn't been kidding about the final part of the program being a bitch. It was hard for Leo not to get frustrated with every passing day that he couldn't get the final piece completed, but King did everything he could to make sure Leo had what he needed—plenty of water, food, snacks, and sleep, despite Leo trying to argue with him about "going a little longer." King did his part by wearing Leo out good and hard every night. After more than one round of King pounding Leo into the mattress, there was nothing but soft snores coming from his sweetheart until morning.

The guys did their part, keeping Leo in good spirits throughout the month of January. When February came along, King was starting to get a little stir-crazy himself, mostly because he wanted some time with Leo that didn't include being watched over by NSA agents or Bowers breathing down their necks. Bowers's weekly visits had become a test in restraint for King, and usually involved the guys keeping King away so he wouldn't plant one in the guy's face every time he had a go at Leo for not being done. Everyone was starting to feel it. The guys were missing the men they loved, their beds, their homes. King made sure the guys took shifts, so they got to go home and spend some time with their boyfriends, but this had to end soon.

King checked in with work to make sure everything was okay and that Mason had all the support he needed. King hadn't intended on leaving Mason on his own this long, even if he wasn't entirely on his own. Jay was being a star, helping Mason run a tight ship, despite his little altercations with Ryden. Apparently, Jay and Ryden didn't see eye to eye on a lot of things, but Mason suspected it might be down to something sparking between the two. King hoped whatever it was sorted itself out, because the last thing he needed was a damned office romance, especially involving his irreplaceable executive assistant and the hot-headed Marine. No one needed Jay breathing fire and snapping people's heads off. King promised he'd deal with it the moment he was back at the office.

Leo came up for air, and cookies, getting up from his chair to stretch his delicious little body, his shirt riding up to reveal all that tantalizing skin, his lounge pants dipping dangerously low, exposing a patch of skin King loved to nip at. King stood, and Leo threw up a finger. "Nope."

"What?"

"You sit that sexy butt back down, soldier. I have work to do, and that's not going to happen if I get distracted by your sexy muscles."

King grunted and dropped back down onto the couch, arms crossed over his chest. Just a few more hours until bedtime. Since when was he so impatient? He'd spent *days* in hiding, through all kinds of hellish weather and abysmal terrain, barely moving a muscle, waiting for his target, and he couldn't wait until evening to pounce on his boyfriend? King scoffed.

"I can wait."

Leo rounded the couch, his eyes narrowed. "That so?"

King lifted a brow. "You forget who you're talking to. I once conducted a fourteen-hour interrogation nonstop, without so much as breaking a sweat. Hell, I've been inter-rogated. I didn't break then, and I won't break now."

"I see." Leo took a seat on the coffee table in front of

King, his arms on his legs as he leaned forward to study King. "Nerves of steel, huh? Immovable."

"Yep."

"So, if I um—" Leo got up and straddled King's lap. "—did this, you'd be fine?"

"That's right." King didn't so much as budge. He prided himself on his resolve. When he put his mind to something, no one—*Fuck, that feels good.* King gritted his teeth but remained unmoving as Leo cupped him through his pants, his lips inches from King's. Oh, so that's how Leo wanted to play this. Okay, he was game. "Just know that when I get my hands on you tonight, you're going to be begging me for mercy."

Leo's smile was wicked. "You mean like you're going to be doing in a minute?"

"We'll see about that."

"We sure will," Leo said with a shrug, licking a trail up from King's bottom lip to the tip of his nose, making King swallow hard. "Maybe I'll break you, maybe I won't. But I'll have one hell of a time trying." Leo slipped his hand up under King's shirt. "What if I unzip you right here and suck your dick?"

Little shit. Leo wasn't going to win this.

"No? Okay, what if I sit back, and give you a little show? Pull my cock out, get myself off, come all over my hand with a dildo up my ass."

King jerked. "What? You have one? How do I not know this?"

Leo shrugged. "I was saving it for when it was just the two of us."

The thought of Leo on the bed writhing with pleasure as King jerked him off and fucked his tight little hole with the dildo had King jumping to his feet, Leo wrapped around him. With a hand under Leo's ass so he wouldn't fall, King walked him over to his desk and deposited him on his chair with a growl.

"Looks like I learned something new about you," King grumbled.

Leo blinked at him. "That I like sex toys?"

King almost choked on air. "That. And, good God, you're evil. Sure, you just get back to work while I take my blue balls back to the couch with the image of you and that thing shoved up your ass. Fuck me."

Leo's cheeks went bright red, and his smile faded, his tongue poking out to lick his bottom lip. "Would you, um, ever consider that?"

King leaned in, his grin wicked. "For you? I'll think about it. Have fun coding with that hard-on."

Leo's glare was adorable, and King chuckled, placing a quick kiss to Leo's lips.

"Shit, guys, I'm sorry for interrupting."

They turned to Jack, who stood at the top of the stairs.

"I just got a hit on something." Jack motioned behind him, and they hurried after him down the stairs to the dining room, where the guys were still gathered, only this time they were huddled around Jack's laptop. They made room for King and Leo next to Jack when he resumed his seat.

"Thanks to Leo, we've had access to all the analysts in the bunker, along with whatever they've been working on. We set up an algorithm to analyze their activity and alert us when something out of the ordinary happens on their end. Until now, it's mostly been little things, like Harold checking his social media accounts—he's a bit of a d-bag, but came back clean—or Miranda sending her mom an encrypted email to let her know she's okay. Those are false positives, and the system knows to ignore them unless certain words or phrases trigger an alert. Anyway, one of the analysts triggered an alert after sending an encrypted message hidden within their code to an outside source."

"Who?" King asked.

"Heather Wallace."

"I knew it!" Leo thrust a finger at the screen and the profile of Heather that popped up.

King turned to him. "You did?"

"Yes! I should have known. It was so obvious. How could I not have seen it? It was right there in front of my face, or rather in front of *her* face. Oh, that sneaky sneak."

King peered at him. "So you think she's behind all this?"

"Absolutely."

"What evidence do you have?"

"Evidence? How about my witnessing her evil with my own two eyes?"

"What did you see?"

"Remember when you asked to borrow her headphones?"

"Yes."

"When you walked away, you should have seen the way she stared at your ass. Her eyeballs were like laser beams. *Pew!* Right at your butt. Like she wanted to snuggle with it. She doesn't get to snuggle with it. Only I do!"

King stared at him. "I'm sorry, what?"

"Whoa, back that pony up," Ace said, his lips twitching from how badly he clearly wanted to laugh. "So, what you're saying is, Heather is obviously working with the Russians to kidnap you because she stared at King's ass."

"She didn't just stare at it, Ace. She was *studying* it." Leo spun around and marched across the room before marching back waving a finger at no one in particular. "Yes, he has a fine ass, but that ass is not yours, Heather! You don't get to take a mental picture of it and store it away for later."

"Leo. Sweetheart." King brought Leo's marching to a halt. His indignant expression was very cute.

"Hm?"

"Her staring at my ass, does not make her one of the bad guys."

Leo narrowed his eyes. "Well, it makes her guilty in my book."

"Oh boy." Joker patted King's shoulder. "Good luck with that."

"Leo. Darling. Love. Please focus." King quickly held a finger up to stop whatever Leo was about to say. "Think about it. Are you really prepared to send someone to prison for treason and a host of other crimes because they stared at your boyfriend's ass?"

Ace popped up behind Leo, smile huge. "Boyfriend?"

"Now is not the time," King warned, his gaze still on Leo.

"Gotcha." Ace disappeared, and King gave Leo a pointed look.

"Well?"

"Fine." Leo rolled his eyes. "We'll just have to find some 'evidence.'" God help King, Leo had actually used air quotes around the word. With a quick kiss to Leo's brow, King turned back to Jack.

"Do we know what the message said or who she sent it to?"

Jack nodded. "Our decryption program is working on it now, but Heather's got some pretty mad skills. Not as good as Leo, but she's good. It's going to take a few hours."

King nodded his thanks, and the guys went back to

their posts in the apartment downstairs with the exception of Ace who dropped down onto the couch when his phone rang. With a big dopey smile that could only mean Colton was calling, Ace tapped the screen and put the phone to his ear. "Hi, baby." The color drained from Ace's face, and King went on high alert. "Baby, slow down. Tell me what happened?" Ace started pacing as he listened before coming to a halt. "*What*? Calm down. Are you okay? Good, that's what matters. Who's there? Ryden and Mason? Where are they? Can I talk to one of them? No, that's fine. Just stay inside the house, okay? Yeah, I'm coming, baby. It'll be okay. You're okay. I love you." Ace hung up, and the fear in Ace's eyes had King immediately at his side.

"What is it?" King asked.

"They found a bomb under Colton's car."

"What?" King put a hand on Ace's shoulder, offering comfort, and hopefully calm. Ace needed to use his head now, even if his heart was most likely going into overdrive.

"Colton was going to meet his father for lunch, and you know Sanford always double and triple checks everything before he lets Colton anywhere near the car. Anyway, Sanford was running through his regular checks on the SUV, and he found the bomb. It doesn't have a timer or anything, so my guess is it's rigged to go off when the car door opens. Colton called Mason right away. He's there with Ryden and a shit-ton of our guys. Colton's freaking out."

"Go," King told Ace, cutting him off before his best friend could protest. It wasn't the first time Colton had been targeted. The timing was for shit, but King wasn't going to take any chances. "Take Lucky and Joker with you. Keep me posted."

Ace nodded. He brought King in for a quick embrace. "Watch your back."

King gave him a final squeeze before releasing him. "You too."

Ace had the same feeling he did. It didn't bode well, but there was nothing they could do. King wasn't about to leave Colton out there, vulnerable and distraught without Ace. Whatever the reason behind this latest development, they'd get to the bottom of it.

TEN

WATCH YOUR BACK.

The subtle warning from Ace to King hadn't escaped Leo's attention. Something was wrong, and it had nothing to do with the bomb under Colton's car. At least Leo didn't think so. What if someone was trying to get to him? Leo was terrified for Colton. Maybe it was all unrelated, but Ace warning King meant he thought it could be. Was it the same men who were after Leo?

"Shit, this is my fault," Leo said, taking a step back.

"Hey, no," King argued gently. "None of this is your fault."

"What if it's the men trying to kidnap me? What if my being at Colton's house for Christmas put him in danger? What if they found out where I was and thought I was still there?" Leo started pacing, but King quickly put a stop to it.

"Leo, we can't allow ourselves to get caught up in the what ifs, okay? Until we know more, let's not speculate. The guys are going to get to the bottom of this. Just like those bastards showing up at the bunker wasn't your fault, this isn't either. We will deal with it. Tell me you understand."

Leo nodded. He knew King was right, but it was hard not to feel guilty. Colton had been kind, insisting they were going to become good friends and that Leo was welcome to visit anytime, talking about how he was looking forward to seeing Leo at their weekly Sunday dinners. Leo had been dumbstruck by the invite until King nudged him, asking if he'd consider it. As if Leo would turn down the chance to become a part of King's family.

King pulled out his phone, set it on speaker, and after the first ring, Jack answered. "Hey, did Ace fill you in?"

"Yeah, he just left with Lucky, Joker, and Chip. I'm going through Colton's security feeds. The cameras must have picked something up. If I find anything, I'll let Ace know and then report back to you."

"Great." They heard Red's muffled voice in the background. "What did he say?"

"He said to tell you he's making dinner and we'll bring it up in about half an hour, but to call if you need something sooner."

"Okay, thanks." King hung up, following Leo, who took off upstairs. "Leo? What's wrong?"

"I have to finish this. I can't keep putting everyone's life in danger."

"Hey, hold on a second." King took Leo's arm, bringing him in close. "I thought we agreed this wasn't your fault."

"No, I know that, but the longer this takes, the longer everyone I care about is in danger. There's something that's been bugging me," Leo said, taking a seat in his chair.

"What's that?" King was looking around the room, like he was trying to figure something out.

"Why haven't they tried again?"

King turned his attention back to Leo. "What?"

"The Russians or whoever sent them. Why haven't they

tried again? Let's say they did go to Colton's because they found out I'd been there. Why now? Why haven't they shown up here? It's been almost two months. Are you telling me they just gave up?"

King considered his words. "Maybe. After what happened at the bunker, maybe whoever was working with them bailed, deciding it wasn't worth the risk."

"You don't believe that," Leo said. "I know you don't want me to worry, but I'd rather know the truth, no matter how ugly."

King swallowed hard, then nodded. "You're right. I don't think they gave up. I don't have the answers to your questions, but we need to remain vigilant. I'll call Bowers and let him know what's happening with Colton. It might not be connected, but I'd rather him and his men be on alert." He removed his phone from his pocket and frowned. "I have no signal."

Just as King said the words, a shrill alarm went off, and Leo spun his chair toward his desk.

"What the hell is that?" King asked, his hand on Leo's shoulder.

"That's my security system. It's been breached."

"What? How the hell is that even possible?"

Leo brought up his security system interface, feeling sick to his stomach at the sight of intrusive code wreaking havoc. He felt like he'd been violated. Someone had come into his safe space, into what was his, a part of him, without permission. No one should be in here. Leo tried his best to regain control, but there were so many damned things going wrong at the same time, too many fires to put out. Where the hell was it coming from? *First things first, focus on the most important part.* It looked like they were making their way through his defenses, one piece at a time. If he could just head them off.... He went into the admin area and gasped. The little piece of coding jumped out at him. The ears, the whiskers....

"Oh my God, it's them."

"Who?"

"Codey Cat. The coder I told you about. The one who disappeared. But... how? Why? This makes no sense." Sense or not, he had to try to stop them. "They've disabled all my fail switches. They're... in everything. Oh my God, they're in the AC vents." Leo shot away from his desk, a chill traveling up his spine. "King, they've taken over the whole building. It's too late to stop it." Whoever was doing this had gotten in way before the alarm went off, discreetly deactivating one section at a time without alerting him. It was only because they'd tripped the alarm connected to the elevator that he'd been alerted, but why? If they'd been so careful before? Whoever had done this was good, *really* good, and now someone was on their way up. "King, some-one's coming."

"Okay, we're getting you out of here." King grabbed his hand, and they turned in time to see Heather reach the top of the stairs, a small army of men behind her.

Leo froze. "Heather?" *Wait....* "You're Codey Cat?"

Heather shook her head. "I'm so sorry, Leo." Tears streamed down her cheeks, and she moved to one side as men flooded the room; none of them were Bowers's agents or soldiers.

The ventilation system. If Bowers and his men weren't up here, it meant they were out for the count. *Oh God, Jack and Red. Please let them be okay. They had to be okay.*

"What did you do to them?" Leo demanded, trying to get around King, who'd pulled Leo behind him and was moving them farther back into the room.

"They're alive," Heather said with a sniff. "Just out. Except for him." She motioned toward King. "I'm so sorry, King, but he said you'd get in the way."

Leo's heart jumped into his throat. "No."

"Leo, stay back," King ordered, removing his gun from the holster he always wore as half a dozen men wearing military-style uniforms with no insignias charged King. One of them grabbed Heather and put a gun to her head, shouting at King in Russian and motioning for him to put his gun down.

"King, you have to do what he says," Leo said, flinching at Heather's cry.

"You're my priority," King replied through his teeth, his eyes on the approaching men.

"Please don't let him kill me," Heather begged.

Leo grabbed King's arm. "King."

"They're not going to kill her, Leo. They need her. Why do you think they brought her up here? Get behind the futon." King fired at the men in the room, and Leo ducked behind the futon like King asked. King was right. The guy holding a gun to Heather pushed her behind the kitchen counter. King didn't miss, but the problem wasn't his marksmanship—it was his lack of ammunition and the army of men that continued to flood through the doorway.

Leo felt helpless. Each guy was twice his size and obviously trained. King had taught Leo some self-defense but nothing that would be enough to take down any of these men. What the hell could he do? *Do what you do best, Leo. Think. Come on.* He couldn't leave King in their hands.

King used everything in his arsenal to take his enemies down. He didn't hesitate, didn't pause to take a breath or even blink, grabbing everything within reach and turning it into a weapon, from a book sitting on the coffee table that he slammed into one man's windpipe, to one of the hand weights he swiped up off the floor to swing into another man's face. Leo cringed at the sound of breaking bones. Blood splattered across his furniture and walls. One man jumped onto King's back, and King flipped the guy over his shoulder onto the coffee table, smashing it to pieces, before he spun and slammed a fist into another man's face. One, two, three hooks into another guy until he collapsed, King's knuckles bloodied and bruised. The fifth guy hit the floor in a heap, and four more men launched themselves at King.

"No!" Leo tried to think, but how could he when the man he loved was being viciously attacked by a small army? There were too many of them. Not even King could fend them all off. The floor was littered with bodies, some life-less, others out cold. Three huge men rushed King from behind, another four from the front, the hideous sound of fists pounding into flesh echoing through the room as King roared, determined to smash through his attackers, ignoring the hits he received in the process. A punch landed across his jaw while he was busy throwing another guy across the room. King staggered but quickly recovered, ducking under another fist, rolling, and popping up behind the man. He kicked at the side of the guy's knee with his boot, followed by a punch to the side of the head.

"Take him out! For fuck's sake, it's one guy!"

Bowers stormed into the room, and the truth of who had betrayed them momentarily caught King off guard, enough for someone to shoot him in the leg.

"No!" Leo screamed and fought furiously against the men who rushed him. "King!"

"Leo," King growled, pushing himself to his feet. He stumbled but managed to take two more men down before another shot rang out, and then another. King stumbled toward Leo, only to have Bowers kick the back of his injured leg before grabbing a fistful of his hair.

"No!" Leo shook his head, tears filling his eyes. "Don't! Please!"

King grabbed Bowers's wrist and threw his elbow back at the same time, twisting, and taking advantage of Bowers doubling over from the pain in his groin. King growled, punching Bowers in the stomach and pushing himself to his feet, but he was rushed by two men, and slammed into the wall, his pained scream shaking Leo down to his core. King held on to his side as his legs gave out and he hit the floor, his leg, side, and shoulder bleeding. The same two men rushed toward him, and King got to his feet again, pushing away from the wall, and fighting despite his injuries. If he kept this up, he was going to bleed to death. A fierce punch to the jaw and another kick to his injured leg had King down on one knee. Several men attacked at once, punching and kicking.

"Please, stop!" Leo shouted. They were going to kill King. He looked around, frantic to find something, *do* anything. He'd never been more terrified in his life, but King needed him. Bowers shouted at the men to finish King off as he marched over to Leo, grabbed his arm, and dragged him toward his desk. Leo swiped up his bag of snacks and held it out to Bowers.

"Goldfish cracker?"

"Are you fucking kidding me with this right no—"

Throwing the bag in Bowers's face, Leo used the maneuver King had taught him and snatched Bowers's gun. He spun on his heels and faced Bowers—gun aimed at his own temple.

"Stop!" Bowers threw up his hands. "Everyone, stop!"

The room stilled.

"Get away from him," Leo spat out at the men crowding King. He felt sick to his stomach, and it took everything he had to keep his hand from shaking.

"Leo, don't," King wheezed, sucking in a sharp breath and wincing. His gorgeous face was bloodied, one eye shut, the other showing ugly splotches of red from the popped blood vessels. He was battered, bruised, and bleeding, yet he was trying to push himself to his feet, his boots sliding on the puddles of blood beneath him. *His* blood.

Bowers held his hands up in front of Leo as he edged closer. "Leo—"

"Don't come any closer!" Leo removed the safety, and Bowers's eyes went huge. "My father is a General, asshole. You think I don't know how to use a gun?"

"Okay, all right," Bowers soothed. "Come on, you're not going to do this."

"Fix him," Leo demanded, pointing at King with his free hand.

"That's not going to happen," Bowers replied, and Leo's heart slammed in his chest when King started sinking farther to the floor. He was on the verge of passing out.

"You're not listening," Leo shouted. "If *he* dies, you get nothing! And my guess is, if you get nothing, the men you're working for will make sure *you* die." He knew how this worked. Human lives meant nothing to the kind of people who were after the program.

"Look, I know he's your friend—"

"He's more than my friend," Leo growled.

Bowers squinted at him. "What?"

"You heard me."

Bowers looked from Leo to King and back. "Shit."

"Yeah. You've fucked yourself over. Now. *Fix. Him.*"

"Leo, no," King wheezed. He coughed, sputtering

blood, and a tear rolled down Leo's cheek. Leo wanted nothing more than to go to King, but he couldn't take his eyes off Bowers, not until he got King medical attention.

"You want me to do this? You fix him up and you don't lay another finger on him."

Bowers cursed under his breath. "Fine." He nodded to a small group of men, and they carefully lifted King. One of them opened the futon, and they laid King down.

Two of the men left, and Leo figured they'd be coming back with medical supplies. Leo edged closer to King.

"What are you doing?" Bowers demanded. "You're getting what you want. Now give me the gun."

Leo placed the gun in the waistband of his pants. "This is my insurance policy."

"You think I'm going to let you get near him with a gun?"

"Look at him," Leo spat, throwing a hand in King's direction. "He's barely conscious. You really think he's going to do something?"

"Yes. It's what he's fucking trained to do! He'll die protecting you."

"Just give me a minute! Okay?"

Bowers threw up his arms but motioned for Leo to go ahead. Leo knelt by King's side, needing to touch him, but not sure where he could so it wouldn't hurt King. He took King's hand in his and brought it to his lips for a kiss.

"We're going to be okay, Ward. I promise."

King nodded. He murmured something, but it was too quiet for Leo to hear, so he leaned in, his ear close to King's lips.

"Get us out of this."

Leo pulled back, his eyes filling once more. "Me?"

King nodded again. This time when he spoke, the words were clear as day. "I trust you, and... I love you."

Calm. Keep him safe. Calm. Keep him safe. King....

Leo wanted to sob, but he wouldn't give in to his emotions in front of that bastard Bowers. This was only for them, for him and King. "I love you too, Ward," Leo said, then kissed King, promising him without words that he would be strong for the both of them, that he'd take the trust King had in him and find a way to get them out of this. King no longer had to be the strongest man in the room. He had Leo. With King's muscle and Leo's brain, they'd be a force to be reckoned with. King's head lulled to the side, and Leo cupped his face. "Ward. Stay with me. Please."

Bowers appeared and checked King's pulse. Leo wanted to hiss and claw at him like a feral cat, or better yet, fire a couple of rounds into him, see how he liked it. How dare he lay a hand on King?

"He's alive."

Leo glared at Bowers, venom dripping from his words when he spoke. "Lucky for you."

"My, my, haven't we grown a spine. Green Beret rub off on you, did he? Well, he certainly rubbed something," Bowers said with a snort.

Leo stood and headed for his desk, pretending for all the world that he was in control and calm. He kept his hands balled into fists so Bowers couldn't see them shake. "Tell your guys to wait downstairs."

Bowers laughed. "Yeah, fuck no."

The men Bowers had sent for medical supplies returned, and at his okay, went over to King, but not before Bowers took one of their guns and holstered it. The men got to work on King, cutting through his clothes to get to his wounds.

Leo took a seat in his chair and motioned around him. "Where the fuck am I going to go? And I sure as hell am not leaving without King, so your goons can wait downstairs. How do you say, 'don't touch my shit' in Russian?"

Bowers peered at him. "You've gotten mouthy, too. I don't think I like it."

"I don't think I give a shit," Leo ground out. He narrowed his eyes at one of the men pulling on surgical gloves. "You better know what you're doing."

"Relax, Juliet. Romeo's in good hands. Lyosha was a medic for the Russian Army. You have my word."

"You'll have to excuse me if I'm a little underwhelmed by your assurances, given the circumstances." Leo glanced over at Heather, who was sobbing quietly. Whatever her involvement, she either never expected things to take the turn they had or she was being forced into this. Time to find out.

"Why is she here?"

"To make sure you do what you're supposed to do." Bowers turned to his men. "You, bring me the laptop. The rest of you wait downstairs." They did as Bowers ordered, and he handed the laptop to Heather, who set it on the kitchen counter. She stood behind it so she was facing Leo.

"How is she supposed to check my work without Jarvis?"

Bowers frowned. "Who?"

Leo rolled his eyes. "Jarvis. My coding software. I created it specifically for this program. She needs Jarvis to access what I'm coding. What, you thought I'd create a top-secret government program on Windows?"

"He can install it on my computer," Heather said. "It's secure."

"Then get to it. Fucking nerds and their comic book bullshit. Just get it fucking done," Bowers growled.

"There's one little problem," Heather said. "I need to reopen the connection."

"Absolutely not." Bowers shook his head. "You open a connection, and he sends an encrypted message out to his boyfriend's Green Beret buddies."

"Oh, you mean the ones you sent *four hours away* to Ponte Vedra?" Leo snorted. "Yeah, that's really going to help. Nice tactic, by the way, getting the guys out of here. But without an internet connection, I can't upload the software onto her computer."

"Can't you stick it on a USB drive or something?"

Leo stared at him. "Um, no. Sorry, Agent Smith, but we can't transfer the Matrix onto a USB stick. It's a highly sophisticated AI program. We're not backing up your documents folder." If looks could kill, Leo would have vanished in a puff of smoke. Leo turned to meet Heather's gaze. "I won't let anyone else get hurt. I promise. I want to end this."

"Jesus Christ. Fine." Bowers studied Heather before moving his hard gaze to Leo. "She's going to get you back online. If I catch even a whiff of you calling the cavalry, I'll make sure they slowly bleed your boyfriend to death. Then they'll chop him up into little pieces and mail him to his family."

"I know what's at stake," Leo spat. "Let me do my fucking job." He nodded to Heather. "Get me online, and let's get this over with." While Heather typed away at her computer, getting his system back up and running, Leo focused on Bowers. He couldn't watch them working on King, on the way they dug around in his open wounds to remove the bullets. All he could do was be thankful King was out cold and couldn't feel pain. It suddenly dawned on

Leo. He couldn't believe he hadn't pieced it together sooner, but how could he, without knowing Bowers was the one who'd betrayed them?

"The breach at the bunker wasn't an attempt to kidnap me. You wanted to compromise the location."

Bowers leaned against the counter next to Heather, his grin smug. "Figured it out, did you? I thought you were supposed to be a genius?"

Leo gritted his teeth but didn't reply. He was pretty sure his "fuck off and die" face said it all.

"I needed to get you somewhere less secure. What better way to do that than a security breach?"

"Which is why you didn't put up much of a fight when King suggested bringing me here."

"You boys made it too easy, Leo. I mean, really."

"Let me guess, when they come looking, you'll have your scapegoat."

Bowers shrugged and looked over at Heather. "We had a good run, sweetheart, but someone's gotta go down for this, and it won't be me. Hurry it up. I don't have all day." Heather glared at him but kept her mouth shut. "Harold was supposed to take the fall, but he started to become a pain in my ass, always sticking his nose where it didn't belong. Guy had a hard-on for you. Must be the glasses. The gay boys really dig that geek chic look, huh? I don't see it, but what the hell do I know about why you people like anything."

"Wow, you actually went there with the whole 'you people.' Guess I know who *you* voted for."

"You're a funny guy, de Loughrey. You're online. Get to it."

Man, he wanted to stab the guy in the eyeball with a spork.

"So with no Harold," Leo prompted, "that's where Heather comes in."

"We picked Heather up three years ago. Wow, three years. My, how time flies. Maybe not for her, since she's working off what would have been a very long prison sentence. It was either work for us or get to wear a very nonflattering orange jumpsuit, and orange is definitely not your color, sweetheart. Not with that red hair."

"Let me guess," Leo said with a snort of disgust. "You gave her another choice. Do this or go to prison."

"She's a smart cookie, aren't you, sweetheart?" Bowers ran a finger down her cheek, and Heather recoiled, her face expressing her desire for him to be struck by lightning, set on fire, and have his dick incinerated to nothing but ashes. At least that was Leo's take on it.

Leo spun to face his computer. "Why did you wait so long?"

"Because you wouldn't finish the fucking thing," Bowers muttered, coming to stand next to him. "When Heather said you had the fifth piece and just needed one more, I figured it was time for a little encouragement. If you haven't noticed, I'm running out of time, and patience."

Leo logged in to Jarvis, aware of Bowers hovering over his shoulder. A few keystrokes later, his software's messaging window popped up.

"What is that? What are you doing?"

Leo looked up at Bowers like he was an idiot. "Giving Heather permission to access my software. Jesus, Bowers, do you know anything about this shit? You think software created to handle a program like the one I've been working on is going to have open access so anyone could get in? What if it fell into the wrong hands? Isn't security your job?"

Bowers pointed his gun at King. "Call me stupid one more time and I put a bullet in your boyfriend. You think I want to be working with you fucking holier-than-thou nerds?" Bowers's nostrils flared, his near-black eyes filled with unbridled anger. "No. This is my punishment. You make one mistake and suddenly every assignment is babysitting little shits like you."

This project was groundbreaking. How was it a punishment? He supposed it would be to someone like Bowers, who was most likely used to field work. Leo took a page from Heather's book, sending an encrypted message hidden within the code that would supposedly allow her access to his program. In truth, the software he was sending was a dummy, a sort of mirror to the real thing. It would look and act like the program, but none of the changes would affect the real program. It would do what Leo wanted it to do, including making Bowers believe he'd completed the code. With Bowers hovering over Leo's shoulder, he couldn't get a message out to the guys, but Heather could. He made sure to discreetly alter the transfer speed on his outgoing upload, slowing it down. The transfer window popped up, the green bar moving gingerly, but not slow enough to make Bowers suspicious. "What happens to us?"

Bowers shrugged. "Not my problem."

"Really? You're just going to let us go?"

"Like I said. Not my problem. Now those men downstairs? That's a different matter. Once the program is done, packed up, and ready to go, I'm out of here."

"I can't believe you sold our government out to the Russians," Leo muttered, shaking his head. He needed to buy them some time, to figure something out. The guys might be four hours away, but the Kings owned a chopper. Leo was under no illusion the guys weren't already hauling ass over here, providing Heather sent them the message he begged her to. Even *if* Heather sent the message, it still left a lot of unknown variables, such as the message getting to Ace and the guys in the first place. How long it would take them to get here was another unknown. Without information on exactly what type of helicopter the Kings had, Leo couldn't get a time of arrival. He had to think of something else. Leaving their fate to the guys wasn't an option, but it was hard to think with Bowers watching his every move. He'd only be able to stall for so long.

"Lyosha, get yourself cleaned up. Bathroom's right there. Then stand guard with Osip," Bowers ordered. "Wounded or unconscious, I still don't trust that cocky bastard."

"How is he?" Leo asked the large man, ignoring the glower he received.

"He will be fine. For now. Bullet went straight through the shoulder. Removed the bullet from his leg, and the third bullet did not hit any organs. He has the best stitch work and is bandaged. If he dies, it will not be from his wounds."

The implication in the asshole's words wasn't lost on Leo, but he said a little prayer of thanks anyway that Bowers had at least kept his word, saving King. Not that Leo still wouldn't shank them all if he got the chance.

"So what's the going rate for our country these days?" Leo asked, as the green bar came dangerously close to finishing. Fuck, he was running out of time. If Heather didn't play ball, he'd be out of it. *Play ball....*

"You've seen it for yourself. Our government is broken. The ship is sinking, and I'm not going down with it. I'm taking my money and buying some deserted island some-where to live the rest of my life in the sun, sipping cocktails and getting laid."

"A vacation getaway? Seriously?"

"You're not listening. This country is going to crash and burn. It's only a matter of time. Look at your boyfriend. When he and his friends got back, who took care of them? No one, because Washington didn't give a shit. They're too busy with their little pissing contests to care about what happens to guys like him, like you, like me. I gave everything I had, sacrificed my family, my life, and because I'm not willing to bend over and take it up the ass—no offense— I'm demoted to babysitter, threatened with permanent desk duty."

"I'm not sure what disturbs me more, that out of everything you said, the thing you thought I'd be offended by most is in reference to taking it up the ass, or that you're prepared to do exactly what you're accusing *them* of doing. It could mean the end of this country. You're not only opening the door to every threat imaginable. You're handing them the grenade to blow it all up. Innocent people will be hurt."

"Haven't you heard? We're already at war. Might as well join the winning side."

"And you think they're going to go, 'Hey, thanks for the treason. Here's your bags of cash. Enjoy your island'? Come on, Bowers. You know better than that."

"How about a little less mouth and a lot more typing."

The green bar finished, and Leo's time was up.

"Avengers are en route," Heather said, and Leo's heart leaped into his throat. God, he hoped that meant what he thought it meant. *Thank you, Heather.*

Bowers peered at her. "You mean Jarvis. Avengers is the op name."

Heather rolled her eyes. "Whatever. I don't follow that comic book stuff. Isn't Jarvis part of the Avengers?"

Leo held back a smile. He could have kissed Heather for being so convincing. "If you're talking about the movies, then technically yes. Tony Stark and Bruce Banner uploaded Jarvis into the synthetic body Ultron created. He then became Vision."

Bowers looked from Leo to Heather and back. "This is why you nerds don't get laid."

"First of all, that's stereotyping and so eighties-teen-movie. Second of all, my boyfriend's a Green Beret, so I win any argument on that front."

Heather snickered, and Bowers's scowl turned fierce. "I might reconsider the whole 'not shooting you two in the head' thing."

Leo leaned forward, reaching beneath his monitor, and found himself face-to-face with the barrel of Bowers's gun.

"Steady there, hotshot. What do you think you're doing?"

"Relax. I'm getting my stress ball." Leo plucked up the little black handball and showed it to him. "See?"

Bowers peered at the ball before moving his gaze to Leo. "What are you going to do with it?"

"Um, relieve stress? That's how stress balls work."

Bowers motioned to the screen. "All right, smartass. It's done. Now get to work."

Leo grunted, squeezing the black ball in his right hand, his knee bouncing. "Is she set up?"

Bowers muttered something under his breath and returned his gun to the holster attached to his tactical vest. He went to stand beside Heather, and Leo glanced over his shoulder to do a quick scan of the room. Lyosha and Osip stood in front of the bookcase housing his collectibles. The room had been destroyed during King's epic fight. The coffee table was in pieces around the living room area.

Bowers now stood to the right of the kitchen a few feet from the open doorway that led downstairs.

Think. Leo squeezed the ball in his hand. He glanced at King and froze. From Bowers's angle, he couldn't see what Leo did—King tapping his pinky finger.

King was awake.

ELEVEN

IT WAS ONLY a matter of time.

King could feel the shift in the air, along with the agonizing pain shooting up the left side of his body from the three bullet wounds he'd received. At least he wasn't bleeding out anymore, and on the plus side, it was his left and not his right. If he wasn't so weak from the blood loss and the beating, Bowers would already be dead, but there was no way he could get up and take down those two bastards before Bowers got a shot off. Not in his condition. There was also the little matter of the small army downstairs.

Leo had played this smart, and King was so proud of him. His guy had expertly turned the worst of a situation to his advantage as much as he could. Knowing Bowers needed him gave Leo leverage, and with that he'd cleared the room, limiting the number of hostiles for when they made their move, which would be soon. Leo was stalling. No way he was about to give Bowers the program he'd been working on. Judging by the looks Heather was giving Leo and the fact she hadn't ratted him out said she was eager to get out from under Bowers's thumb.

King did a quick assessment of his injuries. His body screamed with pain, his muscles ached, he could barely see from one swollen eye, and the second he moved to get up, he'd most likely tear through his stitches. But he could do this. He *would* do this. King gritted his teeth, his mind and body preparing to take action, because the last of Leo's resolve was about to snap.

Bowers was yelling at him.

"Stop yelling," Leo said through his teeth, but that only made Bowers yell louder. Hands balled into fists on his legs, Leo looked Bowers right in the eye and yelled, "Penny!"

Everything that came after could only be described as orchestrated chaos, a series of events happening in rapid-fire succession as well as simultaneously.

Mouse Trap.

On hearing Leo's command, King rolled off the futon and hit the floor, ignoring the pain that coursed through his body at the sudden movement and the jolt that reverberated through him when he landed. As King rolled, Leo's ball hit one of the large glass display cases on the bookshelf, shattering the glass into millions of pieces and sending the sharp projectiles into Osip's face. The man screamed, grabbing his face, and jerking to his left where he slammed into Lyosha. The ball was back in Leo's hand as Lyosha tried to move out of the way of his falling comrade only to trip on one of the coffee table's legs.

With a roar, Lyosha fell head-first into the kitchen counter, knocking himself out and scaring Heather, who screamed, momentarily startling Bowers, giving Leo enough time to shout.

"Baseball!"

Penny, drop. Baseball, catch.

Bowers spun toward Leo in time to get smacked in the face with the handball rebounding off the wall to the guy's left, all while King caught the gun Leo had tossed him in the seconds Bowers had been hit with the ball. King fired one round after another into Bowers, the blows from the bullets hitting his vest sending him stumbling through the open doorway behind him, curses filling the air along with the thumping of Bowers tumbling down the stairs. King spun and fired a round into Osip who'd decided to charge him, the bullet to the head killing him instantly.

"Heather, let's go," Leo ordered as he ran over to King, helped him to his feet, and put an arm around him. They hurried for the balcony doors, and Leo slid one open just as the thundering sound of helicopters filled the air. Heather closed the door behind them, and they ran for the end of the expansive balcony, bullets tearing into the glass behind them and hitting the pillars as the horde from downstairs emerged.

"Looks like the boys brought the cavalry with them," King shouted over the whirring of helicopter blades. Either Ace and the guys had notified the General or Heather had, because along with the black Four Kings helicopter, three military choppers approached from the sides. Ace, Joker, and Lucky, wearing full tactical gear, rappelled down ropes attached to the chopper. As soon as they were cleared, the Kings chopper moved out of the way and another took its place. Boots hit the rooftop balcony from all sides, the men returning fire the moment they were free from the ropes. Ace turned to Leo, his smile huge as he shouted over the cacophony of gunfire and helicopters.

"Your dad's an awesome guy."

Leo returned Ace's grin. "I know."

"He wants us to follow his guys back. He's going to meet us wherever that is after he chews some asses. He is *not* going quietly into the night after this clusterfuck." Leo nodded, and when Ace moved his assessing gaze to King, fury filled his gold-green eyes as he took stock of King's injuries. "They've got a medical team waiting. We'll head there first."

"I'll be okay," King shouted. "Find Jack and Red. I think Bowers pumped something into the vents to knock them and the others out."

Ace turned to Lucky and Joker. "You heard him. Go get our boys."

Joker and Lucky took off, and Ace turned his attention back to King. "We should go. The guys can hitch a ride." He went to tap his earpiece, but King stopped him. "You need to find Bowers."

"I will. *You* need to get patched up."

"They've got Bowers," Leo said, stiffening beside King.

They turned to the small group of soldiers heading in their direction, Bowers restrained and in tow. The guy looked pissed, a little worse for wear, and was limping, but he was in one piece, which was more than he would have been had King gotten his hands on him. He'd kind of been hoping Bowers would have put up more of a fight, but the guy wasn't stupid. Bowers clearly didn't want to die, though considering where he was heading, death would have been a better option, in King's opinion. The wind picked up, and one of the Army choppers perched near the balcony's railing.

"What about her?" Ace asked King, motioning to Heather, who stood shivering and hugging herself.

"Put her on the chopper with Bowers."

"No," Leo said, his expression hard.

"Leo, she betrayed you," King ground out.

"She had no choice, King."

"There's always a choice."

Leo's nostrils flared, and King cursed under his breath. He wasn't going to win this. Leo believed Heather to be an innocent victim, and maybe she was, but King would need to see proof of that.

"Fine. Ace, she rides with us. Don't let her out of your sight."

"Got it," Ace replied.

The soldiers escorting Bowers nodded to Ace, who returned the gesture, before they shoved Bowers toward the awaiting helicopter. A couple of soldiers grabbed him and hauled him on board, then pushed him down into one of the seats and secured the seatbelt around him. As soon as the chopper cleared, the black beast belonging to the Kings took its place, and just in time too, seeing as Joker and Lucky appeared with Jack and Red.

Relief flooded through King. They were okay. Jack and Red ran over when they saw him, and Red checked him over.

"We need to get you to a hospital," Red said, his eyes filled with concern.

"There's a team waiting." Ace took hold of King's arm, Lucky the other. "Jack, Joker, you guys hitch a ride with the General's guys. We'll get King to the black site." Everyone had their orders, and King gave his weight to his brothers now that his adrenaline was plummeting and Leo was no longer in danger. He made sure Leo was on the chopper first before he let the guys help him in. He dropped into the seat beside Leo and put his arm around him, holding him close against his good side. It was almost over. Leo laced their fingers together and kissed his temple. It felt good. No, it felt amazing. The doors closed, and they took off, nothing but blue skies ahead.

With Leo at his side and his brothers surrounding him, King surrendered to his exhaustion.

———

WHEN HE WOKE, he was reclined in some kind of hospital bed, hooked up to machinery monitoring his vitals, a saline drip attached to his hand, with the IV in his other hand delivering a nifty painkiller.

"Hey, handsome."

King smiled at the familiar voice. He liked that voice a whole lot. Actually, he loved that voice. "Leo," King murmured, his throat dry and rough. He hated the mind fog that came with morphine. He preferred the pain, but he had a feeling Leo wasn't going to let him get away with toughing it out. Neither would his brothers, for that matter. He'd probably get a lecture from Red, or worse, Ace. He certainly didn't need that.

"I've got some super yummy ice chips for you."

King grunted and held a hand up for the little plastic cup. "I'm not dying," he grumbled, ignoring Leo's chuckle. He was so beautiful. "You're so beautiful."

Leo's warm brown eyes sparkled from behind his glasses as he smiled lovingly at King. "Aw, and you're even more adorable when you're high."

"I'm not high." King sucked an ice chip into his mouth, his movements slow, like he was moving through Jell-O. "I hate Jell-O."

"Okay, then. No Jell-O for you." Leo ran his fingers through King's hair, and King hummed. He closed his eyes.

"*That* I like. What you're doing now." He leaned into Leo's touch and gently took hold of his arm. "Come 'ere."

"Come where?" Leo asked, laughing softly. He leaned in and kissed King. It was feathery soft, and King wanted more. He wanted Leo closer. "Easy there, stud. You're lying in an infirmary bed with three bullet holes in you, in case you forgot. No sexy times for a while."

King huffed out a breath. "Well, that sucks." The room was large and painted white, with four more sets of beds, all empty, and medical equipment. "Where are we?"

Leo shrugged. He took a seat on the edge of King's bed. "We were only in the air for, like, twenty minutes, so still in Florida, I think. Dad was here when we arrived, though."

"Shit, your dad is here?" King jerked his arms forward to sit himself up and hissed at the pull from the IVs.

"Whoa there, soldier. Where do you think you're going?" Leo asked, trying to get him to lie back.

"I can't let him see me like this."

"Like what? Like you took on an army and were shot three times trying to save his son?"

The scowl King received was *fierce*. Okay, yeah, maybe he wasn't going anywhere.

The door opened, and the guys came in, Ace's smile wide when he saw King. "Look who's finally awake. Hello, sleeping beauty." King narrowed his eyes at him. "Glad to see your delightful disposition remains intact," Ace added, his grin wicked.

"Leave him alone, Anston." Red nudged Ace to one side so he could check King's vitals. "The guy just fought his way out of an impossible situation. How the hell did you do it?"

Feeling more lucid, King shook his head. "I didn't."

"What?" Lucky frowned, confused. "But you were beat to shit and shot. Leo said you fought a small army of men."

"That part is true, but I wasn't the one who got us out." King smiled warmly up at Leo, his heart swelling with pride. "That was all Leo."

Everyone gaped at him before their stunned gazes moved to Leo. Ace was the first to speak up. "How?"

Jack gasped, his smile huge. "Mouse Trap!"

King chuckled. "Yep." He kissed Leo's hand, loving the way Leo blushed at everyone's awed expressions. King knew the feeling. He was in awe of Leo as well. "Leo lined up all the pieces, waited for the right opportunity, then let it loose." Leo reached into his pocket and pulled out the little black handball. He tossed it to Jack, who caught it. "Leo was the one who got Bowers to send his guys downstairs, and convinced Heather to send out a distress call. He kept Bowers busy and none the wiser."

"How did you get Bowers to cooperate?" Lucky asked Leo.

Leo cleared his throat and averted his gaze, knowing that was the part King was *not* impressed with.

"He put a loaded gun with the safety off to his own head. Something he will *never* be doing again."

"Shit." Joker shook his head. "And you guys say I'm crazy."

"You are," Lucky said with a snort before turning his attention back to Leo. "Nice work."

The guys all chimed in, coming over to congratulate Leo and pat him on the shoulder, the back, or the cheek. It was obvious Leo was moved, his eyes glassy as he thanked everyone. King was a little misty-eyed as well. Must be the morphine. Yeah, definitely the morphine.

Ace put his hand on King's good shoulder, relief and

affection written all over his face. "I'm glad your grumpy ass is okay. Why don't you get some rest, huh? We're going to meet with the General, get debriefed. I told him you'd be along as soon as you were able."

King nodded, appreciating Ace's understanding. The last time King had been in a hospital, he'd woken up to learn the mission had failed and half of his brothers were dead. Not wanting to face the General like this had nothing to do with proving his masculinity or fearing he'd be showing weakness. It wasn't about ego. It was about finally leaving the past behind him and moving forward, but to do that, he couldn't be the same guy he'd been back in that hospital bed. He didn't want the General associating him now with the man he'd been, because he wasn't the same guy. Some things about him would never change, like keeping the memory of his fallen brothers alive, fussing over the ones who brought so much love and joy to his life, and being a grumpy ass. He'd never stop doing whatever it took to protect his family. What *had* changed, was the knowledge he no longer had to shoulder the weight of the world on his own.

The guys left, and Leo kissed him sweetly. This one man had changed his world completely, yet the best parts remained. King parted his lips, inviting Leo to deepen the kiss. He cupped the back of Leo's head, murmuring an "I love you" before he drifted off to sleep.

The next time he woke, he was ready, and thankfully Leo didn't argue. King had to wonder if Ace had said something, because Leo got him out of bed and didn't ask questions as he helped King out of the hospital gown and into a clean pair of black tactical pants, black boots, and a black henley. A pair of crutches had been left by his bed, and King took one, adjusted it for his height then placed it under his right arm. Leo stood in front of King, the adoration in his eyes stealing King's breath away. Leo kissed him again, short and sweet, but no less amazing.

"Whatever happens, remember that when it comes to me, he's a dad first and a General second. He respects you and admires you, Ward, just like I do. I'll be right here waiting for you." Leo took his hand, and together they left the infirmary. A couple of armed soldiers stood outside the door, and Leo turned to one of them. "Mr. Kingston is ready to see General de Loughrey."

The soldier nodded, and King left Leo with a gentle squeeze to his arm. He headed down the corridor of the black site—not all that different from the one where he'd first met Leo. The irony wasn't lost on him. Except this time instead of being led into a bunker, he was shown to an empty room with only a one-way mirror on the right side of the wall showing the interrogation room that held Bowers on the other side. His wrists were in cuffs secured to the steel table in front of him by a chain, and his feet were secured to an iron loop in the concrete floor.

"Ward." The General's smile was warm and welcoming as he held out his hand. King took it, taken aback when he was pulled into a tight embrace. The discomfort to his shoulder was well worth it, and he returned the big man's hug, receiving a gentle pat on the back before he was released.

"Sir. It's good to see you again."

"It's good to see you too, son. How are you feeling?"

"Better. Thank you." For the first time, King noticed the resemblance between the General and his son. The General was a much bigger man, tall with wide shoulders and salt-and-pepper hair, but he had the same boyish smile as Leo, along with that mischievous twinkle in his brown eyes. Eyes that were sharp and currently assessing him.

Not ready to address the matter of Leo just yet, King turned to face the mirror. "Has he said anything?"

"At the moment he's more terrified of the man who hired him than he is of us, but that'll change very soon. We're moving him off US soil."

In other words, Bowers was about to disappear.

King narrowed his eyes at Bowers. The guy couldn't see him, but Bowers would know he was here. "Promise me you're going to bury him in some hole where no one will ever find him."

"You have my word. I'm not going anywhere just yet."

"Does that mean you're not retiring?"

"They might be forcing me out, but it's on my terms. I'm pulling in every favor owed to me to make sure Leo is safe, and that this kind of thing never happens again. Bowers might not be talking, but thanks to Heather, we have intel on a small cell of Russian spies we believe were behind this. She's been communicating with us from the moment Bowers started blackmailing her."

All the pieces fell into place. "The encrypted message Jack found, the one she'd sent out.... She wasn't communicating with the Russians; she was communicating with you."

The General nodded. "Heather's a good kid. She'd made some stupid mistakes, but her working with the NSA instead of being prosecuted should have been a good deal for her. We've renegotiated the terms of her contract, and she'll be working for my people now. Thanks to her, we have a team closing in on the Russian cell as we speak. Of course the Russian government is denying everything. I won't go until I put down the bastards who hurt you and my son."

King was touched to be included, but what mattered was that Leo would be safe. "What about the program? Leo's been worried about it."

"Really? Because he told me it was a complete failure." The General gave him a knowing smile. "It's been destroyed. I'm sure we can find other ways to protect our country without turning our own citizens into suspects."

King opened his mouth to express his relief, when Bowers stood, his gaze focused on the mirror. "I know you're there, Kingston. How'd the General take the news that you're banging his son? Bet that wasn't what he had in mind when he asked you to guard his son's body."

King balled his free hand into a fist, telling himself not to let Bowers bait him because that's clearly what he was doing.

"How was he, King? Bet he jumped at the chance to get fucked by a big bad Green Beret. Was it easy? Did you take advantage of his vulnerability, or was he so damned eager for your cock that he gave it up at the drop of a hat?"

Thanks to the hefty painkillers in his system, King managed to storm out of the room, despite his crutch. He ignored the General calling out after him and slammed through the door to the interrogation room. He grabbed Bowers by the neck, his teeth gritted as Bowers gave him a shit-eating grin.

"What are you going to do? Are you going to torture me into confessing all my sins?"

King barely flinched, but it was enough for Bowers's smug grin to grow wider.

"Yeah, I know all about your little trip to London. Hey, I'm not knocking what you did. The guy had it coming. You put a serial rapist behind bars. By the time the guy gets out, his dick will be too shriveled and useless to do much of anything with. If he makes it that long."

"What's your point?" King growled, shoving Bowers down into the hard metal chair.

"My point is, you're not Captain America, are you? Too much blood on your hands. Do you think you're really the kind of guy the General wants for his son? He hid the kid, for fuck's sake. To keep him away from all our fucked-up government shit, and there ain't no one that fits the bill more than you, my friend."

"You're right," King said with a nod. "I'm not perfect, and maybe Leo does deserve better. You should be thanking him."

Bowers snorted. "For what?"

King loomed over him, his gaze never wavering. "He's the reason you're still breathing through your nose. See, I'm a better man because of him. Now if you'll excuse me, I have a beautiful man who loves me waiting for me, and the rest of my life to look forward to. Enjoy the fiery pit of hell that's about to become your new home." King turned to leave, then paused. "What the hell." He grabbed Bowers's hand and broke two of his fingers, Bowers's scream echoing through the room. With a satisfied grin, King headed for the door.

"What the fuck happened to being a better man?" Bowers spat after him.

"Guess I'm more of a work in progress."

Leaving Bowers to curse him and his ancestors, King rejoined the General in the viewing room and came to stand beside him. They watched as Bowers screamed and ranted at the top of his lungs, calling King every name in the book.

"He's wrong, you know," the General said, putting a

hand up to stop King's protesting. "When I was informed my son would be working on a project for the NSA and Pentagon, you came to mind immediately. There was no one I trusted more to look after him, and no one who is better suited for Leo."

King stared at the General, too stunned to speak. When he finally found his voice, he spoke up. "He's... incredible. I didn't take advantage of him. I fell in love with him, and I'm going to do everything I can to be worthy of that love. He does make me a better man."

"You're a good soldier, always were, always will be, but most importantly, you're a good man. There is no one who would fight for my son the way I know you would. Leo is a genius, but as I'm sure you've seen, he needs someone who can help him with other aspects of his life. To make sure he doesn't get lost in that big brain of his. No one understands him like you. Not even me. You two need each other." The General put his hand on King's good shoulder, giving it a squeeze, his eyes filled with emotion. "He loves you, Ward. You should have seen his face when he talked about you. Thank you. For making my son happy. It's all I ever wanted for him."

King swallowed hard. "I have to tell him."

The smile fell from the General's face, and he dropped his hand. He released a heavy sigh. "Ward...."

"Please. I love him. If he and I are going to have any kind of future together, it needs to be built on trust and honesty. I can't carry that weight anymore, and neither should you."

The General seemed to think it over. He closed his eyes for a heartbeat before meeting King's gaze and nodding. "You're right. I know you are. Go on. He's waiting for you.

I'll talk to him later. Guess we're going to be seeing more of each other."

The thought made King smile. "I'm holding you to that."

King excused himself and found his way back to the infirmary. The moment he stepped inside, his arm was full of Leo. His sweet man's urgent kisses made him laugh, and he hugged Leo to him, mindful of his side as he savored the taste and feel of Leo's plump lips on his. When they were forced to come up for air, King led him over to the row of chairs at the end of the room resembling a sort of small waiting area.

"Leo, I have to tell you something."

"It can wait. I want to know when we can get out of here." Leo went to stand, but King gently stopped him. He laced their fingers together, his heart in his throat.

"No, it can't. It's important. Please."

Leo slowly sank back down, his eyes filled with concern. "Okay."

"What do you know about your mom's death?"

Leo flinched. "Why are you asking me that?"

"Please, answer the question."

"That she was in Syria working on something classified for her job. There was an accident. An explosion on site, and she was... caught in it."

King nodded. "I know you're going to have questions, but please, hear me out until the end, okay? It's important. Can you do that for me?"

"I'll try," Leo replied quietly, his rapt attention on King.

"Thank you. Your mother was part of a covert operation put together by Washington and the CIA to gather intel in Syria along with Mossad operatives. They had suspicions of a facility being built for military purposes, and intel from both groups confirmed workers from North Korea were helping to build a nuclear reactor. There were complications during one of the raids, and your mother's cover was blown. She made it to a safe house, and although the US government had already stated it wasn't willing to take any military action, your father wasn't about to abandon her."

Leo's eyes widened, his expression one of stunned disbelief and his skin losing some of its color, but as promised, he remained quiet, so King forged ahead. "We weren't supposed to be there, but we had our mission. Get in, find your mother, and get her out. A backup team would be close by in case we needed it.

"The thing is, my unit and I were supposed to be the backup team, but our commander and the General went way back. The commander wanted to be lead team on this, but he would accept being backup if I wasn't on board with taking the lead. It was up to me. He knew if I accepted, the rest of the guys would follow. How could I say no? We had to try. I approached the guys, told them about the mission and that I was in but that I understood if they weren't. This was a black op, and if it went sideways, they might never see their families again." King swallowed hard, closing his eyes for a moment, reaching deep for the strength he needed to break Leo's heart. "They didn't hesitate. If I was in, so were they. Despite the risks, they wanted to bring her home."

"What happened?" Leo asked, his voice barely above a whisper.

"Someone betrayed your mother, and we arrived at the safe house just as Syrian intelligence got to her. We were ambushed." King released a steady breath, his eyes shut tight as he tried to forget the smell of burning flesh, his eyes stinging from the dirt and dust, throat raw from the smoke as he bled out. "I was pretty sure I wasn't going to make it out of there, but Red was determined to save my ass." He opened his eyes, his gaze on his and Leo's intertwined fingers. "When I woke up in the hospital, your dad was there. He told me your mother was dead. She'd been killed at the safe house. The backup team had been too late to save her, but they managed to get us out and avoid an international incident." King felt the dam break, and he choked on a sob. "I'm so sorry, baby, I tried. We all did."

Tears streamed down Leo's cheeks, and he pressed his lips together, shaking his head. "No."

"I'm sorry."

"Stop," Leo pleaded. "Did you betray her?"

King's head shot up, and he stared at Leo, the anger in Leo's eyes catching him off guard. "What?"

"Did you betray her, Ward?"

"Of course not."

"Then why the hell are you feeling guilty for something you had no control over?"

"Didn't you hear me?" King grabbed his crutch, and pushed himself to his feet where he started to pace, albeit somewhat awkwardly. "We failed. *I* failed." Not only had he cost his men their lives, but it cost Leo his mother. King couldn't even begin to fathom how a grief-stricken General had broken that news to a tiny Leo.

"Stop," Leo snapped, stepping in front of King and taking hold of his arms. "How is any of this your fault?"

"If I had said no, stuck to being backup, maybe she'd still be alive, maybe they all would be—"

"Enough. Whether you went in as lead or backup, there was no guarantee what would happen. You had your orders. Your unit was going in regardless. You said it yourself. Backup arrived too late, so you would still be blaming yourself for her death, for not getting to her in time. There's no winning for you in this situation, Ward. Maybe your men would have survived this op, or maybe you would have lost men trying to make it out or on another op. My point is there's no way of knowing what could have happened at any time.

"You and your men risked everything to rescue her. Even now, if anyone found out what really happened, you, Ace, the guys...." Leo put his hand to King's cheek. "Is this what was holding you back?"

"You knew?" Maybe Leo didn't know exactly what King was hiding, but he'd known something was wrong.

"Every time you got close to opening up, you'd pull back. Did you think I would blame you?"

"I wanted to talk to your dad first. He was trying to protect you." King let out a heavy sigh. "And yes, a part of me thought that you wouldn't want anything to do with me if you knew the truth, but falling in love with you... I had to tell you."

"Maybe it's time my dad trusted me to take care of myself. I don't blame you, Ward. How could I? You're even more amazing than I thought you were. You risked your life to save my mom. I'm so sorry you lost your brothers, but that wasn't your fault. They loved you. How could they not? I mean, seeing how Ace and the others are with you, it's so obvious. Tell me, if one of them had approached you asking you to save someone they cared about, would you even have hesitated?"

King shook his head. "Never."

"See? I know my telling you not to feel guilty isn't going to stop you from feeling it, but what was it you said to me recently? You always have a choice. You, your brothers, had a choice to go in first or wait. They were good men, and they chose to risk their lives to save another. For that, I will always be grateful to them." King wiped a tear from Leo's cheek with his thumb.

"I love you, Ward. You are the best thing that's ever happened to me. I'm not going to lie. I come with a hell of a lot of maintenance. 'The Manual for the Caring and Feeding of Leo' is hefty. Like unabridged-encyclopedia long. I used to use mine as a step stool when I was a kid, course the thing was heavier than I was so you could hear me pushing it across the floor from a mile away. What was I saying? Right, yeah, see, that. I'm not like everyone else, but if you think you're up for it, I can guarantee no one will love you more fiercely than me, and I won't let you go skulking back into your shadows. According to Ace, I seem pretty good for you. What do you say? Is there room in your life for an awkward geek with anxiety issues, who can't cook, and has a penchant for fish-shaped snacks?"

King wrapped his arm around Leo's waist, bringing him in close. "What you think are your faults, are part of what makes you amazing, Leo. I fell in love with all of you, and in return you haven't just given me your beautiful heart, you've given me an amazing gift."

"What's that?"

"Joy. Not that I wasn't happy with my life, but Ace was right—God help me—something was missing. *You* were missing. I'm not perfect, and I don't need to be. I might still carry the guilt from what happened that day in Syria, but for the first time in my life, I feel like it doesn't define me. That I can move forward with my life and enjoy all the good in it. You gave that to me, Leo." King brushed his lips over Leo's, loving the way Leo opened up for him.

Together they completed a whole. For all of their vast differences, no one was better suited for him than Leo. As King kissed Leo, losing himself in the warmth and love of the wonderful man in his arms, King knew he'd do everything to hold on tight to the love he'd found. Maybe the good in him *was* wrapped in a rough exterior, like the diamond in the rough Pip had been convinced King was, but that was okay, because the people who mattered most in his life loved him the way he was.

EPILOGUE

TWO MONTHS LATER

PERFECT.

King stood back to admire his handiwork. He was probably as excited about this room as Leo.

The moment Leo had stepped foot back into his apartment he'd started tapping anxiously at his leg as he walked around, until King brought him into his arms and asked him to share his thoughts. What followed was a ramble of epic proportions that ultimately equated to Leo not wanting to live there anymore. After what had happened there with Bowers, he no longer felt safe. And while he didn't know where to go or what to do, he knew he wanted to be closer to King. Finding Leo a new place where he felt secure would have been a challenge, to say the least. Then it occurred to King that the safest place for Leo would be in King's home.

Leo had blinked up at him, his beautiful face a picture of bewilderment until it finally sank in that King wanted him to move in. Deciding to live together after a few months might seem quicker than the average couple, but they agreed they weren't exactly average. King knew Leo was it for him. It had taken him this long to find the right someone to lose his heart to. And for Leo, King was everything he wanted and needed. He adored King, loved his family, and together they made one hell of a team.

After Leo jumped on him, assaulting him with kisses followed by one of the best blow jobs King had ever had, King got the ball rolling. He took care of the arrangements and sold Leo's apartment to a friend of Leo's sister who'd just started a new job not far from there. The only belongings Leo wanted to take with him to King's house were his clothing, collectibles, electronics, and snacks. He'd never considered most of the furniture his, so he didn't have any trouble leaving it behind—except for his computer chair. King had a feeling that thing was going to be with them for a very long time.

King had been a little worried about what Leo would think of his house. It wasn't on the beach, but sort of in the middle of a forest, surrounded by nothing much but trees. It was a big house, but nothing extravagant. Comfort and simplicity had been his goals when he'd redecorated after inheriting the home from his parents after they were gone. There were a lot of good memories in this house, and some difficult ones, but it was a family home, where the guys walked in as if it were their own place. They came at all hours, hung out, and shared meals.

Leo hadn't simply loved the house, he settled in like he'd always been there, stating he was sorry but was having an affair with King's couch. The plump cushions, softness, and size had been the downfall of many, so King didn't fault him. The one thing that stood out to King was that Leo needed a new safe haven within the house. A little nest that was all Leo's. So King had asked Leo to create a 3D rendering of what he'd want his new room to look like, and King had recreated it exactly.

He stood back, admiring the navy-blue paint on the walls, with the thick white stripe running along one wall near the ceiling before it dropped down at an angle on the right wall and then again on the third wall until it reached the door.

The furniture was all black and silver, with Leo's L-shaped desk in the corner along the right wall with his favorite chair, his computer, multiple monitors, and equipment. Beside it was a set of metal drawers. In the center of the room to the left of the desk, King had mounted the large flat-screen TV, and underneath the TV a two-shelved TV stand housed Leo's various game consoles and Blu-Ray player. A comfy black couch and coffee table that had a *Game of Thrones* map embedded in the surface completed the space. The left wall had floating bookcases that King had installed, where Leo's collectibles were painstakingly displayed. Everything was exactly to Leo's specifications.

The only thing missing was Leo. Where had he gone off to?

"Leo?" King walked into the hallway when he heard a crash from the direction of his office.

"In here," Leo called out.

King found Leo in his office on the floor, several boxes scattered around him. He hurried over to help him up. "You okay?"

"Yeah, sorry. I was trying to store some of these boxes in the closet like you said I could, but I couldn't reach the very top, so I stood on my toes, and well, the step stool took offense."

King chuckled and picked up one of the boxes. "Just tell me where you want them to go, and I'll put them up there."

"Sure." Leo handed him the boxes one by one, and King put them up on the top shelf that he'd emptied for Leo. They were mostly collectibles Leo didn't need to have displayed but didn't want to get rid of.

"What's this?" Leo asked, removing a box from the middle shelf. He picked up one of the tins. "Altoids?"

"They're for pocket-size survival kits. I've been making them for the guys since our first deployment."

Leo returned the box to the shelf and removed one a lot more beat-up. King swallowed hard, knowing what was in it.

"These look really old. They're stained with dirt, and is this... blood?" Leo's head shot up, his eyes wide.

"Those belonged to the guys," King said quietly, taking the box from him. "I know it's morose and messed-up, but their families didn't want them, and I couldn't bring myself to throw them away."

Leo gasped, looking horrified by the idea. "Throw them away? Why would you do that? They belonged to your friends, your brothers. You put them together for the guys, and they carried those kits on them. It's a part of them."

King was taken aback by Leo's words.

"What?"

"My last boyfriend became my ex when I refused to get rid of them. He thought it was creepy."

"If he couldn't understand what these meant to you, then he didn't deserve you." Leo shrugged. "His loss, my gain."

King's lips spread into a soft smile. "Thank you."

"You're welcome." Leo placed a kiss to King's cheek, and King found the courage to give Leo what he'd been holding on to for a few weeks now.

After returning the box of kits to the shelf, King pulled out another box. "This one has kits for Ace and the guys."

"Wow, there's a lot of them."

"Two is one, and one is none."

Leo cocked his head to the side. "I never thought of it like that."

"Always have a backup," King said, removing one of the tins. He handed it to Leo, who with a bemused smile opened it.

Leo laughed as the first item on top was a tiny packet of Swedish Fish.

"In case your blood sugar drops."

Beneath it was one of Red's favorite Bravery Bandages —the bandage looking like a military medal that read "brave little soldier"—and underneath that was a compass, whistle, flashlight with the Four Kings Security crest, a low-profile flash drive, a cloth to clean his glasses, and....

"Chapstick?"

"It's extremely valuable in survival situations. You can start a fire with it, prevent blisters, stop small cuts from bleeding."

"Thank you." Leo beamed at him, and King's heart did a flip. Every day he grew more and more in awe of Leo. "Question."

"Yes?"

"Why the pink rubber band around it?"

"That would be Ace. He entered the wrong SKU number during his last stationery order at work and we ended up with thousands of pink rubber bands."

Leo laughed. "That's amazing." His laughter faded, and he smiled lovingly at King as he placed the tin in his pocket. "I'll always have it with me." He wrapped his arms around King's neck. "Thank you. For everything."

"Of course. Come on. Your office is all done." King popped a kiss on Leo's lips and laughed at Leo's excited happy dance and loud "*whoop*." He hadn't let Leo see his progress so he could surprise him once it was complete. "Close your eyes."

Leo did as he asked, allowing himself to be led into the room. King closed the door behind them and let out a breath. Even if Leo knew what it looked like, since it had all come from his mind, the reality was always different.

"Okay. Go ahead."

Leo opened his eyes and gasped. "Oh my God!" He slowly walked farther into the room. He ran his fingers along the edge of his sleek new desk, turning this way and that to take in everything. "Ward, this is...." His eyes glittered with unshed tears. "No one's ever done anything like this for me."

"Come here. Let me love you."

Leo darted over, and King kissed him, feeling every ounce of love pouring out of Leo.

"Thank you," Leo said when he pulled back.

King opened his mouth to reply, but Leo held a finger to King's lips. His free hand cupped King through his jeans, and unable to help himself, King groaned and pushed his groin shamelessly against Leo's hand, needing more. Damn, that felt so good.

Leo rubbed King through his pants as he nipped at King's jaw. "I think someone deserves a treat for all their hard work." Leo moved his hands to King's belt, unbuckling it before pushing his pants down to his thighs along with his underwear, his already hard, leaking cock jutting up, begging for attention. Leo wrapped a hand around King's thick length, drawing a gasp from him.

"I love how *big* and strong you are."

Leo sank to his knees, and King gripped the edges of the couch as Leo licked up the pearl of precome at the tip of his cock. King released a groan, his grip tightening as Leo moved his hand to the base of King's dick before those plump lips wrapped his hard length in slick heat.

"Oh God," King groaned, placing a hand on Leo's head as Leo sucked, licked, and laved every inch of King's erection. Leo pulled away only long enough to wet his finger before he swallowed King down to the root. King bucked his hips, curling his fingers in Leo's soft hair. Who said DIY didn't have its rewards?

King dropped his gaze, loving the decadent sight of his cock slipping in and out of Leo's pink lips. When Leo slipped a finger between King's asscheeks, the tip teasing his hole, King almost came right then.

"I love how you make me feel," King said, panting. He thrust his hips, fucking Leo's mouth, his body shivering from the sensations Leo brought him with his talented tongue. "Leo," King warned. He wasn't going to last much longer.

Leo pulled off him and stood, his lustful gaze aimed at King before he brought their mouths together in a searing kiss. Reaching into his back pocket, Leo pulled out a packet of lube. *Saucy little minx.* He put it in King's hands and grabbed a fistful of King's shirt, his swollen pink lips curling into a wicked grin. Leo switched their positions, his eyes never leaving King as he undid his own belt and pushed his pants and boxer briefs down to his ankles. His beautiful, hard cock had King's mouthwatering.

"We should break in the new office," Leo said, his voice husky and laced with sex as he turned around and stuck his ass out in invitation. Leo whimpered, wantonly undulating his hips as he stroked himself.

King wasn't about to let him off that easy. Getting down on one knee, King parted Leo's cheeks before spearing Leo's hole with his tongue.

"Oh my God!" Leo bucked his hips, and King wrapped a hand around Leo's cock, stroking him as he continued to lick, nibble, and tongue Leo's puckered entrance. Leo moaned and writhed, his hips moving frantically as he fucked King's hand. His body trembled, his pleas growing desperate.

"Ward, I can't...."

King stood, tore through the packet of lube, and slathered himself up good. He prepped Leo as fast as he could before lining himself up, then pushing in slowly. His muscles strained as he sank inside Leo inch by inch until he was balls-deep inside him.

"You feel so damned good," King growled, wrapping an arm around Leo's chest, his other hand jerking Leo's cock as he plunged in and out of his ass. Leo folded down over the couch, and King followed, his chest pressed to Leo's back as he pounded into Leo, deep and hard. Their panting breaths and the sound of skin slapping skin filled the otherwise silent room.

"Ward," Leo moaned. "I'm gonna come."

King slid a hand around Leo's neck, and Leo turned his head so King could ravish his mouth, stifling his cry as King hit his prostate. Leo came hard, squeezing around King's painfully hard dick, and King's roar when he came was lost inside Leo's sweet mouth. He thrust several more times before collapsing on Leo.

"Best. Day. Ever," Leo panted, and King chuckled, carefully pulling out.

King groaned at the feel of his come slipping out of Leo. Man, he loved knowing he was the only one leaving a part of himself in Leo. "Hold on." He pulled up his pants and went over to the set of metal drawers, the top drawer containing wet wipes.

"Don't worry, I'm not going anywhere," Leo said with a blissed-out hum.

Chuckling, King cleaned Leo up, then tossed the wipe. Leo straightened his clothes, turned, and kissed King.

"You know what would be even more awesome right now?"

His love was a creature of habit, and seeing as how it was lunchtime, it didn't take a Leo to figure out his sweetheart was hungry. King tucked Leo against his side and walked with him out of the office and into the hall.

"Time for a bacon, lettuce, and avocado bagel and Goldfish crackers?"

"Make that six, and one for you if you're hungry," Ace called out from the living room.

King smacked Ace upside the head as he walked by on his way to the kitchen.

"Ow, what was that for?"

"What have I said about boots on the coffee table?"

"Shit."

King chuckled when Leo rounded the couch, greeted the guys, and then jumped to land between Jack and Ace, his two favorite people next to King. Leo loved all the guys, but over the last several weeks, he'd bonded the most with Ace and Jack. Jack because he was the only one who spoke Leo's language when it came to all things computers and tech, and Ace because he made Leo laugh and was always finding new ways to torment King. For all his juvenile antics, Ace was a very smart man. Smart and intuitive. He was the only one besides King who'd quickly figured out how to read Leo and seemed to know what to do to help.

The guys were all great, but it was different with Ace. It always had been.

King got to work frying up bacon and prepping all the sandwich stuff, when Leo called out over his shoulder, "By the way, your title of Captain America has been revoked and given to Red."

King frowned at him. "What? Why?"

"Because after seeing you in action, it's pretty obvious who you are. I don't know why I didn't think of it sooner, but then I guess when we first met, I didn't really know you, but now it's so obvious."

King eyed him warily. "I'm listening. Wait, where did Ace go?" Oh, this couldn't be good. He hated that Ace could do that. Disappear in the blink of an eye. No good ever came from Ace pulling a vanishing act. He was worse than Leo.

Ace popped out from behind the counter, arms out. "Ta-da!"

"What the hell are you wearing?" King peered at the two comic book characters on Ace's T-shirt. He knew one of them was Spider-Man; the other one was....

"My new ship," Ace declared. "That's what the kids call it."

King stared at him. "What's happening right now?"

"Ship," Leo pitched in cheerfully. "It means relationship. It's when fans want to see certain characters in a relationship. Hence, Spideypool!"

"Spider-Man and Deadpool," Ace explained, motioning to the two characters on his shirt tangled together in Spider-Man's webbing.

"It's totally a thing," Leo added.

"Deadpool? Really?" King shook his head. "I don't see it."

"Come on, Ward. All the dudes you took down by your-self, your getting boners over weird things like my brain, and the fact that you kept fighting despite having been shot three times and beat up by a small army?" Leo jumped over the couch, his smile huge. "It's a perfect fit! Wade Wilson—Ward Kingston. Come on. He was even Special Forces!"

"But he's a smartass," King argued.

Leo's eyes widened, and he threw his hands out at King.

"I'm not that much of a smartass."

Ace snorted.

"Deadpool also never shuts up."

"Okay, so you're a bit less talkative."

"I'm too broody," King pointed out."

"What? No, you're not. You laugh and smile all the time. Ace is broodier than you. Okay, maybe he just pouts more." Leo waggled his eyebrows, and King sighed.

"Really?"

Leo nodded enthusiastically, and King knew he wasn't going to win this.

"Fine."

"Also, Ace is Hawkeye."

Ace spun to face Leo, and King barked out a laugh. "*What*?"

"Who am I?" Lucky asked, heading over.

"You're totally Wolverine."

"Yes! I am a badass!" Lucky wiggled his fingers in Ace's face and stuck his tongue out at him, then laughed when Ace smacked his hand away.

"Aw, come on, Leo! I thought we were friends? How come Lucky gets to be Wolverine, and I'm a purple-suited Katniss Everdeen?"

Leo took a seat on one of the kitchen stools while Jack, Joker, and Red joined them at the counter, Red coming around to help King in the kitchen. "First of all," Leo said, "Katniss Everdeen is a badass. Second of all, so is Hawkeye. The movies don't do him justice. Sure, when you put him next to huge-ass superdudes with powers, he doesn't seem like a badass, but he totally is. He's also a rebel and has mad skills with weapons. Lucky has to be Wolverine because the guy is seriously scary when you put a knife in his hand. Have you seen the way he chops veggies?"

"Who am I?" Jack asked, taking a seat next to Leo.

"You're Tony Stark, obviously." He and Jack high-fived before Leo moved on to Joker. "You're totally Gambit. I mean, what better weapon for you than exploding playing cards."

Joker nodded his approval. "Sweet."

"Come on," Ace pleaded, shoving Jack out of his seat, so he could sit next to Leo. With a chuckle and roll of his eyes, Jack slipped into the next chair. "I'll even take Black Widow."

"Sorry, she's already taken."

King shook his head in amusement, removing the bacon from the pan as Ace continued to argue his case on being assigned what he believed would be a more appropriate superhero. Red came to stand next to him at the stove, his smile warm.

"He's a perfect fit, isn't he?"

King glanced over his shoulder at his family. Lucky had an arm around Leo's shoulder while he teased Ace, who had a hand to Joker's chest as he explained how Joker should be the Hulk. *That* wasn't going to end well. Jack laughed his ass off at his best friend's unimpressed expression.

"Yeah, the guys love him." King turned back to Red.

"That too. What I meant was that he's a perfect fit for

you." After stealing a piece of bacon, Red joined the others in teasing Ace.

King started to get to work on making their sandwiches, his eyes lifting to meet Leo's. The happiness and love reflected in those big brown eyes squeezed at King's heart. Thanks to the General, they were able to start their lives together without having to look over their shoulders.

General de Loughrey had been true to his word, and after pulling every string he had, every favor owed, Leo was safe. If the government wanted something from Leo, several security measures had to be put in place for them to simply speak to him, and part of those security measures included King and his brothers-in-arms. There'd be no black ops, no secret government projects. If they wanted advice or to hire Leo, it would have to be on the up-and-up, and on Leo's terms. Leo was back to freelancing, which lately included doing a fair amount of work for Four Kings Security now that he'd found a kindred spirit in Jack. The two of them had way too much fun coming up with new security systems.

With it being a Saturday, King wasn't surprised when the doorbell rang, and Lucky opened the door for Colton, Laz, and Mason, the last of whom he kissed in greeting. The room erupted into cheers at the arrival, and King had never been happier.

"Hey, Wade. I mean, Ward," Leo teased.

King wrapped Leo up in his arms and brushed his lips over Leo's. "Very funny, smart guy."

"That's me." Leo hugged him close, melting into King's embrace. "I love you."

"I love you too." As he kissed Leo, surrounded by the boisterous cheers of his brothers, of his family, King thought about his life and how he'd always seemed at war with something—his guilt, his past, his demons. It was time for him to stand down. Although he would always protect those he loved, his war was over.

King was finally home.

The shenanigans continue with Jack and Fitz's story in *Stacking the Deck*, the first book in the Four Kings Security spin-off series, The Kings: Wild Cards, available on Amazon and KindleUnlimited.

Want to read about the Kings attending Spencer and Quinn's wedding? Check out *In the Cards* available on Amazon and Kindle Unlimited.

Haven't read Spencer and Quinn's story? You can find *Beware of Geeks Bearing Gifts* on Amazon and Kindle Unlimited.

A NOTE FROM THE AUTHOR

Thank you so much for reading *Diamond in the Rough*, the fourth book in the Four Kings Security series. I hope you enjoyed King and Leo's story, and if you did, please consider leaving a review on Amazon. Reviews can have a significant impact on a book's visibility on Amazon, so any support you show these fellas would be amazing.

What's next in the Four Kings Security Universe? Read Jack and Fitz's story in *Stacking the Deck*, the first book in the new spin-off series The Kings: Wild Cards, available on Amazon and KindleUnlimited. Want to binge-read the Wild Cards series? Check out the Boxed Set on Amazon and Kindle Unlimited.

Want to stay up-to-date on my releases and receive exclusive content? Sign up for my newsletter.

Follow me on Amazon to be notified of a new releases, and connect with me on social media, including my fun Facebook group, Donuts, Dog Tags, and Day Dreams, where we chat books, post pictures, have giveaways, and more!

Looking for inspirational photos of my books? Visit my book boards on Pinterest.

Thank you again for joining the Kings on their adventures. We hope to see you again soon!

ALSO BY CHARLIE COCHET

Shifter Scoundrels Series

Co-written with Macy Blake

FOUR KINGS SECURITY UNIVERSE SERIES

Four King Security

Four Kings Security Boxed Set

Black Ops: Operation Orion's Belt

The Kings: Wild Cards

The Kings: Wild Cards Boxed Set

Runaway Grooms

THIRDS UNIVERSE SERIES

THIRDS

THIRDS Beyond the Books

THIRDS: Rebels

TIN

THIRDS Boxed Sets

OTHER SERIES

Paranormal Princes

Soldati Hearts Series

North Pole City Tales Series

DID YOU KNOW?

If you own a book or borrow it through Kindle Unlimited, you can get Whispersynced audiobooks at a discounted price. Interested in audio? Check out the Charlie Cochet titles available on Audible.

ABOUT THE AUTHOR

Charlie Cochet is the international bestselling author of the THIRDS series. Born in Cuba and raised in the US, Charlie enjoys the best of both worlds, from her daily Cuban latte to her passion for classic rock.

Currently residing in Central Florida, Charlie is at the beck and call of a highly opinionated sable German Shepherd and a rascally Doxiepoo bent on world domination. When she isn't writing, she can usually be found devouring a book, releasing her creativity through art, or binge watching a new TV series. She runs on coffee, thrives on music, and loves to hear from readers.

www.charliecochet.com

Sign up for Charlie's newsletter:
https://newsletter.charliecochet.com

amazon.com/author/charliecochet
facebook.com/charliecochet
instagram.com/charliecochet
bookbub.com/authors/charliecochet
goodreads.com/CharlieCochet
pinterest.com/charliecochet

Made in the USA
Las Vegas, NV
13 January 2024

84313759R00173